T0035519

Manuel Rivas

The Last Days of Terranova

Translated from the Galician
by Jacob Rogers

archipelago books

First published in Galician as *El Último Día de Terranova*
by Penguin Random House Grupo Editorial
First Archipelago Books Edition, 2022
Second Printing

Library of Congress Cataloging-in-Publication Data available upon request.

Archipelago Books
232 3rd Street #A111
Brooklyn, NY 11215
www.archipelagobooks.org

Distributed by Penguin Random House
www.penguinrandomhouse.com

Cover art: *Habitación del viejo marinero* by Urbano Lugris

This work is made possible by the New York State Council on the Arts with the support of the Office of the Governor and the New York State Legislature. Funding for the translation of this book was provided by a grant from the Carl Lesnor Family Foundation. Support for the translation of this book was provided by Acción Cultural Española, AC/E.

This publication was made possible with support from Lannan Foundation, the National Endowment for the arts, the Nimick Forbesway Foundation, and the New York City Department of Cultural Affairs.

PRINTED IN CANADA

For Molist, the bookseller
In memoriam

For Elsa Oesterheld,
another memory on
the Horizon Line

For the booksellers Lola, Begoña, Silvia,
Amparo, and Marta

For Mónica Sabatiello, Débora Campos,
Noemi Fernández, Susana "Tati" Falcón, Mario Greco,
Paco Lores, Carlos X. Brandeiro, and the students
at the Rosa de los Vientos in Buenos Aires.

For Lorena Pastoriza, from the Republic of the Houseless

For the people at La Sala, in Caballito

For Carmen Rama, the Neo-Grecian

The Last Days of Terranova

Total Liquidation

(GALICIA, FALL 2014)

There they are, the two of them, on the rocks beneath the Lighthouse. A man and woman. Clandestine.

I'm facing the sea and I'm afraid that if I turn around, it will all disappear forever, them included. That if I look back, all I'll find is an immense nothingness traversed by the Horizon Line, a fossil with memories traveling along it the way Garúa is doing now, as she rides her bike with a packet of books in the saddlebag. That the Lighthouse will suddenly flash on in the middle of the day, and a fuming ray of black light will cross the city and shine its accusatory spotlight onto Terranova, onto the sign in the window where I wrote: *Total liquidation of all inventory due to imminent closure.*

I shouldn't have written that message.

I can picture the eyes poring over the last of the books, weighing their value, their health, color, musculature, and the state of their spines, meanwhile the books are in a state of shock as they feel the ground vanish out from under them.

I have to go back and take it down. The sign, I have to take it down.

I should lie and write: *Liquidation due to death of owner.* And I should be out there instead, on the front lines.

What are you doing here, Mr. Fontana?

Waiting for death, like everyone else.

That might earn me a round of applause. No, more than that, an ovation. It would ignite a glimmer of hope. I lived that prophecy, I wore it as a badge after I gave up my role as the White Duke: *No Future*. It horrifies me to think we were right. Right. It was the last thing we wanted to be. Like discovering only now that our deliberate grotesquery was a form of beauty. That the layer of grime was a form of protection.

Very poor indeed art thou,
Yet thy home is heaven, I trow...

That prayer always brings me peace. Jacopone da Todi, my poet. A gift from Uncle Eliseo when I was in the Iron Lung:

Bread and water – nothing more
But some herbs – unless, indeed
These a little salt shall need.

I should go back and take down that sign, but I'm too afraid to leave.

I'm composed of water, air and terror. Yet again.

When I was in the Iron Lung at the Marine Sanitarium, the only thing that could quell my fear of death was the gushing of the waves. Poliomyelitis, polio! The affliction was mine to bear, but it dropped on Terranova like a howitzer shell. There'd been a major outbreak, only people hadn't been told. By the time it came knocking, they were shocked to learn that the plague had been there for a long time already, lying in wait. Not only did my limbs lose the ability to move, my entire respiratory system forgot to respire.

The Iron Lung was my salvation.

My body was slotted into a cylindrical chamber, into the machine that spurred it into action, into remembrance. Compressing to let air out, inflating to expand my rib cage and suck the air back in. The only part of me outside this contraption was my head, sealed at the neck. It's strange. You observe the outside world while life, your life, struggles in the darkness. It felt like I was in a submersible, a capsule-shaped vessel made to my measure, where the mirror, placed high enough that I could see without moving my head, was my periscope. From my pitiful, immobilized position, I was often struck by a sensation that I could see things other people couldn't. The invisible.

I shouldn't have written that notice. I shouldn't have put it in the window with that funerary cliché.

I encountered many similar signs on my way to the Lighthouse. The Socrates News Kiosk: *Closing Sale*. Boreal Lamps: *Storewide Clearance*. Ambrosia Sweets: *Everything Must Go*. Even Ovid's Bar, its sign already gone, my eyes protesting as I pass it by. La Donna Moderna Lingerie: *Total Liquidation*. That one stopped me in my tracks. People say that when booksellers go out walking, they only look at bookstores. But not me. I've always spent more time looking at hardware stores, corner stores, toy stores and lingerie stores, especially the ones with mannequins. There it is, my Silk Road. Coquette, The Three Bs, The Glory of Stockings, Chrysalis. And, of course, Dandy Hats. Would you like to try on a hat, Mr. Fontana? I need something Al Capone style, Mr. Piñón. Why of course, we make them just like in Chicago! But today, in front of the window of La Donna Moderna, the mannequins are naked behind the *Total Liquidation* sign. A pause for my unease. And to catch my breath. My memory is an extension of that former respiratory apparatus. In these moments, the distance between the old man I am and the boy I was shrinks to almost nothing. I finally find support on the gallows tree. In the park where they hung A Coruña's hero, the liberal general Porlier—just the end you'd expect for a city's most beloved citizen: death by hanging. And in order to warm his feet and make sure he was comfortable, they burned all his papers, memoirs, manifestos, and even love letters under his swinging body. This tree gives me life. That's why it didn't bother me, that's why it actually brought me joy, the day I heard that vicious whisper at my back: Look how well the fucker limps!

I feel responsible for all these closings. For having written my sign. A rebellion of the eyes. For having stuck my damn paw into the intimacy of words. I should stay open day and night, should hang up ship lights. It's been a long time since I saw young people stealing books. The thrill in their bodies, in their gaze. I have to get back and open the bookstore right away. Someone might be hoping to steal a book. They'll be so crushed. So disappointed.

It's them. The clandestine couple. My company at the edge of the earth.

The three of us are unmistakable. He: the warrior with his long rod, prying barnacles off the rock they call Seagull's Landing. Each time he bends over, he looks like a cephalopod. Taller and taller as he stands upright, he spans yards, like a vertical extension of the horizon. He keeps netted bags around his waist to store his plunder. The moment one bag is full, he tosses it to her, to the tiny woman. Normally they're connected by a rope. That's how I'm used to seeing them, an outlandish amphibian with two bodies. As for me, the crippled catcher on the Horizon Line, what am I to them?

I know the answer: someone witnessing something he shouldn't, from a place he shouldn't be.

An old, fallen angel on crutches. A liquidation.

The reason they're by themselves on the rocks, why no other fishermen are there to get in their way, is the weather. A deluge is coming. You wouldn't think it now. The sea looks agitated, but more fragile and bitter than powerful and angry. Spitting and regurgitating foam, quivering and cracked all over, it looks as if it's about to break open.

The predictions are much more precise nowadays. Soon, I'm guessing in two and a half hours, a crowd of people armed with recording devices will flock to the Orzán Esplanade for its wide-ranging view. There's an explosive cyclogenesis brewing. In other words, a deluge, maybe even an inundation. But both of those terms have fallen into disuse, like ancient fears.

I have no doubt, though, that what's coming for Terranova is an inundation. That's the word I use when anyone asks. It wasn't easy for me to admit that tragic fact. It felt like too exceptional a word; I was almost ashamed to use it. But when I say it out loud, I realize that the only one who trembles at the sound of it is me, or rather, me and Terranova itself. What happens, happens in the present, but when I talk about what's going on with us, about my diagnosis, I can tell that they hear me as a mere whisper from the past.

I see my uncle Eliseo brandishing one of his hundred umbrellas on the Horizon Line. He must be worried I'll throw myself off. Hey, my boy, don't tear yourself down! I'm too old to commit suicide, Uncle. He always calls me that, *my boy*, and it must be because I'm on my crutches again. Ever since the assault against Terranova began, I've felt I needed them. The doctor says it's post-polio syndrome. What it is, doctor, is an inundation. Hey Fontana, why don't you buy one of those motorized wheelchairs, asked Old Nick of all people, the very landlord who's in the process of evicting me. I gave a Neo-Grecian reply, a response worthy of Polytropos's son: Because I want people to gawp at the bulging muscles of an old man after he casts off his rags.

Are they new? Uncle Eliseo asks me from the Horizon Line.

They're Canadian, Uncle. And jointed. Canadian crutches!

Excellent! Then don't lose heart, my boy. What was it Will said in *The Tempest*?

That what's past is prologue, Uncle.

And he leaves, comforted, convinced that, should the need

arise, a safety net woven from poetic threads will be there to break humanity's fall.

Poor Will. Poor Eliseo.

All the news outlets are talking about an explosive cyclogenesis, an iron sea with waves over thirty feet tall. If it doesn't happen, if the sea doesn't live up to that expectation, the people with their phones and cameras at the ready will be furious: What a rip-off! Nature is a joke! It's been almost a hundred years since the Futurists declared that Electricity had shorn nature of all its majesty. Nowadays, the grandchildren of Filippo Tommaso Marinetti mash the buttons on their PlayStation's war games. *La guerra è bella!* War is beautiful! If I'd written a song like that, maybe The Urchins would have found success.

Epopopoi popoi! shouted Potentially Dangerous Nacho, the head of a gang that runs around Hercules Tower, as he walked his Potentially Dangerous Dog.

Popoi popoi!

I changed directions but responded. Just this once, I responded. He's probably one of the only people in this city who remembers I was the lyricist for The Urchins, a band that carved out a place for itself in the metal scene until people realized that we weren't metal, that the song "Cross to the Jaw" was only a metaphor. It was my fault: me and my goddamned need to appear cultured. I laid it right out, in an interview, I said that "Cross to the Jaw" was just a metaphor. Wait, what? It's a metaphor? At our next show, someone hurled a metaphor so potent it put a gash in the singer's head. That's how our mythical status tanked, spilling down the proverbial drain. Now I only write songs as I walk, using my crutches to provide a rhythm and interweaving the inspirations I've picked up at random and stored in my hospice, like the mad poet Jacobo Fijman:

This poor hospice of my life
housing nothing but chance!

They're still at it with the barnacles. As always, he moves with amphibian ease. When he bends over and attacks the rock with his scraper, he looks like a sea creature that has surfaced to do battle with the land. He scrapes off a row of barnacles and slips them in the sack at his waist. Wearing his dark neoprene suit, sequestered, his arms moving frenetically, he looks like a massive gannet. Every time he stands up, he appears immensely, impossibly tall, only to quickly retract into his tough, lean, flexible body. But there's nothing anchoring him to the land. If it had eyes, even the sea would notice the anomaly. And it does.

I picture The Wave. Not a wave, The Wave. The Glutton. The sinuous movements of a force on the prowl, self-aware, camouflaged among the waters. I can hear the ultrasound of its growl, the primed position of this hydraulic engine under the placid surface of the water.

I watch it happen. The woman moves back, but only an inch, paralyzed by shock when she notices how, after diving into the massive, unexpected wave like a gladiator with his scraper, he's not where he was. He's missing. There's no man. Nothing but the foam left by the wave.

I make a phone call. One of those three-digit numbers. My clumsy fingers. You don't have booksellers' fingers, you have the fingers of a dockworker. Maybe, but you don't know what it's like to move books around in the Sanctum Regnum. All the protein, fat, and carbohydrates you have to expend. But memory has its tricks. The number for the police comes to me, 092. I'm so agitated that there's no need for theatrics, but I say that two people have disappeared, a man and a woman.

Here it comes. The Rescue Helicopter.

She's at the edge, the foam lapping at her feet, shouting with her hands cupped around her mouth. The wind and noise from the blades slap away the words and names, interrupting their trajectories mid-flight, and all I hear are cries, squeals, disjointed screams.

Appearing to have disappeared, devoured by The Glutton, he

shoots out and scrabbles up the rocks; his feet are hands and his hands are claws. He reaches her. Places his hands on her spherical belly. The world should stop for an instant, I think to myself. The churning birds in the air. The Helicopter. The police siren. There should be times in this life where we have the chance for a freeze frame.

They take off running along the sea of grass, its green flattened by the buffeting winds of the spinning blades. They grab each other's hands, let go, grab each other's hands again. They fall, get up. They rush across the alder fields leading to Lapas Beach.

They disappear.

And not just from my line of sight. I can tell from the confused, uncertain trajectory of the Rescue Helicopter that they've disappeared for everyone. The rescuers seem to be taking one last look before they go back to the base, and a few moments later, they flit by with the scrutinizing frustration of a dragonfly now that their mission—whatever it was—has been thwarted.

The sea was getting ready to claim them, but in the end, it was the earth that swallowed them up.

The first policeman to get out of his car could tell I was agitated and tried to calm me down.

Don't worry about them. They're like jellyfish. Transparent. But any day now they're going to be in for a nasty surprise, and not in the water—on land. They don't have papers, and there's some hotheaded guys with licenses who'd love to knock the teeth out of their smiles.

The sergeant came up and greeted me, and not rudely either. Ah, so you're Mr. Fontana, the Terranova bookman!

He, at least, hadn't read the *Total Liquidation* sign.

He wouldn't stop looking at me, a glimmer of curiosity in his eyes: The disappearance of the Monelos River, I'll never forget that essay.

It was a formal complaint.

I know, I still have a copy. I have a copy of all the complaints you've filed. The disappearance of Parrote Beach, the expulsion of starlings from the city sky, the eviction of fishermen's boats from the Marina as a way to make room for aluminum yachts, the neglect of *art-nouveau* buildings, the decrepit state of the old prison... You're right, Mr. Fontana, that prison could be a cultural space. Yes sir, they're like historical artifacts. Your complaints, I mean. An alternative history to this city. To think how much I've learned from them! It brings a smile to my face every time you file a complaint.

I'm glad you've enjoyed reading them, Sergeant, but you should do your due diligence.

Of course, the cases are open, he said, gesturing at some point on high.

Speaking of due diligence, said the corporal, you're going to have to pay for this.

He appeared to be the most veteran among them, his hair white and his tone commanding, not just towards me, but to everyone in the vicinity, including his superior.

Pay for what? I asked.

What do you mean, what? This rescue operation. Do you know how expensive it is to get a helicopter off the ground?

Sure, but it was an emergency. They were drowning. Two people, and one of them was pregnant.

You can write that novel for the government delegation when they send you the bill.

They were in danger! I insisted, looking at the sergeant.

I know, Mr Fontana. You did your citizenly duty, but it's just one of those cases where the regulations have two faces, one human and the other...not so much.

Well, I called the human side!

Don't beat yourself up about it, said the sergeant.

The corporal took down the license plate number on the motorcycle left behind by the clandestine couple. It was an old model, mud-caked and run down. He gazed out at the rocks once he'd finished. The sea was looking choppier. The inundation was on its way.

Now that the sergeant is gone, he said, I have to admit, I like your complaints too. And I'm sorry about the starlings. I didn't sign up to be a human cannon and scare them all off with gunfire. But I do have to disagree with you about the disappeared river. It was just a stream. A shitty little stream.

Corot, Corot, I said nervously. Corot painted streams like that, and they're works of art.

He clicked his tongue and said:

He must not have had anything better to paint.

I started to walk, but I couldn't dispel my unease. The memory weighed heavily on my crutches. Every so often, I used to go down to an underground parking lot where, in a corner, you could still hear the hoarse warbling of the capped water-flow through a wall.

I turned to the corporal. Canadian crutch outstretched, I gave him a piece of my mind:

What do you know, policeman? You've clearly never heard the sound of a disappeared river!

Viana and Crash

It's going to be a quick operation.

They stop the motorcycle in front of the restaurant-bar. He stays on. Map in hand, motor running. An old, rasping, rickety machine that looks like it's kept going out of spiteful self-love. He looks around, the swiveling inspection probably necessitated by his helmet, a great black helm with an illustration of a lightning bolt on the side and a transparent visor in front; a magnificent cosmonaut head on an amphibious body, because the rest of him is still covered in neoprene, the same as it was when he leapt over the Horizon Line: a mythical presence, a clandestine warrior, a body announcing to the world that *The food I bring home depends on my spear*; such a contrast to the dilapidated motorcycle and the incessant grumbling of its consumptive, ill-humored engine. Someone appears in the door to the restaurant: the owner. I recognize him, he's the only one who dresses as a waiter, and he looks both ways down the street and runs his hand over his face, then returns inside. The motorcycle driver gestures in approval, and she, his backseat rider, dismounts, agile but with a plodding grace. Staggeringly pregnant. A few minutes ago, she was running along the grass like a gazelle, ahead of the man, even. But now the bulge is in her body. It's a giant's pregnancy in a diminutive, delicate frame. Her helmet is more comical than his: metal with rags over the ears and the buckles undone. She wears a loose dress and walks like someone who's just lost her slippers. The backpack on her is far from small, and she hunches over from the weight. As expected, she heads towards the door of Restaurante Gambernia, then suddenly turns around, lights a cigarette, and blows out a volcanic cloud of smoke. Wait, look, she's walking towards me, there's no denying it, but she's resolute, all she does is stare, hardening her gaze as she plants herself in front of me, her eyes like embers, the smoke might not even be from the cigarette, it was already lit, but it makes no difference, because then she says:

We had to fork over all our cash to get the Ducati back.

Then, not waiting a second more, she lets loose what she came here to say:

And it was all your fault, asshole!

It took me a moment to get going; stammering can be my most fluent language. She already had her backpack halfway open, shoving it in front of my face so I could smell the visceral, animal stench of the sea.

We lost the barnacles too. And it was your fault! You should open a jinx store instead. You're one of those guys who has to jump out into the emptiness to feel full.

I was struck by the image. Empty fullness, full emptiness. Her voice was harsh, a bit gravelly, but not unpleasant. I felt the lash of guilt in my leg and grabbed my crutches. Words can cause such pain. It hadn't been in my body, that jinx, until she'd come along and slathered it on me like grime. I never thought I'd be a magnet for bad luck. Damn it all to hell. I was the one who'd come out on the wrong side of things after what happened at the Lighthouse! Another box ticked on my résumé as an expendable. I'd take revenge by showing her the art of falling. I'd tell her the saddest story, sadder even than Pedro Oom's tale of the little bunny, the orphan bunny that thought its mother was a beautiful collard green, the bunny that, when famine set in after the plague of locusts, started to nibble and nibble away at its beloved vegetable mother. There I'd been, stuck in the Iron Lung, when my uncle Eliseo, Pedro Oom's abject comrade, made me cry. Or rather, not just me, but the other polio-argonauts: the three hunchbacked girls, the nurses, the entire ward of the Sanitarium. It was amazing how believably Eliseo had played all those roles. Even the mother collard! She said to the little bunny: You lived in my breast for a time, and now it's time for me to live in you.

I was going to make the clandestine girl cry with my abject tale until she'd shed the last tear in the history of weeping.

But I didn't say anything. I didn't tell her that story. The word of the dead. I'd sooner gnaw out my own gums than cause someone that kind of grief. People say that books can't change the world. I disagree. Just look at me, they've given me quite the beating. But I'd still forgive anything for a stack of them. I wonder how many must have traveled in the trunks of the emigrants in *Vidas secas,* Barren Lives, the novel by the Brazilian writer Graciliano Ramos, about a starving family in the backcountry that has to eat their own parrot because it's all they have. They eat the bird because it can't talk; or at least that's what they tell themselves in order to stomach its meat. And why can't the parrot talk? Because neither the parents nor children ever speak. Though it may not have spoken, the parrot did reproduce sounds: it imitated their dog Baleia. And why don't they eat Baleia? Because, besides being skin and bones, she has a name. You don't eat an animal with a name.

If I had to emigrate, one of the books I'd put in my trunk would be Julius Fucik's *Reportáž psaná na oprátce,* Notes from the

Gallows. Now that one really did change my life, and even my gait: Let sadness never be linked with your name.

Damn it, why did I write that sign? *Total Liquidation at Terranova.* Here I am, the king of sadness. My ass settling right onto the needle in the haystack.

That's how I've felt for some time now, ever since the ultimatum. An evicted Ecce Homo, with nothing to his name but his crutches. And now this. A clandestine, pregnant girl with fiery eyes, the girl I wanted to help, staring daggers at me and gutting me with her knife-sharp words.

I looked up at the sky. All Saint's Day. The day when people flock to the cemeteries. And my favorite day, because it marks the return of the starlings. I can remember my father Amaro on the terrace: Here they come, all the way from Stonehenge! His rapt smile. The infinite flock drawing a protective fiction in the sky. Do you know what they're doing? It might seem unfathomable to us, but they're forming the image of a giant, monstrous bird to scare off predators. They've been putting on that play at sunset for millennia. All the many starling compositions in the sky over the bay. During their migrations, we'd close Terranova early just to attend the performance. Us, and anyone else interested. Look over there! Four hundred starlings are about to create an eagle like a Ben-Day dot illustration in the comic-strip sky. Bravo, bravissimo! But there's nothing to see at today's sunset. Where's the Star Man?

There's a star man, waiting in the sky, lulla, lulla, lullaby! A veiled sky, that's what it is, with a procession of stormy clouds in its wake. It's incredible how nature manages to heed the saintly calendar with all its nebulous iconography.

She brought me back to the world, snapping her fingers in my face.

What did you find in the sky? You were humming!

She was smiling.

We lost the barnacles, but after we escaped, we went back for this. I know you like them. You're an Urchin.

What does she know? How does she know? No, there's no way she could know that I wrote the lyrics for The Urchins. She probably hadn't even been born yet. But they always send my heart racing, sea urchins. Eliseo said he'd once seen the most joyous interjection, a textual delight, watching a boy hang a sign in a Paris shop window: *Les oursins sont arrivés!* The urchins are here! The feeling of being able to read Mr. Proust with a certain stalking irony, like an urchin with its spines, its Aristotle's lantern nibbling into the center of the stunned madeleine.

I inhaled memory. A handful of sea for my deep memory. There was a time when you dreamt of breathing, remember? That could be a good sign for Terranova: *The urchins are here!*

I don't have any money, I said. I live like the King: not a dime on me.

She laughed. Wow, I thought to myself, night and day. So her rage was all just an act.

The truth is, you give us good luck. Every time, too! Whenever I look up from the rocks and the foam and see you there on the cliff, with your crutches, I feel safe. There's our limping angel.

I'm more of the old Poseidon, or Lear, however you like, the crazy cripple who pacifies the sea. I tried to call for the Rescue Helicopter, but as always, I was clumsy with this junk phone. I dialed at random. 092. And, at random, I got the police. I always hit the mark with my random tries. I thought you were in danger, that you were going to drown.

Yes, she was quick. In movement, in speech, in blinks. Her very skin gave off an animated air with its layers of tattoos. The colors of her various ages. Letters, anagrams, tribal images disappearing into climbing vines. I even noticed some ancient cave paintings like the Rolling Stones tongue and the Los Suaves cat. And a winged horse. Not a Pegasus, something more childlike, maybe an abraxan from the Harry Potter series. We sold lots of those books. It was back during the housing bubble: the bestsellers came in on pallets. I remember it clearly because it was the last time that tides of kids flowed into Terranova. There were so many that Lezama, Antigone, and Captain Nemo, the nocturnal store cats, which the kids saw as cult figures, were forced to stay awake during the day, and our dog, Baleia, even stopped gnawing on her *saudade*, perfectly happy to drop that bone for a moment. The animals in Terranova are the bearers of absences. And where animals are happy, so too are people.

But people don't deserve that sign. Ever since the recession and the lure of the big malls, the palefaces may have disappeared, but the redskins will always be around. Then there's the wilderness. The unexpected vine that started growing in a crack on one of the walls, two floors up, and climbed until it reached the attic window. It was easy enough for it to lie in wait for the right moment, with that prehensile passion vines have, and I'm sure it helped that the attic window was broken. It'd been that way for years. When the glass installer came to fix it, Eliseo stopped him. It was no accident that it was broken; there was some expressive intentionality to the fact. Whether you saw it or not, it was a sign. A minor work of the avant-garde. A tribute to "The Broken Window," a story by Emilia Pardo Bazán, about emigrating to the Americas. It was the best story of its kind. The three of them, Amaro, Comba, and Eliseo, all agreed on that much. Bazán had fashioned an epic out of the mundane image of a broken attic window, at the same time as she portrayed the singular enigma of the human animal: the emigrant who returns to his homeland with untold riches and an obsessive longing to sleep where he once slept, beside the broken window, meanwhile the cold seeps into his dreams and the wind howls in his head.

After the vines, which I tried to guide with a trellis, came the robins. First was the female, who built the nest. I'm impatiently awaiting the starlings. If not a whole flock, a half dozen would do. I should make some holes and alcoves in the spheres left over from Terranova's early days. There's a flock of bats in the Penumbra, protecting the most vulnerable books from woodworms. Eliseo always said they were from the School of Bats at the Johannine Library in Coimbra.

My most recent discovery was a toad, right in the corner with withered constellations of globes, noisemakers, windmills, an occasional broken toy and some damaged nativity figurines, among them mutilated shepherds, women who'd lost their pitchers and animals displaying the stupor of the abandoned. Curros Enríquez? I thought that might be a good name for the toad. Neruda? No, I know! Francis Jammes, the great hermit. My father had so much respect for him. He once told me: This was the man who wrote a manifesto, "Le Jammisme," rejecting proselytism. We have one of his books in the Pinhole Chamber, *De l'Angélus de l'aube à l'Angélus du soir*, From the Morning Prayer to the Evening Prayer, in its 1920 Spanish translation by Díaz-Canedo... Right beside *Barco sin luces,* A Lightless Ship, by Luís Pimentel. I'd put both of them in my luggage, in my emigrant's trunk. Are you Pimentel? No, I'm Teixeira. Teixeira de Pascoaes. Oh, Teixeira, how my uncle loved him. Pure adoration. He was constantly talking about going to Amarante and climbing the Serra do Marão. He told me how one day, when he was at Café Gelo in Lisbon, among the surrealists, Mário Cesariny had said: Pascoaes is the great poet, I have nothing against Pessoa, but to me, Pascoaes is the old man on the mountain, the magical figure. And there was a farmer who spoke the highest praise one can speak of a writer: Who's that man with fire spouting out of his head?

I'm lucky to have such a toad in my home. A toad that lives a hundred years. To hell with Total Liquidation! I'm going to go find a copy of *Saudade*, there must be one in the Penumbra. We'll drink a few drops of *saudade*, our terrible longing, with *A velha lembrança gerando novo desejo*. Old memories awakening new desires. That's what my sign should say. I'll send it to Helena at Ferman Printers, and she can print it on the old Minerva machine, in Ancient Roman type, with a futurist asymmetry on the blades of the baseboard. Signed Teixeira de Pascoaes, in jagged Sex Pistol-style lettering.

But getting back to the winged horse, I've read that series. I like to read bestsellers, or sometimes I like to. It depends. I guess what I mean is, I like to know what I'm selling. Whether it's wheat or chaff. Cecilio, the journalist, another someone who hasn't come by Terranova for a while, used to tell me he'd started trying to separate the wheat from the chaff. He only wanted to publish the wheat. He was coming to pick up a special order, *Die letzten Tage der Menschheit,* The Last Days of Mankind, by Karl Krauss. He called me the next day. It was a joke, a reminder of the fateful call that had tormented my father his whole life: You're living on borrowed time, Fontana!

But this time he was out of ammunition, troubled, downcast. Listen to Krauss: Take one step forward and keep quiet.

Don't turn off the light, Cecilio. To hell with the electric company.

This time, the phone truly smelt burnt.

Goddamn journalism! It's a worse poison than cocaine. Cynics can't do it right, humph. I guess Kapuściński was a failure! All he wanted was to do a satire and the entire fucking office took it seriously. The most beautiful profession in the world. Another clown, that García Márquez! He'd look great as provocative graffiti at the School of Journalism. You know the first thing a journalist has to learn nowadays? How to get his head up nice and far up his ass. And be a champion of cynicism.

Write all that, Cecilio, and I'll read it tomorrow!

Oh, get fucked by a swordfish. And he hung up.

It really has been a long time since I've heard from him.

She's still there, what luck. Dark hair, light eyes. I think one is a bit lazy.

Are you okay? She asks.

Yes. My mind wanders sometimes.

You need to get that checked out. Your head's probably out of whack.

My head is perfectly fine, I say with too much conviction. I just get distracted. Do you remember when there were flocks of starlings in the sky?

She looked up. Couldn't locate the memory. Shrugged.

No. Yeah. Maybe.

If you'd seen them, you'd never be able to forget it, I can promise you that.

I take care of cats by the Dock. I bring them food. They say they're going to wipe them all out.

I directed my attention to her black cat tattoo.

Do you like it?

Yes. But I'm not so sure about the winged horse. I prefer my horses wingless.

The wings are to cover up a name I had tattooed there, she said in a bitter whisper. Like it was secret.

Listen, I told her, the two of you need to be very careful. The sea is dangerous even when it's asleep. Brave souls are its favorite food.

She came a bit closer, as if she was sniffing, sussing something out. She didn't touch me. It felt as if the whiskers of the tattooed cat were brushing against me.

We're always in danger, she whispered in my ear. And then, in a louder, more playful tone: Sea or no sea, we're always in danger. We should have a Rescue Helicopter hovering above our heads all day long.

The guy, getting impatient, shouted from the motorcycle.

Leave the old man alone, Viana!

She flapped her hand at him, as if to say you-stay-there-and-shut-your-trap.

She said:

He's not built to die.

Who?

Him, Crash. My boyfriend.

I felt a pain trying to claw its way up over the wall of my Deep Memory. I knew that phrase. I'd heard that diagnosis before.

How do you know he's immortal? I asked.

I don't know about immortal, but that's what the doctor said: He's not built to die.

It's too bad I didn't go to that doctor, I said. Which doctor is it, if you don't mind me asking?

The prison doctor. The kind who looks at your head. Crash was in prison a while back. We made this little thing during a visit.

She brought her hand to her belly and tapped on it with her fingers, like someone stirring a hidden companion awake.

And it's a good thing for us he's not built for it, she said calmly. He has to go off to battle soon!

To battle?

Now, yes. Now she hurries. Starts to run. Goes into Gambernia. Disappears into a darkness punctuated by the gleam of a television. The warrior on the Ducati remains upright, impassive. At the ready. Lightning on his helm.

I'll have to go to battle soon, too.

Now I Go Hide as Before

(MADRID, FALL 1975)

Today, it's the safest place in Madrid.

We'd fallen asleep, still dressed, on the worn green carpet, so resistant in its decrepitude that it looked like a floor of tundra, complete with clumps of grass, moss and lichen. The room was like an abandoned theater set where the only thing that remained, as a kind of veil against the outside world, was a set of thick, heavy black curtains that refused to open, seeming to stay up purely out of hatred for the light. Only in the mornings, on the floor by the windows, did the curtains allow the smallest pittance of sunlight to creep in.

We were in an apartment on Calle de Manuel Silvela, in Madrid. It was daybreak on November 22nd, 1975.

I got up, took a few hasty, pattering steps in search of my body, and headed to the bathroom. Once inside, I immediately popped an Upper. And another. I didn't want her to see me with amphetamines. Not Uppers, not Speed, not Dexadrine, nothing. I was going to subsist on air, water and light. I was going to be a bird and a fish. I was going to be an amphibian. But today, I needed an Upper. And another. And a hit or two of Speed.

She and a friend were in the bathroom here yesterday developing photos. They'd left out the cameras, enlargers, trays, and red-paper-wrapped bulb. An Argentinian journalist, she told me, who had to finish his assignment urgently and couldn't do it where he was staying, a guesthouse on Calle del Pez. I'd agreed, why wouldn't I? My roommates, all students, had already left Madrid. I myself was going to get out of town the very next day on the Atlantic Express. At least, that was the plan.

I'd wanted to leave beforehand, like everyone else. To get away without begging bread for the road. If I hadn't, and this is the truth, it's because she appeared. She had appeared, then disappeared. And now here she was again.

Franco's funeral was tomorrow.

I should have made something for breakfast, but it had been ages since I'd set foot in the kitchen. It was the most ill-humored part of the house, its wide cupboards and cabinets occupied by a resentful emptiness that made you feel as guilty as if you were hunger incarnate. The main bathroom evoked the *saudade* of a wealthy spa, only for that luxurious feeling to dart away, pale and naked, the moment you turned on the faucets and heard the asthmatic groaning of their ancient pipes. Otherwise, the once stately apartment seemed perfectly ready for a second, bohemian life. The missing furniture and paintings had left marks of barrenness, geometrically perfect discolorations that had been there for so long it seemed as if they'd been put there on purpose, an aesthetic that matched the posters and the crude art of the bed frames and shelves we brought in with us. We'd found the place through a contact of Manuel de Inés, one of our roommates. The rest of the building was still inhabited by families with long lineages. We didn't cross paths, didn't see each other. There was a set of stairs on the second floor that led to a service exit, which we generally took instead of the elevator. We were children of the night, of another planet. To put it in the words of David Bowie, The White Duke, my other self, our home was Gnomar, the land of the Gnomes.

But it wasn't the safest place in Madrid, said Estela. Because back then, Garúa was Estela. And when she first appeared in my life (my life!), her name was Beatriz. The friend who'd come to develop photos had called her Mika. No, it was Tana. And when he'd said goodbye, it was: "Ciao, China Doll!"

I was at Café Commercial as the White Duke, reading *The Catcher in the Rye* by Salinger, a contraband edition from Terranova, the first Spanish translation, titled *El Cazador Oculto*, The Hidden Hunter. I had one eye on the words and another trained on the folks who were coming into the light of the café as dusk fell. Garúa was making her way towards the second floor, already a few steps up, when she whirled around and approached me. She didn't fall into the arms of the White Duke or admire the green lock of hair on his head or the lipstick on his lips or the makeup around his eyes. She simply stared at my book. That manner of looking. Squinted eyes squinting harder upon further scrutiny, not believing what they're seeing, the cover absorbing her full attention, because it had an eye with an iris like a bullseye. This is from Libros del Mirasol! Let me see that, she said, as she tore it from my hands. I knew it—printed by the Compañía General Fabril Editorial in Buenos Aires! Are you...? No, I'm not Argentinian. And I've never been, I found it in a bookstore. I could have called it *my* bookstore, Terranova. But no, the White Duke liked to retain a certain air of mystery.

My father worked at Fabril Editorial, she said. He was a typographer. The way he ran his fingers over the letters made me feel like they belonged to him. I'm serious: I didn't just think that, I really felt it. Libros del Mirasol! They published Calvino, Brecht, Miller, Dylan Thomas, Alberti, Pasolini, the two Marguerites, Duras and Yourcenar...and the covers by Cotta—true works of art.

You can hang onto it if you like.

Her attention finally shifted to the White Duke. To my cover. My face.

She was excited, but also perplexed. Before she could say anything, I casually added: I have lots of these, lots of Libros del Mirasol.

Hang on, who are you?

A smuggler.

Garúa stopped by the apartment. She ran her hand down the spines of the Libros del Mirasol. You have the Los Poetas collection too! That's right, the one Pellegrini produced back in 1961, the best of the century, I said with a smuggler's inflection. She read Georg Trakl's poems and stood up, her eyes marked by them the way a transfusion of the abyss will tend to do. Without a word, she went to the living room, splayed herself out on the floor, and started rolling around on the tundra. Slowly at first, then frenetically, until she hit the wall. I waited in my room, unable to uproot myself. I heard her sobbing. Sometime later, she came in with a smile, a pained one, but a smile nonetheless.

I think I'd like to put on some music, she said.

She started to rifle through the piles of records.

David Bowie, Bowie, Bowie, Alice Cooper, Cooper...Is there anything by you?

For the time being, just a single: Side A: "Tumbadiós," Side B: "Epopoi popoi popoi." A tumbadiós is a drink, a cocktail from hell.

Gotcha.

She played them both. Then put on "Epopoi" again.

I like "Epopoi" better, she said.

Sure, everyone likes "Epopoi" better, I said sarcastically. Popoi popoi!

Aquellare, Invisible, Sui Generis, Spinetta...She flipped through the albums, all while playfully swapping the names for others I didn't know. You should smuggle records too, she said. She'd liked what I'd told her about Terranova and the books in the emigrants' suitcases and trunks. You could start your own label, Amphibia. That's it, she said, Amphibia. "Amphibia" would be a good title for an *amour fou* song, I said. A magical, unsentimental kind of love. Like Dita Parlo in *L'Atalante*, an amphibian kind of love! Garúa shot me a sardonic look, then dove back into her river: And "Balada por un loco"? Have them come with their suitcases full of Goyenche's "Balada"! You're a songwriter, aren't you? Or you want to be. You could stand to learn a lot from Goyenche. And from tango, dangerous tango, with lyrics by Discépolo and Horacio Ferrer. Or how about "Acquaforte" by Marambio? Did you know

Mussolini banned Acquaforte in Italy? He said it was an anarchist's tango. "Es medianoche," "El cabaret despierta…" She gazed inquisitively at Frank Zappa and the Mothers of Invention: one of my prized possessions, *Weasels Ripped My Flesh*, its cover showing a guy shaving his face with a weasel in place of a razor. She put "Stairway to Heaven" on the turntable. She sat down on the bed with the album case, *Led Zeppelin IV*. She stared at its image of a framed painting of a man with a bundle of sticks slung over his shoulder, hung up on a wall with peeling wallpaper. She sang along, she knew the lyrics well.

What about Mercedes Sosa? I'd really love to hear something by "La Negra" Sosa today.

I laughed, and, trying to mask her annoyance, she said: What's so funny?

I don't like folk. I mean, all that folk crap, not folk itself, just all that folk crap.

Now it was her turn to laugh, and she wasn't masking it: *Che*, your stupidity is showing!

I mean, I meant, what I meant is that I don't like the singer-songwriter style, professional protest songs with prologues that sound like sermons, and so on. I realized immediately I was prodding her on purpose. Why was I trying to provoke her? This was one of my more finely developed qualities. Needling a person

I was attracted to. And what I'd just said was the exact kind of nonsense I myself hated hearing. If someone had said something like that to me, I'd have had to repress an urge to shout *Viva Verdi!*

That's what Príncipe Galín himself had shouted at a prohibited concert in Santiago de Compostela. The auditorium was already packed when the government order came down to suspend the concert. It was a form of provocation, and it always resulted in the same sequence of events. The crowd would cry "Down with the Dictator," or its humorous offshoot, "Down with the Diptater!" which rankled the authorities even more. Then the police would charge. Chaos would ensue. Punches, baton blows, and a row of broken, swollen bodies and badges on the ground. But that day, Príncipe Galín stopped the awful cycle for a moment. He was a freethinker who'd lived in exile in Paris and, once he was back in Santiago, had achieved some success in the practice of a historical form of student resistance known as "Productive Leisure," which I myself had engaged in before my miraculous rise to the roof of the cathedral, the act that had led to my expulsion from the City of God. Anyway, Príncipe Galín, with his cantor's qualities—a fifteen-note range!—was getting ready to start his performance when the government delegate announced the suspension of the concert. That's when Galín shouted *Viva Verdi!* into the stone amphitheater, and my, was it a marvel to hear the crowd take up the slaves' chorus from *Nabucco*, to hear "Fly, thoughts, on wings of gold" take flight, to feel that the air itself had a spirit, and that the people, in the most natural way possible, were singing with that same spirit—style and protest merging into one and embodying the very question posed by the song: "Golden harp of the seers of old, why do you hang silent upon the willow?" What I should have said to her? You're right: Viva Verdi!

She continued to rifle, her fingers moving instinctively as she sang something which, I now realize, was one of the sounds of the Horizon Line.

I take out my little music box
whenever I'm down.
Not for anyone's sake,
just because it ends my frown.

She flipped rhythmically through the records. Dylan's first album. She had found something she liked. She flapped it so hard in my face that I could feel a breeze.

Dylan is Dylan. That's not folk!

"Song to Woody." Woody Guthrie! She exclaimed.

Woody played his songs on top of train cars, I declared in a radio announcer's voice. There was a message written on his guitar: This Machine Kills Fascists. He walked a hard road. That's not exactly folk.

Blah, blah, blah.

I'd been caught. I could confess to her that whenever I heard Mercedes Sosa sing the poem, "To My Brother Miguel," by César Vallejo, with the lines, "Now I go hide as before," I'd forget to breathe, I'd feel an urge to get on my knees, I'd be overtaken by a yearning for the Iron Lung. "And I hope that you will not find me." But I'm the type who keeps up the act. What does my machine kill? My Machine Kills Happy Times.

You're a jackass!

I'd never heard the word used so intimately. It circled me, that word, and threw a cross to my jaw. I liked the tone. I liked the accent. I liked the cross. I liked it all.

She put Nico on.

"I'll Be Your Mirror."

She walked out, left the door cracked, and, back in the dark, empty living room, a sliver of light crept in with the music, altering the space such that the threadbare, carpeted floor now evoked a paltry, suburban park, its fields scar-pocked and littered with dry patches.

Still dressed, she lay down in that outdoor realm. The music, too, pushed the light slowly, murkily along. I could see her eyes twitching.

"I'll be your mirror."

I lay down beside her, lacing my hands behind my head as a pillow.

What was it like, the sky she was looking up at?

I knew the song, I'd dissected it. I was a lyricist, in spite of my growing insecurity about my practice, my growing doubts about my talent.

"Let me stand to show that you are blind."

How do mirrors breathe when they sleep?

I went looking for a blanket to drape over the mirror. The temperature had shifted a few days earlier. Madrid was frozen.

We saw each other several days in a row, but always away from Gnomar. At the Filmoteca, for a showing of *L'Atalante*, at an exhibition about Spanish Surrealism at Galería Multitud, eyes bulging at the glow of what had been buried, someone whispering: They made off with our subconsciouses, too! We even worked together for a few days, conducting surveys for a home appliance company. People responded positively to the Crippled White Duke and the Argentinian Girl. We'd have lunch at Casa Domingo, behind the Plaza de España, a dingy eatery in the back rooms of the tallest skyscraper in Madrid. The waiter was a Portuguese boy who spoke like a grandfather and always treated us with a noble cheer, as if we were touring artists. Out of nowhere,

Garúa disappeared, until we ran into each other again at that same eatery in mid-November. She'd cut her hair. She'd gotten thinner, and it seemed to me that her voice had changed, and that the weight missing from her body had entered her words.

Today, the safest place in Madrid is by his casket, she said.

Her friend, Tero, El Negro Tero, as he introduced himself, was coming back to develop more photos. With a colleague and better equipment. Madrid was the center of media attention. He had an important project on his hands. An exclusive. He couldn't say any more.

Not that I wanted to prod any further. I went along. But with one condition.

I'm not going to see the mummy, I said. I read in the papers that there've been lots of heart attacks, and if that's what happens to the *franquistas*, imagine what it'll be like for me.

We're not going to try to get inside, are you out of your mind? We'll be there today for the procession in the streets, like any other couple in mourning. But none of that White Duke stuff. Put on a coat.

I got myself in gear with a hit of Speed. And another.

We agreed not to talk much. We'd keep our eyes and ears open, while making sure not to be uncovered as spies in the funereal bushes, morbid tourists trying to catch a glimpse of the tyrant's corpse. We'd exchange the occasional look of sympathy. It was an act. We put on a show. All the way down Paseo de la Castellana, Cibeles, Alcalá, Sol, Arenal…

It was cold. We huddled closer and closer to each other. Hands, arms, shoulders. Before the procession reached the Palacio Real, we branched off towards the Campo del Moro.

And there, at twilight, to the west, was the Horizon Line.

Cheerily, she said:

I wish I could ride my bike along it.

And I'd ride on the back with my lifts.

Jackass!

That was the first time I located Terranova for her. Do you see it up there, on the Horizon Line, with the red cloud shingles?

When we reached the apartment on Manuel Silvela, the last slivers of light were retreating under the curtains. No one was there. The big exclusive was underway.

We dropped our coats.

She brought her hand to my forehead and kept it there for a few seconds. Suddenly she pushed so hard that I lost my balance and fell over. She got on her knees. Bared her teeth at me. Leapt at me, brought her claws to my face. And I crawled backwards until my back found something to lean up against. I tried to growl, but all that came out was a guttural whimper, a moan. I laughed, but she didn't. She slithered towards me. I mimed her movements. We were two animals, amazing! I whinnied softly. We touched foreheads, retreated. Came back, rubbed our necks against each other's. Bit each other's hair, ears. Leapt over each other. Fled from each another. Looked for each other, sliding along the tundra, chasing the other's scent. Spitting on each other. Licking each other. Panting. Hands on our hearts. Exhausted.

Lying face-up.

Take me to Terranova, please.

It was more than I could bear to hear.

And I was scared.

The Foundation

(GALICIA, SUMMER 1935)

There was a bottle on the center of the table. While their father navigated the future, Eliseo found himself inside the bottle, trying to keep his head above the water. Their father wanted Eliseo to be a man of the sea. But a Nautical man of the sea. This was the way he talked, the Ponte style, a form of personal precision. A Nautical sailor, not a serf with the rope forever around his neck. Among fellow sailors, the saying always went: There are the living, the dead, and then there are sailors.

Eliseo's tale captivated me. That's how I saw him—inside the bottle, his head bobbing above the water. He was always like that. The stories he told were happening. Were going to happen. And it was that day that the dream of Terranova, of the bookstore, was born.

Nautical studies had been eliminated in Galicia during Primo de Rivera's dictatorship. Antón, who preferred to work on Basque ships—less servitude, he said—had pulled some strings to find Eliseo a place to live in Bilbao, which still had a Nautical School. He wanted for Comba to get her studies too. It didn't matter in what, the important thing was that she got them. Eliseo kept his mouth shut. They were eating. He had already gotten his studies. More than any of them. He had challenged himself to read every book and literary magazine that passed through the hands of his teacher and friend Amaro Fontana, Polytropos, which meant that he could never stop reading, because Amaro was, at that time, a secondary school teacher of Greek and Latin and, more importantly, a member of the so-called Star Generation, not to mention being an active collaborator in the Seminary of Galician Studies, a collective of young researchers spanning every field imaginable, like avant-garde encyclopedists. The Seminary was headquartered in the Pazo de Fonseca building at the University of Santiago and functioned as a kind of research network that encompassed the whole of Galicia. Amaro and Eliseo became inseparable. Amaro, the teacher of the pair, directed one of the teams that worked in a "rainbow" style, making developments in the fields of geography, biology, linguistics, musicology, ethnography, and archeology in a single unified space. They would set out to gather knowledge every weekend and holiday. With every free hour they had. Work was their leisure.

What do I have to do to work with you? Eliseo had asked.

How's your eyesight?

Good, the young man had responded, intrigued.

Alright then, the only thing you need to do is to bring an ocular supplement.

Amaro was well known at the University due to his passion for the *Odyssey*. He'd been given the honorific, "He Who Knows Odysseus Best." The title wasn't without its irony because he'd never been one to hide his proficiency. Like Odysseus, he was infatuated with the act of speech. It was more intoxicating to him than wine. Whereas others chose alcohol, storytelling was his poison of choice. And Eliseo imbibed his tales. On the topic of surrealism, which had exploded like a pollen bomb in the air, Amaro Fontana told stories about an avant-garde movement that was founded in Brazil by Oswald de Andrade, who had penned the *Anthropophagic Manifesto*. And he told them that the date which de Andrade signed as the completion of his manuscript was the 374th anniversary of the day the Tupí Indians had made a meal of Bishop Sardinha. In Amaro's telling, the bishop stood at the helm of the first ship clutching a hyssop in his right hand, ready to crack the evangelizing whip at this people and land that has remained concealed from us to this very day. When the Bishop was spotted by the Tupí watchman hidden on shore, the watchman called out: Here comes our food, all happy and hopping up and down!

That's what I feel is missing in your bishop André Breton, Amaro had said to Eliseo. A bit of Tupí humor.

The one who laughed loudest at the story of Bishop Sardinha was Henrique Lira, "Atlas." It was a sunny Sunday afternoon. They had been working at an archeological dig since crack of dawn. Atlas had never attended University, but he was well-known and admired within the Seminary's cultured milieu. As far as Amaro was concerned, his knowledge far surpassed that of an ocular supplement. He was from Chor, where Amaro himself had been born. They were childhood friends, albeit from quite different social backgrounds. Amaro was from the Big House and Atlas from the blue house, a tightly sealed stone structure with its windows and front door painted the indigo hue of rowboats. He was a stonemason, and they all saw his talents for themselves that Sunday: he could move a boulder with no more than a gentle nudge of his fingertips.

It was also Atlas who had found the Thunderstone. The hand axe. The Paleolithic hatchet.

And Comba? Comba said she'd like to be a bookseller. To own a bookstore like La Fe. A bookstore? Wouldn't you prefer a piano? Antón spoke like that, in Certain Point, after his own fashion, but he always knew what he was saying.

What's Certain Point? I asked Eliseo.

It's the place where surrealists go to talk, my boy. In Certain Point de L'espirit. Your grandfather wasn't a surrealist, but he spoke in Certain Point.

And he continued with the events of that summer in 1935.

Antón insisted on the piano because when Comba was little, the piano at one of her schoolmate's houses had left a deep impression on her. And her mother, Nina, had laughed. She was a seamstress. She had a special knack at making costumes for boys and girls during Carnival. The year before, she managed to costume a full half-dozen Harlequins and Colombinas for the Artisan's Circus.

A piano? I'd have to sew costumes for the entire city. And you know the kinds of things people wear here. The men go as show-girls and the women as gigolos. Better if you take singing lessons, darling, vocal cords are free.

But Antón had a logbook in his head where he kept a register of everything. He cast his nets into the sea, figuratively speaking, with the hopes that he would pull up a piano one of those days.

A bookstore?

That afternoon, they went to visit La Fe, on Rúa Fermín

Galán. It was the first time Antón Ponte had ever set foot in a bookstore. And he left wanting to see every single one in the world. He gaped at the façade of La Poesía. Good wood, he murmured, good wood. For him, no architecture could compare to naval architecture. Our store, he said boisterously, should be like a boat. They visited the Lino Pérez bookstore, which doubled as an art exhibition space. Opposite it was Canuto Berea's music shop, the first Music Warehouse in all of Galicia, founded in 1836. It was a vast, ground floor shop with a heavy shadow at the back, but not so heavy as to hide the light emanating from the wood of the stand-up piano, and Terranova's quartermaster made a beeline for it like someone rushing to a long-awaited date. During his weeks at frigid sea, his daughter's infectious dream became his too. The cranes didn't lift any pianos out of the water, but there were moments in their work routine in which the sliding of a finger along an icicle would produce the whisper of a note, a sound that reverberated all the way to Nova Scotia and changed the very coloration of the sea.

Antón gazed at the piano with the secret hope that simply doing so would make it his, but the salesman wedged his way in as if he was afraid of being left out. The piano, as is often the case with the instruments in music shops, seemed more like an esteemed guest than an object for sale.

It's a Collard & Collard, sir. *The best!* he exclaimed in English.

It looks like good wood.

I can tell you without exaggeration: it is impervious to wrong notes.

What kind of wood is it made out of?

In this class of piano, sir, the hammer is higher up than the keys, which provides the player greater confidence.

He leaned on the word *confidence*, which made it seem more significant than it probably was. The salesman wore a three-piece linen suit with a color scheme that called to mind rocks, lichen, and moss. That was the detail that most stuck out to Nina and Eliseo. She, because she loved the texture of fabrics so much that she had to repress an urge to run her hands over his suit. Eliseo, because he'd been envisioning just such a suit for a very long time, though his would be made of Hebridean linen.

He'd even gone so far as to venture into Iglesias Tailors, on Rúa Rego de Auga, to get a quote. The tailor told him that they would have to talk before he could give an answer. They sat down. Resting on the glass table between them was a fabric sampler in the format of a textile book and a copy of the magazine *Alfar*, headquartered in nearby Cantón, which happened to be the magazine where Eliseo first encountered André Breton's writing, an encounter that left him convinced that the Frenchman was a ventriloquist giving voice to his own thoughts, that the words in that magazine were already imprinted in his mind, and as proof, that he could murmur along before he read: I know the desperation in his magnificent verses; in his magnificent verses, desperation is meaningless. Yes, he had to translate himself, to translate the things he carried in his mind, he had to write them down and show up to *Alfar* in person, to burst into the office of the director Julio J. Casal, also the consul to Uruguay, and hand in his magnum opus: This is my book, *A Rosa dos Ventos,* Compass Rose, Mr. Casal. Add me to your list of earthquake navigators. It was already imprinted in his mind; he had only to write it.

The magazine published new writing with a seismic impact, but what particularly called out to Eliseo were the ad pages for transatlantic navigation companies. Royal Holland Lloyd, The Liverpool, Brazil & River Plate, Compagnie de Navigation Sud-Atlantique, Compañía del Pacífico, Norddeutscher Lloyd. All of them with the same tagline: Immediate Departures from the port of A Coruña. Next to *Alfar* was another magazine, one that Eliseo had never heard of, with the kind of cover that can make a person forget their surroundings, the only door they can think of opening in that moment. *Minotaure.* It was a reproduction of a book composed of several layers of different materials: a paper-cut of the mythological bull-man superimposed on lace cuttings and leaves, all overlaid on a piece of ridged cardboard and held together with thumbtacks. He felt an immediate urge to run his hands over it.

It's a history-making edition, *Minotaure*'s first, said Iglesias the tailor. It's from '33, it came out two years ago now. It was the beginning of Picasso's union with the surrealists. And what did Picasso do? He gave new life to mythology. The Minotaur is on the alert, dagger in hand. Iglesias held up the magazine: It's perennially new! Or to quote Tristán Zara, I love an ancient work for its novelty.

The Thunderstone, Eliseo blurted out. The hand axe. It's a perennially avant-garde tool. And he brought his hands together, mimicking its almond symmetry, the wrinkles of his fingers, knuckles, and veins acting as its bezel, the meeting point of his two hands as its blade, his fingernails as its teeth.

Iglesias the tailor looked inquisitively at the archeological wonder that had just sprouted from within the mind of Eliseo's hands.

Come again?

A Paleolithic tool that we found during an excavation for the Seminary. Truthfully, it looks like a stone heart. Something made to bring pleasure, not death.

Mystery is always an aesthetic matter, Iglesias murmured.

Night was falling. The tailor stood up and turned on the lights. Eliseo pulled apart his hands like someone cutting off a trance. The tailor sat down again, looked Eliseo straight in the eyes, and asked:

So, young man, what sort of suit are you looking for?

Antón and Eliseo were meant to go to the port together to greet some of Antón's acquaintances on the Basque ship making a pit stop on its way to Newfoundland, that is, Terranova. Eliseo was coming from a rehearsal. He walked down the harbor pretending to be Charlie Chaplin, practicing. His face was still caked in white makeup, with the exaggerated features of a clown.

Beat it, his father said. I don't want you coming up!

Eliseo explained where he'd come from, how he hadn't had time to change, how Chaplin, in *The Immigrant*, and so on and so forth...the onslaught of the waves, of chance. All in Certain Point.

Fine, but I don't want you to come up. I don't want you on that boat, I mean it.

He was a peaceful man with a harsh lexicon.

Get out of here! I don't want them to see you.

What was going on? Eliseo knew that priests weren't supposed to board ships, but he'd never heard of any such superstitions regarding clowns. It didn't occur to him that the issue may have been contempt, or Antón's not wanting to feel humiliated in front of his friends. His father had a great fondness for music. He respected the arts. And all of them, Nina and Comba included, had gone to see Chaplin at Kiosco Afonso. Antón had laughed as loudly as anyone else in the crowd.

But his father didn't want him to board the boat in costume.

And he said something very uncharacteristic of him. Because Antón saw it as a terrible insult to be called a *bichicoma*, a term which Newfoundland fishermen had taken from the English expression "beach comber." In the eyes of these men, who'd practically grown up at sea, it was the worst kind of disgrace: you were a shirker, you weren't willing to get wet.

That was before Antón set out on what would be his last voyage.

He said: Swear to me you won't make a life in the sea! That you'll never work, Eliseo!

This was a disturbing thing to hear coming from him. He spoke the words through gritted teeth, hard as bone. Eliseo was afraid that what his father was really doing was relegating him to the status of a *bichicoma*. A deadbeat. But what his father was saying, with a palpable disquiet from the depths of his eyes, was something else entirely. It was an order.

Completely stunned, Eliseo replied: I'll become an artist, father!

He followed that with a confused jumble of words, which Antón seemed to think was perfect.

That's exactly what I wanted to hear, he said.

He coughed. It was a cavernous cough. The sound of a man coughing within the deepest reaches of himself. That's what Eliseo remembered about their farewell at the port. How his father had stopped himself from coughing by tensing every single part of himself: his fists, his teeth. By sealing himself away. Phthisis. Tuberculosis. The sailors had requested measures to detect these illnesses and provide treatment. The company's response: What do you think this is, an ocean liner?

He'd done his work and that of others. Extra jobs like slicing and gutting the fish, on top of his position as quartermaster. And they paid him for these side jobs in dollars. Every time they stopped to restock on coal, he'd collect his pay. He put away every penny he could. He had a mission. It couldn't wait. Anytime he coughed, if he tasted blood in his mouth, he'd stick his fingers inside to warm them up. He was quick, and his hand obeyed his eyes. But that lightning hand would freeze up sometimes, and a frozen man was dead weight on a boat. His only choice was to prick himself with a needle. Fingers and toes. To revive himself with his own blood. Then Antón's lightning hand went right back to gutting the fish. Until the blood dropping into the gelid air, mixing with the blood on his hands from the fish innards, had started to come from his chest.

They held his funeral in Newfoundland. It was thanks to those savings, those side-jobs, that Comba was able, years later, to open the bookstore that went by the island's Galician name.

In the center of the portrait gallery on the wall, between

Ernest Hemingway and the Galician sailor-poet Manuel Antonio, hangs the photo of Antón Ponte.

And this one, what did he write? A customer asked one day.

It's the only time I can recall Eliseo being at a loss for words. Inside his bottle, struggling to stay afloat. A solitary Chaplin on the pier, sopping wet in the rain. The gullet of the disappeared river eroding his makeup.

Him? He wrote *The Last Days of Terranova.*

Old Nick

(GALICIA, WINTER 2014)

I'm looking at the sign in the door to Terranova. The despondent handwriting is mine.

Yes, I have to take it down before the people from the funeral home come around. But they're already here. That's not a car, it's a tank. More and more people are being transported in those vehicles nowadays. When you walk down a street with your Canadian crutches, one of these big cars appears and you can feel the heavy machinery of History at your back. You feel the impatience of Saturn, the turning gears of Chronos, and you try to quicken your pace: if only you had a white flag in your hand, or a red cross on your back! And you walk until you reach the safe harbor of a doorway, while the steamroller continues on its path and belches out a message from its exhaust pipe: You're living on borrowed time!

Father and son. Both wearing dark Ray-Bans. Attending the funeral together. A solemn visage. He didn't pick up my calls. And on their last visit, when they informed me they wouldn't be renewing the lease, he'd let his son do the talking. Baleia was the only one who got up to receive them, with a peremptory courtesy. Animals don't like dark lenses.

Mongrels everywhere, as usual!

You mean the books?

Don't joke, Fontana. You're in no position.

It turned out that I wasn't the affected party, the victim, on the verge of being made superfluous, a pariah, an exile, a retiree, a homeless man, an ex-man, a buried man, a banished man, a forgotten man, a man erased, no, the affront was to him, and he stood there fuming with a sulfurous rancor. After so long hiding behind his father's coattails, his time had finally come.

Pick out a book, Nicolás! We've got to keep Terranova afloat. We've got to look out for each other. I'll be picking out something from the Club del Misterio. Any new releases, Mr. Fontana?

And my father ceded the floor to Eliseo, who was bustling in and out of Penumbra with a tentative step.

Kiss and Kill, by Ellery Queen!

Eliseo liked to proclaim the titles of hard-boiled novels, mimicking the musical drone of the *volantes*, the street book salesmen who wore suspenders with a horizontal board attached as a kind of display case. Eliseo himself had been a *volante* for a spell, when Terranova first opened its doors.

Where do you get all these treasures?

They wash in with the tides, Mr. Hadal. Fabril Editora, under Muchnik's care, accomplished more in two years than most publishers do in a hundred. There's one good thing about emigration for you: we're a nation of many suitcases.

Ah, Buenos Aires! He'd have to return one day. Even if only to spend an hour on the corner of Corrientes and Esmeralda.

And Eliseo returned to boast: A street corner in Buenos Aires is a universal place.

Kiss and Kill. The title stuck with me, because Eliseo would employ a version of it on his way out the door, especially when he could see I was in a bad mood and hard at work on my Olympia typewriter: Clack and kill, Vicenzo! Kiss and kill. Clack and kill. I liked Mr. Hadal. I knew he owned the building, I knew he'd come for his payment, and to snoop around while he was at it, a kind of ritual of possession with his son behind him, but he popped in in such a way that it seemed as if his real purpose were to buy one of those hard-boiled Club del Misterio novels. I was a fan of the club, too. *Kiss and Kill*. Clack and kill. Years later, when I dove into my father's secret journals, *Mnemosyne in Hispania*, one of the many blows to my heart came from seeing his unpublished essay, "Miguel de Cervantes and the 'Hard-Boiled Novel.'"

I miss Guillermo, the homeless man who would stop by every so often to sell me some "abandoned" book which he himself had swiped from our new release table the day before. He would read it first, before returning to sell it to me. I'm offering you a real bargain here, Maestro. And then, in a booming voice, he would put a question to me:

Damn, Fontana, why don't you write a bestseller one of these days?

The songwriter in me hadn't died. In fact, it was coming up with lyrics that led me to the hiding hole of poetry. But after the cross to the jaw, I couldn't write lyrics anymore. There was a line, a line separating the accessible from the inaccessible, that had to be crossed. I couldn't cross it; I wasn't brave enough. Maybe if I'd had the Thunderstone in my hand, I would have been. But the Thunderstone had been returned to the earth, where it belonged. I could specialize in stupefying lyrics. Even lyrics with a cursed semblance. Back then, there was still some money to be made in music. I could do it. But I tried once and the words burst in my hands like a firecracker.

My father had a nickname for Mr. Hadal, the building owner.

He always leaves happy, Old Nick!

Why do you call him that? asked Comba.

It's an antiquated name for the Devil. Have you still not realized he's the Devil?

During one visit, a few years after Amaro died, Hadal Sr. said to me: I know your father had a nickname for me. I never let on that I knew, but he wasn't wrong. Aside from being educated, your father was also quite wily: he managed to get along with the Devil himself.

There are plenty of devils out there, I said.

Yes, but he knew the hierarchies of the Sanctum Regnum. Your mother too. You should listen to her.

That was around the time that the conflict arose. My parents had undertaken lots of renovations before they opened Terranova, with Old Nick's approval. They even uncovered treasures that had been concealed out of bad taste, like the art-nouveau tile floor. But time is always in the background wearing things down, and the damp on Rúa Atlantis never quits either. Things began to deteriorate. While Comba was alive, at least as long as she was lucid, there was a rapport, a certain level of respect. But one day Comba climbed up to the attic and never came back down. She didn't lose her memory so much as she picked out a single one, a seasonal memory, the springtime of her life. She would sit beside the broken little window and sew costumes. Costumes for me. Costumes for the cats. Costumes for everyone.

She lived in her youth. In the days when she sewed with her mother in their house on Rúa Sinagoga. Suddenly alarmed, she would say:

Are they behind the wall, are they hidden?

Who, mamá?

Who else? Eliseo and Amaro. They're not supposed to come out until I give the all-clear.

They'd spent a few years as "moles," never leaving the house, or only leaving dressed as women to be sure no men's clothing was ever left lying around waiting to be washed or dried, and on slower days they would make handcrafts like little birch clogs, or shell-encrusted boxes, or basic toys, in the workshop that they expanded when they opened Terranova and its sphere factory. I should go back to making spheres and clogs, ships in bottles, lighthouses. Costumes.

They love each other.

Of course they do, mamá.

They love each other so much, they really do. With them, it's true love.

Her voice threaded like a sewing needle, joining the disparate pieces.

I love them too. That's why I have to look after them. And that's why I'm going to marry Amaro. So that we can all be together forever.

My parents were married in 1947, a year after Comba opened the bookstore. In 1942, a Purging Committee had ordered Amaro Fontana's expulsion from the teaching corps: *Severance from service and a drop in the hierarchy.* Eliseo moved in with them at Terranova, on Rúa Atlantis, 24.

Old Nick was real. I realized that when Hadal Sr. started saying no to everything. No to every proposal for a renovation. He would put off every decision with an apology and never allow me to touch anything. He refused to take any initiative but didn't let anyone else take it either. Old Nick reached his full power, though, in the conjunction of the elder with the younger, with Little Nick, who underwent an astounding mutation from wimpish to arrogant. Not Uppers. Not Speed. Not X. Not Crack. Not even a handful of Dextros combined with a line of Coke could bring about such a shift. I'd quit amphetamines and the rest of that trash a long time ago, when I rediscovered my respiratory system and the sea air rushed into my brain. Looking at Nick Jr., though, I couldn't help but wonder what chemical substance the underworld had concocted this time around, unbeknownst to me. A rhetorical question. There was no new mega-amphetamine. It was a mixture of fast-paced living and greed.

I was looking right at it.

It was him, the Perfect Synthesis, who told me that my time was wearing out.

Time never wears out, Hadal, I said with my eyes to the sky.

Maybe not, but patience sure does, he said.

Whatever grain fell from the horses' troughs was for the sparrows, I said just to say something. Now the horses eat every last bite, even what were once the sparrows' crumbs.

Be realistic, Fontana, said Nick Sr. It brings me no joy to shut down a bookstore like Terranova. But that ship has sailed. It's a new era. Spare us the theatrics. We'd like to avoid all the drama of throwing you out. Why don't you go live in the country? You deserve a calm life. You have a house in Chor, don't you?

Vintage Old Nick. He knew perfectly well what had happened in Chor. He knew that Aunt Adelaida and the Aviator had sold the Big House. He himself may have had a hand in it. He knew, he must have known, that I'd inherited nothing. But I should be grateful! For one thing, there were all the maintenance costs that my aunt and uncle had been saddled with since my grandparents had died, and beforehand, for that matter. The new roof was worth more than the entire estate. Chor would hardly have been more than a pile of rubble had it not been for them, and I shouldn't even get them started on the electricity bills! I asked about the painting, that little landscape painting with a lightning-split oak tree that my father said may have been done by Ovidio Murguía, the Romantic painter, and the Aviator burst into a cackle.

That painting was sold off to pay for Expectación's cataract surgery. Didn't the old witch tell you?

No, the only thing Expectación had told me was that she didn't much like the world after her eye operation.

What about the icons in the chapel? One was very valuable. The Our Lady statuette, the Annunciated Mary.

Another cackle: The pregnant Mary? It was a copy. A bad one, at that—it couldn't have been more than twenty-five years old. Lord knows where the original is! It's probably in the iconography black market, off in Brussels or somewhere like that. Blessing some mobster's house.

Chor no longer existed for me, but I didn't tell Old Nick that. All I said was: I'm going to take down that sign.

What sign?

The liquidation sign.

Perfect Synthesis interjected himself between his father and me. He looked down at me from on high. The mutation had caused him to grow several meters taller.

He dispensed with the formalities: It's over, you old fucker! If you don't want to take the easy road, we'll have no choice but to have you thrown out. And I promise you you'll be better off leaving on your own two feet. You've turned this place into a hovel for animals and…undesirables. Hadal Properties has a new partner. A majority stakeholder. And he's powerful, real powerful. He's what we in the business world like to call a "killer."

He turned to face Old Nick. Let's go, Dad! If the Master were here, he wouldn't be sitting around listening to some geezer talk about horses and sparrows.

The Master?

That night, I heard Baleia whimpering.

Baleia V, I should say. For as long as Terranova has been open, there's always been a Baleia.

My father saw *Barren Lives*, which features the dog Baleia, the mother of all the Baleias, as a Biblical graft. In the same way that *The Plain in Flames*, *Masters of the Dew*, and *The Kingdom of This World* were grafts. He would haphazardly graft these pieces into his Bible. They came from the copies that lived in the intimacy of Penumbra.

Baleia's whimpers were low, but long. She sometimes whimpered like this in her sleep, caught in some historical nightmare, maybe, a nightmare from the universal memory of the Baleias.

She didn't bark. She spoke the language of eyes, ears, and tail, she was pure expression, but it seemed as if she'd renounced the act of barking. This made her whimpers more disconcerting than howls.

At that time, I was sleeping in the loft, in the bed beside the broken window. Every so often a sphere would roll across the floor. Somewhere nearby, in the night, Teixeira the toad hopped around, relocating the stars.

But now Baleia was trying to communicate something on the ground floor of the bookstore. Not loudly, though, it was more like a lament and a call. I became worried. I jammed on my miner's headlamp, the one that guides me through the endless nights, and I grabbed my Canadian crutches and made my way down the steps as I hummed something to soothe Baleia and calm down the rest of the store. Not that anyone else was giving any signs of restlessness. Goa, Sibelius, and Expectación were asleep, or, to put it another way, they were in dreams. They had found, in Terranova, a refuge where their sleepless nights could be recouped.

There was no sign of violence in the shop window or front door. Baleia rubbed against me, moved forward, nodded her head. She was trying to tell me something, to point out a path, and I followed her until she planted herself in front of the door to the Pinhole Chamber.

She panted, and the more she panted the more she whimpered. Scrawny, curly-haired Baleia. Every hair on end. And all around us the cats prowled in disinterest, with the skepticism of nocturnal idols.

I opened the door.

She looked younger. Almost childlike.

Don't call the police, Fontana!

Don't worry, I said. I won't call the police, or the Rescue Helicopter, for that matter.

She was lying on the couch, with her head facing the Lighthouse and the North Star. Eyes, nose, cheeks, mouth. Everything was easier to perceive in the night with my headlamp. It seemed as if her body had shrunken over the course of a few hours, since I'd seen her with her urchin-filled backpack. This tightening of the skin on her face, shoulders, and arms accentuated the spherical shape of her belly. Her hands, resting at her sides, seemed longer and bonier, like wicker stalks.

We have to call an ambulance, I said. You need to go to a hospital!

No, Fontana, please wait!

Where's your boyfriend, Viana?

He had to run away, he's hiding. They're after him.

The police?

No, not the police this time. They want him to be a replacement again.

A replacement?

They want him to go to jail for someone else, you know? That's what a replacement is. It's how we met. In prison. I was a replacement too.

You were in prison?

No. I was a different kind of replacement. I pretended to be a girlfriend. That was part of how they paid you for taking the hit for someone else: a guy named Boca di Fumo, in our case. Crash accepted the charges, the witnesses corroborated it, and he completed the capo's sentence. That was the deal.

But they paid him, right? How much did he get for it?

All he asked for was an electric guitar. He'd wanted a Stratocaster since he was a kid. One like Jimi Hendrix's.

A guitar, eh? An electric guitar and you.

Yeah. They paid me to attend the visits. Once a month. I was getting money like a prostitute, but I liked him from the very first day. He was so sweet to me. Sweeter than anyone's ever been. And I fell for him. It got to where I couldn't wait for the day of the prison visits to come.

You're very brave, I said.

I'm not. I'm afraid all the time.

Of this Boca di Fumo guy?

Well, him too. But I'm afraid of everything. That's why I'm so aggressive sometimes. I'm the one who wanted to have a baby, and now I'm afraid of it being born. Just the thought of being happy sends me into a panic. Every time I've ever been happy, I've woken up and found myself in a *nasa*. Do you know what a *nasa* is? An octopus trap, yeah. And octopuses are supposed to be super intelligent, right? Oh, and you know what? Even beauty terrifies me. Let me tell you a story. One day, we took the bus from A Coruña to Fisterra. It was Crash and me and a friend people call the Bar Hound. As we got closer to the coast, the water and sky looked like they'd been set on fire. It was amazing. We took each other's hands, we kissed. But then things got weird. Someone started crying. It started as a whimper, but built up to full-on sobbing. And it was contagious. Everyone on the bus started to look out the windows in terror. We begged the driver to stop. We were all banging on the windows, until he had no choice. He let us off. Some threw their arms around each other. Others got down on their knees.

That must have been when the *Casón* shipwrecked, I said, that ship with the chemicals on board. It exploded at sea.

No, this was much later, there were no chemicals. It was just the sunset. It was like a natural wonder.

A Man Erased

(GALICIA, FALL 1955)

Amaro had to go to the Big House in Chor to settle some matters with his parents. He took me with him.

We could hear the intermittent cracks of rifle fire.

They're hunting pests.

My father was furious.

That word, *pests*, was how they used to refer to the fugitives, the ones who had fled to the mountainsides around the time of the Civil War. Once they finished off the human pests, they moved onto the literal kind. The ones that had lived in the mountains for time immemorial. There was money in it. Back then, they'd pay you to turn in a fugitive. Now, they'll pay you to hunt wild animals. And not just wolves. Pit-digging as a method of hunting entire packs of wolves was banned in the nineteenth century, following the enlightened reasoning that it was a primitive practice. But it was a hell of a lot more civilized than what came after. Before, the locals would corral a wolf into the pit by making a ring of noise, a fence of intimidation erected by shouting, banging sticks on pots and pans, and waving around flaming torches, if it was nighttime. They'd lead the wolf into the trap. And it would die there. Skewered. A cruel death. The scene hardly distinguishable from the Stone Age, the era of the hand ax. Of the Thunderstone. But now they're after total extermination. They've created organizations for that express purpose: Provincial Committees for Pest Extermination. Philip IV murdered a bull with a harquebus, just for fun. And a bishop once excommunicated rats from the Church. But where, when, had a society been so savage as to decree the total extermination of a wild animal species?

My grandparents listened to Amaro's pleas in silence. Grandma Balbina had rushed to close the doors to the sitting room, but Grandpa Edmundo said: Best leave the doors open, that way no one will try to listen from the other side.

As we left, my grandfather said:

Calm down, son! There are still lots of hiding places. Sometimes ignorance takes the day.

I don't think we were ever so close to one another as that day, with everything that happened afterwards, on our way out of Chor.

We were on the bus. It made a stop at Praza Lar de Lama. The church courtyard was strewn with dead foxes. I looked through the window. It was drizzling. Drops slid down the glass, making the outside world look unreal. We were being shielded by a self-conscious, amniotic rain. Someone outside shouted: Fifty-seven foxes! Nearly everyone got off the bus to get a closer look. My father took my hand. His was cold and clammy. He'd taken mine out of a protective instinct, but also as if pleading for help. I searched for his eyes, but they were full of tears behind his glasses, the eyes of a blind fish.

The driver called back to let us know he was going to get a move on soon, so if we wanted to get a look, we should step off now. There was, he said, a whole heap of dead animals, not just foxes: weasels, martens, and things like owls and magpies too. Even a golden eagle! The eagle of Mount Pindo. She'd had a name. They'd called her Xoana. The driver wasn't going to get off, though. He didn't like the smell of death. He lit a cigarette and took a series of long, thick drags that looked to me like the word bubbles in comics, except that his were filled with silence.

My father said, in a weak voice, more to me than the driver: We're not getting off either, are we? Then he murmured something that rose from some place deeper the back of his throat: *Epopoi popoi.* He squeezed my hand. Fingers covered in dense black hair, fingernails long as claws, tips frozen. I returned the gesture by wrapping my hands around his to warm them up. I felt like my father needed to be protected.

He rarely came to visit me in the Iron Lung. Comba came every day. Eliseo, almost every day. My uncle didn't go on any trips during that time. The only one of us traveling was me, in my *Nautilus*, beached on my seaside ward in the Maritime Sanitarium. Your father sends kisses, Comba would say. But I knew that he wasn't one for such affections. He'd offer up a cheek, but never return the customary kiss. However, when he embraced, the few times that he did—the kinds of embraces particular to Terranova, especially the ones given to the people who came from Abroad—and Abroad must have been boundless, so many folks came from there, because we didn't say Exiles or Emigrants, we said folks from Abroad—those embraces were so deep they left an imprint of themselves suspended in the air, the memory of the connection. And he'd be transfigured; he'd cast off the shell he was curled up in and start to bustle around the moment people arrived with their luggage—emigrants who'd made the trip all the way back from the Americas, the false backs of their suitcases hiding tons and tons of "messages in a bottle": banned books and foreign titles that hadn't been published in Spain. He was always overjoyed to welcome the smugglers who returned from Portugal with Torgas, or "Heaths," wrapped up in blankets the color of canvas: Here comes *A Criação do Mundo*, Mr. Fontana, The Creation of the World! What day is it? *O Terceiro Dia da Criação*! Ah, if we're already at the third day, then all's well!

These "Heaths" were books by Miguel Torga, books that the author had self-published in Coimbra, among them his *Diarios*. They were a harvest that never failed to bear fruit, and for my father they were never tomes or volumes, always "Heaths," because contraband was a sensory experience for Amaro, and he took a tactile pleasure in touching the living beings that had just traversed the Miño River into Galicia. An even more distinct delight, restless and alert, radiated from him when the drivers of refrigerated trucks returned from their Paris routes with a cache of books from the banned anti-Franco publishing house Ruedo Ibérico. This "seafood" was rushed into the freezers of the Hidden Land. But the Ruedo Ibérico era was much later, in 1965. By that time I'd started to amble around Terranova on my first crutches.

The rare days when he came to visit, almost always Sundays, Amaro drooped under the weight of his shell. Eliseo told me abject tales, like the one about the heroic little rabbit that ate his collard-green-mother, or the story of Job—the tragedy of Job, the comedy of Job—putting up with all the misfortune God meted out to him. But there was no comedy in my father. Slotted in my cylinder, with my head peeking out, I could see him in my mirror, and he looked older, smaller, blurrier, and more distant to me, like an observer who takes pride in his dispirit. While Comba made an effort to laugh, to exaggerate the signs of improvement in my traitorous body, he seemed on the point of disappearing, of being erased.

He'd experienced that before. Erasure. He'd gone to give a talk at the Casa da Cultura in the San Carlos Romantic Gardens. He'd been hesitant, but then his providential friend Verdelet from Madrid had undertaken a mediation, so they'd asked him to talk about the beloved Galician poet Rosalía de Castro. With that, he accepted. After the introducer's long speech and ceremonial greeting to all the notable figures present, Amaro expounded on one of his texts as simply as he might have the Prismatic Stone. Audience members were on the edge of their seats as they listened to his lecture, and when he finished, their applause was more than impassioned, it was sorrowful. He'd titled the lecture "'La Straniera' and Rosalía." The government censors had required him to provide a synopsis before the talk, and he stuck rigidly to the script. But, from what I've heard, reading it to oneself was an entirely different experience than hearing him read it aloud.

Rosalía de Castro had been sixteen when a potato blight led to the famine of 1853. The landowners had hoarded their grain reserves while thousands of famished rural families clawed on the impassive wooden doors of Santiago de Compostela, begging for crumbs. During this crisis, the Church and the Powers-that-Be chose to look away, but the young woman's gaze was so intent she could see even the invisible. She heard a melodious cry outside the door to her home. It was a boy from the street, who'd nothing more to his name than his hair, his bones and a song that shook the very stones in this ancestral, mossy city. Rosalía took him into her home, clothed and fed him and sat him by the fireplace. She asked him to sing one of his *coplas,* his folk songs. Afterwards, she sang a barcarolle, "La Straniera," by Bellini. She was an excellent player of the English guitar. Not to mention the harp, flute, piano, and harmonium. But her favorite was the guitar, which she'd give up years later because her future husband Manuel Murguía, enlightened man that he was, found it distasteful. A pang of that loss can be heard in her seminal poetry collection, *Follas novas*, New Leaves:

Those sweet melodies,
those loving murmurs,
those serene nights,
why are they gone?

The sonorous quiver
of harpstrings and the sounds
of wistful guitar,
who took them?

After she'd finished playing "La Straniera," Rosalía handed the guitar to the boy, who held it tight against his body, trying to extract its soul with his hands.

And that was all. That was all it took. This was Amaro's first public speaking appearance since the war, and he received wild applause and numerous requests for photos from the press. But Amaro wasn't in the photo when it appeared in the newspaper the next day. A friend from the paper said that the director had ordered him erased. I see that bastard Fontana is still around! The director had shouted. No one dared explain to him that this was the same bastard who'd given the speech. Amaro took it in good stride. Friends came to Terranova just to see the Man Erased and joke about how the Regime had made a fool of itself with this paranoid backlash. But his body really did suffer the effects of the erasure. He'd already lived for a time underground, as a "mole." And this time, as soon as he'd stuck his head out to speak about a poet, a boy, and a guitar, he was erased.

I didn't learn this until much later. How my father had been erased from a group photo in the newspaper. Even without knowing anything of the photo when he came to visit me in the sanatorium that day, it seemed to me like someone had taken an eraser to him.

Darling, someone has to look after Terranova, Comba explained.

And he has a hard time with what's happening to you. Not to mention he's got plenty of problems of his own. The diabetes changed his humor. You can't imagine how hard he's working.

I didn't get it. He didn't visit because it hurt too much? And when he did visit, he was the Man Erased? What could he possibly be doing, what was so important about it? I thought back to the day with the pests, to his panic at the thought of getting off the bus.

And I could see he was in pain, that much was true, but also that he was a coward.

The Iron Lung

(GALICIA, FALL 1957)

Night had fallen. I wasn't expecting visitors. The moonlight shone in the mirror of the Iron Lung, offering me a morsel of the sky. It was the closest thing to me. That morsel of sky and the murmuring of the hunchbacked girls.

All of a sudden Uncle Eliseo's thunderous protests barged into my ward.

Non-human persons are not allowed!

The nurse-on-duty was following at his heels: Don Eliseo, be quiet, please. This isn't the Moulin Rouge! This was a recurring theme ever since my uncle had told her how much her beauty reminded him of a vedette, a star, he'd seen during one of his stays in Paris. Well, I'm sure she wasn't exactly wearing a white coat!

Sara, the nurse, had quipped. And Eliseo responded in his troubadour's register: No, Madame of the Dawn, 'tis a pity, but no!

They became friends. I liked that. And I liked Sara, this Madame of the Dawn, her voice, the scent that hung in the air every time she did her rounds. And she found Eliseo funny, in spite of the alarmed look on her face every time he announced he was going to tell a story. Especially if it was a children's story. But she had no patience for him that night. He mustn't go on shouting like that. This was a place full of people who were gravely ill.

Life, that's what's this place is full of, Sara! The outside world is a vast graveyard. The world is sinking like a life raft.

That's too bad for the boy, Sara said, because he's been looking forward to your visit all day, but I'm going to have to ask you to leave, Don Eliseo.

He prostrated himself before her.

I'm sorry, I've come in an expressionist mood today. It's the moonlight!

Now that you mention it, you are looking a little bright around the edges!

They're outside, he whispered, Seit and Zein.

I knew who he meant.

They're outside, on Lazareto Beach, barking at the sea and the moon, holding up the entire universe. Can you hear them?

He was talking about two tiny dogs, male and female, who were inseparable for all their constant skirmishing. Being, Time! This was how Uncle Eliseo scolded them.

What breed are they?

The existential breed, he responded soberly.

Back then, Baleia was at Terranova—the first Baleia, the most languid of them all. And Zein and Seit would run circles around her in an attempt to provoke her ire. But Baleia's melancholy was impenetrable.

The entire ward had its attention fixed on Being and Time.

Pay attention—listen, listen.

He got up. He disappeared from my mirror, heading towards the window. Sein and Zeit were barking, and he spun around to say: Can you hear that, Vicenzo? Can you hear their laments for the last days of humanity?

I've had it, that's enough!

Eliseo sat beside me, obedient, chastened. I was afraid they would kick him out one day and never let him return. But I soon realized that his grave, theatrically solemn voice was a welcome presence at that restless hour in which dreams either make their providential entrance or don't come at all.

Just one story, please.

Fine, but make it short, Eliseo.

This story is a bit childish. Very childish.

Oh, for the love of God! Sara exclaimed, regretting her leniency.

This is the story of a man who feared nothing but wanted to know what it felt like. They told him: Do you really want to know fear? Head off to war and you'll get to know it well. Yet none of the savagery he witnessed there, none of the rivers of blood, exploding dirt, scattered intestines, blistered mud plains, or the fields covered in eyes and amputated hands with their fingers still moving...

Eliseo! Please keep the gore to a minimum!

Less than an interruption, the nurse's voice felt like a necessary graft onto his tale.

He didn't even feel fear, Eliseo continued, when a noseless poet appeared atop a tank hatch screaming, "*La guerra è bella! La guerra è bella!*" Just like that, in Italian: War is beautiful! War is beautiful!

Is all that true? she said.

I made up the part about the nose. But what a futuristic nose it was! The poet screamed: We wish to glorify war, the divine ideal of a cause to die for, and universal contempt for women.

What a swine!

Like I said, he was quite the futurist. In any case, not even this put fear in our man's heart. They told him: Visit the house of the Devil and you'll know fear better than anyone! So he visited the house of the Devil. He arrived exhausted and tumbled into the first bed he found. As soon as he had, pieces of bodies began to rain down on him: arms, legs, innards, a pig's head complete with snout and ears...

A pig's head?

Come on, it's a folk tale. There's a use for every single part of the pig, and one of those is conversation. But for the sake of expediency, let's call it a skull. The man who knew no fear wiped the appendages, bones, extremities, and organs off of the bed. And what happened next? Picture this: all of those scattered body parts recomposed themselves, rejoined, sewed themselves together. It was the Devil in the flesh. But the man who knew no fear thought this was the funniest thing he'd ever seen! Like a circus act. He could hardly contain his laughter.

Wait, so when did he finally know fear?

When he looked in the mirror.

Why? What did he see in the mirror?

Himself. It was just him. There was nothing else there. He was fear.

I don't get it, said Sara.

That was one of Eliseo's typical mistakes. Thinking everyone understood him. As my mother said: Eliseo, where you see a fish, everyone else sees a wet rainboot.

Eliseo dressed like a dandy from a time apart. Neither past nor future. It was a time of his own, simultaneously ancient and modern. On his lapel, he wore a plastic flower which he offered to the nurse that night after concluding his tale.

And he said, with glee: One day the world will be full of these marvels!

And she said: Is this all you brought back with you from paradise?

I'm going to tell you a secret, Sara. In paradise, the flowers fall to the ground; they fall whole, like camellias.

In the ward, beyond the Iron Lungs, was the space where the hunchbacked girls were sequestered, kept out of sight by a drawn curtain. No one ever publicly referred to them as hunchbacked, not even the doctors when they did their rounds, but that was their name, that was what people called the girls when they were out of earshot, or when they thought the girls wouldn't hear their whispers. I guess there could have been boys too, but I only ever heard them referred to as the hunchbacked girls. They were strapped to their beds to keep them from sitting up. Even on Sundays after mass, when the priest would come by with his acolyte to give them communion, they still weren't allowed to sit up.

I once asked Sara why they had to be strapped down like that all the time. I was strapped down too, in a sense, but in my case it was because I couldn't breathe on my own. They could breathe without an Iron Lung, yet they spent years confined to their beds. Sara told me it was for their own good, they had a problem with their spinal column and this was a way to straighten it out.

Will it work?

Sara went quiet. She looked away. Her neck was porcelain white, whiter than her coat, streaked by a blue vein like a mysterious gem affixed to her skin.

One of the days that Amaro came to visit, he also took an interest in the hunchbacked girls. He received a similar response, and I heard him mutter: How awful, how awful!

They got up one night. No one could ever work out how they managed to undo their bonds. There were three of them. And it was three voices I heard, three distinct whispers. Contained, compressed voices, which the night amplified for the Admiral of the Iron Lung. By day, I could hear the voices of the workers at the Oza shipyards. By night, the conversations of the fishermen heading out to sea. On weekends, the music playing at a dance hall. A clandestine couple, hidden away, on the verge of making the entire Sanatorium quake with no more than their moans, with that indescribable sound people make when they're burning to cry out but have to stifle the urge. Like the brakes of a train. And yes, I could hear the train too, the sea and the train and the dance hall band. The embrace of a pair of giants, pounding on walls, making bed frames creak, in the medical staff room, in the train tunnel, in the mouth of the bay. And there I was in the middle, in my Iron Lung, bathed in moonlight. This must have all been the work of the moon. Because its light was so bright that it reverberated through the air.

But that night, I was the only one who heard the three hunchbacked girls. Their whispers simultaneously secretive and animated. It was like listening to bodies that had re-learned to walk. And they learned fast. They reached what I assumed was the window. I could guess why the silence had returned: their hands were clasped in one another's, they were mesmerized by the burning sea, and the rescue ship, and the swaying of the Lighthouse beacon.

And the eldest of them said: It's them, it's the twins!

That escape, the escape of the three hunchbacked girls, should go down as a major event in the history of Spain. Because their condition was also a historical one. Inattentive History had contorted their vertebrae. Conspired against their bodies. I kept my mouth shut. Something inside me told me I should, though my reputation was as a tattle-tale, a gossip, an open book, with my ears everywhere so that I'd never miss a thing, and I had no scruples about exhuming the dead. But I wasn't going to make a peep about what I'd heard. Chaos ensued at sunrise. Alarmed voices. Dashing to and fro. Exasperated shouts.

They've been taken!

Kidnapped!

What if they ran away?

That's preposterous, how could the hunchbacked girls have run away?

Because, in the commotion, the euphemisms and figures of speech went out the window. The girls were deformed, half-anemic, with skin-and-bone legs. They were ignorant of and terrified by the world; they stuttered in their own mother tongue. They were tragic little things, ripe for plucking by the convent.

They were mystical for a long time, after all!

All this until a voice of reason, Sara's voice, asserted itself:

We don't know anything right now. We don't know who they were, or what really went on in their heads. The only thing we know is that they wanted to leave this place.

One of the bloodhounds sent by the management of the Sanatorium reached the conclusion that I, given the placement of my Iron Lung, may have heard something. He was unaware of my reputation as a snitch. Nor did he seem to give any consideration to the moonlit night, which even allowed me to see a bit in my panoptic mirror. He was hopeless as a detective. Children are quick to pick up on the incompetence of adults.

I played my part as the immobile child, as the resident of an Iron Lung. I kept my lips firmly sealed.

But Sara knocked me off balance: Is our intrepid Captain Nemo sure he doesn't have any idea what happened?

I puckered my lips. I dreamt of a kiss out of the movies, so I closed my eyes.

No, he doesn't know anything.

The Resurrection

Yours was the most eagerly anticipated resurrection since the times of Lazarus.

I was down in the dumps, and he found me there. I'd started wanting to be unhappy with my Iron Lung. I wished for the machine to turn human, for it to malfunction somehow.

I was the orphan rabbit, saved by the Collard Machine, but she didn't want to let go of me, or worse, she wouldn't let me move on from her.

Eliseo was a big help with his abject stories. I felt like a character in them.

I was the rabbit.

I was Job the fool.

I was the dead man clinging to the balcony.

And now, it seemed, I was going to be Lazarus.

I'd like you to go, Uncle. I want to be alone.

I couldn't say it to the Iron Lung, but I could say it to Eliseo. Plus, I loved him, and that fit squarely into an abject tale. It was the first time he'd heard me say something like that: I want to be alone.

What a delicious flavor, the salty sweet taste that fills your mouth when it's in conflict with your mind: I want to be alone.

My uncle wasn't much for confrontation. Rather than being asked to leave, he was always ready to take his leave.

I looked in the mirror, past him. The nurse was tense; maybe it was the first time a child had asked to be alone, and she looked at me with a severity bordering on rancor. I could see why. She'd been indoctrinated in the ways of abjection, and I was depriving her of one of Eliseo's tales.

He had no intention of leaving.

As I was saying, Jesus brought Lazarus back to life, Eliseo proceeded, disregarding my plea for solitude. It was the first time I'd ever asked to be alone, and I couldn't have even that. That day, I learned I couldn't be alone just because I wanted to. There was no cost to it. It was no bother for anyone. But I couldn't be alone.

Let's imagine for a moment that Lazarus did not truly want to be brought back to life, Eliseo said. It was a tricky case. In an apocryphal version of the Gospels, albeit one that seems to have hit close to the mark, Lazarus died of his own volition. What does that mean, that he died of his own volition? Well, I guess you could say: he kicked his own bucket. He didn't like the world. Then Jesus Christ came along and, with the best of intentions, brought him back to life. Lazarus' family was ecstatic. Everyone was celebrating except for one person: Lazarus, the resurrectee. He hadn't liked the world beforehand, and he hadn't grown to like it any better since he'd been brought back. He was furious.

But you like the world, don't you, Vicenzo?

And thus, I was resurrected. By a surrealist. An abject surrealist.

The Horse

When I was little, I got a horse as a present. This was before the illness that locked me in the Irón Lung. But it wasn't one of those primitive horses that Amaro and Eliseo made during their time as "moles," or in the early days of Terranova.

Uncle Eliseo had brought it back from the first of his many trips. He was gone a long while. I have a fuzzy memory of that time, but I know Terranova fell into a profound melancholy while he was away. Whenever I asked, they told me he'd gone to France and from there to the Americas. The bookstore regulars, our most trusted customers, either didn't ask or were satisfied with the curt, courteous explanation: He's spending some time in Paris. Oh, wonderful, I'm sure he's happy over there, it's so cultured, and so on and so forth. But there were also the more irascible customers who would demand to know what Eliseo was doing; he's off gallivanting through Europe, and America, sure, but what for? And my father, in irritation, would reply to the nosy customer: If you must know, he was invited by the Surrealist International.

Ah, of course, of course, the Surrealist International! Eliseo always was obsessed with dreams. But that was before the Civil War, no?

I must have been about four or five at the time, and I didn't yet know that they were talking about my father when they mentioned Polytropos, his nickname since university days. It wasn't until later that I became curious about it. There aren't many people with fathers who go by Polytropos. When the time came for us to stop speaking and communicate via the written word, I began my letter: I'm begging you, Polytropos, not to see this as an act of hostility... But on the day with the nosy customer, I didn't have this information. My father was my father, Amaro Fontana, this beloved figure who was always warm with his family and cheerful around friends and animals, at least in general, because he could also be very oblique and sullen, and was known to abruptly cut off a conversation that he felt was approaching rocky territory. He argued with reactionaries and placed high esteem on what he called "dangerous intellect," but he would often turn furious; his blood would boil any time he got into a spat with the sort of man he called "an educated idiot."

I didn't know at the time that my father was Polytropos. But I knew that he was a man of many masks. And that one of them was the barn owl that wakes up hooting:

I'm sure you're aware that in the wake of the war, wherever humanity had not been defeated, civilization took root once again. That's where our dear Eliseo is, ambling around with his subconscious on his sleeve!

This was also the period when the suitcases began to arrive. Rather, people with suitcases full of books, who came from all over the Americas, though Argentina and Mexico were the most common ports of origin. The part about the Surrealist International has always stuck with me, an an amazing project that sent my uncle Eliseo all over the world. A project I also associated with packages.

He said: A little horse from the Pampa, a Cuban Criollo!

To my eyes, its varnished wood was a chestnut skin, complete with a long black mane and white hair that looked more like a doll's, the kind you might find in the window of the Noah's Ark shop, than a wild stallion's. But the fire in its black eyes was proof that this was a wild creature.

I didn't want to ride it.

At first they thought it was some kind of ritual, a game I was playing. They thought I was sizing up the toy. Then they decided it was a whim. A childish notion. Adults don't tend to deal well with obstinacy in children. They all tried to convince me and would even go so far as to plop me onto it. Comba most of all, though she was usually so understanding.

It's a beautiful horse. The most beautiful toy on earth.

Eventually they realized the problem was fear. An unshakeable fear. I was rigid with it, my body wooden, the same material as the horse, and I couldn't get myself into the stirrups. Not that day or any day afterwards. And it stayed on in Terranova, retreating further into Penumbra with each passing day, until it was all the way back in the Magical Labyrinth. Every so often, a customer's child or grandchild would climb astride the horse, which came equipped with a saddle, stirrups and reins, the whole package, and they would gallop frenetically, their back and forth rocking an unintentional insult to me.

Look, Vicenzo. Even the little girl is riding the Cuban Criollo!

Eventually they sent it from Terranova to Chor. They thought the countryside might create one last opportunity for Vicenzo and the horse. But I knew my destiny better than they. I knew what would happen. I knew the horse would seek out Dombodán the moment it arrived, despite all their speculations to the contrary.

Look, he's not scared of it at all!

No, nothing ever scared Dombodán.

And there was nothing Dombodán wouldn't have done for me.

That went all the way to the beginning, when he shared his

mother's milk with me. Though strictly speaking, the credit for that belongs to Expectación, Dombodán's mother and the caretaker of the Chor estate. We were born at almost the exact same time. I was supposed to be born before him, but I think Dombodán came out first to help me through life. Comba had trouble breastfeeding me, the milk wouldn't come. So, Expectación took on a role as a wetnurse. She had milk enough for the both of us. People always talked about how the caretaker's son never cried. Apparently the only one shedding tears was me.

And on the day he came to see me in the Iron Lung, I could tell from the fondness in his gaze that he would have swapped places with me without a moment's hesitation.

He stood up for me. Not once or twice, but constantly. Anytime he heard the words cripple boy or freak or any other insult like that, he would whirl around and spit out curses like a machine gun. I learned a lot just by being around him. When I went off to University, Eliseo gifted me one of his transatlantic treasures from Terranova, *La musa de la mala pata*, The Muse of the Bad Leg, by Nicolás Olivari, but I think Dombodán was my first muse. He never backed down from a challenge. He would say: we'll be done with this quicker than a flip of the hand.

Quicker than a flip of the hand!

He took the first hit in the pigeon loft at Chor for my sake.

There was still life up there. A band of pigeons that maintained the skyways. They still ate baby pigeon at Expectación's house every so often back then before this delicacy came to be seen as poor people's food. The pigeons had disappeared from the Big House, whether in still lives or in moving form. And the two of us were up in the pigeon loft entering an unfamiliar life, injecting something into our veins for the first time. I'd brought the heroin and all the necessary tools; we were going to take the trip together, weren't we, Dombodán? We were going to fly even higher than the loft, we were going to take off from this vessel forgotten on a hill in the gardens, but I felt the cravings, the symptoms of withdrawal before I'd even shot up. The shakes, the sweats. And he, calm as could be, went first to show me there was nothing to be afraid of.

One day the Cuban Criollo was left on the cobbled threshing ground where they used to set the beans out to dry. The summer was coming to an end. The days were mired in a sticky heat. That night, a thunderstorm broke. I must have been the only one who remembered the Cuban Criollo. I got up and looked out the window. And it really did come to life in those intermittent flashes of lightning, among the lifeless heaps of beans.

The horror we felt when we looked upon its shattered remains in the morning had originated with some fear we'd never experienced. A death without a body. A liquid death. A disintegration. But its two eyes remained, a living thing still somewhere in there.

The Manifesto of the Body

I don't know when the break came, but at some point I stopped taking a sympathetic view of my father. Nothing happened; there was, figuratively speaking, no declaration of war, nor did I ever feel he'd mistreated me. Amaro could be aloof and reserved, but he was never tyrannical. He'd have sooner hacked off his own hand than raise it against anyone. But there was also the Polytropos of the debates that raged in the bookstore. In these debates, my father could be, by turns, astute, vehement, ardent, caustic, sarcastic and indefatigable, his entire body implicated in the pleasure of finding a tide-turning argument, a spark in some corner of history, a prismatic stone for his cobbled path. A good literary set-to, to him, was sport, was epic battle. But at other times, in the daily goings-on at Terranova, he would stew in silence or disappear into the Pinhole Chamber, the enigmatic Labyrinth, Penumbra, the Mobilis in Mobili, or into the far-flung mysteries of the Hidden Land.

I wanted to travel in the opposite direction. The promised land I sought, the unexplored territory, was beyond the doors of Terranova. After my time in the Iron Lung, I entered a new stage in the fight against my illness. A military operation had been carried out against my body. An attempt at destruction that I'd almost surrendered to. But after my resurrection, my only strategy, the only training I undertook, was with the goal of becoming independent enough to leave Terranova and blend in with the crowds of people who never set foot in bookstores. The people who would crack open the door, take one look inside, and run off with a look on their face like they'd seen Lucifer himself keeping shop.

I used crutches for a while after emerging from the Iron Lung. It was like learning to walk again. They were made to my measure by a skilled carpenter in Chor who specialized in spiral staircases. They were feather-light, these Feathery Feet of mine. Later on, in my early adulthood, I started to wear platform shoes. The right shoe was much, much taller than the left. As strange as it may sound, I had a hard time giving up my crutches; I felt a kind of autonomy with them, like the starfish that can detach a part of its body as a defense mechanism. Because of the way I moved, I always identified deeply with the twisted figures in the paintings of Francis Bacon. One foot in front of the other in a series of artistic accidents. It took me a lot of work, but after a time my gait picked up a certain flair. One that was admired by children, outcasts, the immature, and animals, that is, by those whose eyes could still see the beauty in wildness.

I became conscious of my body. I felt, all of a sudden, good inside of it. My body was its own manifesto, Uncle Eliseo!

How's your father, Mr. Fontana? Macías, the secondary school director, had stopped me in the hall. Our paths had crossed on my way out of class. Or maybe he'd been waiting for me there. Without giving me a chance to respond, he said: I'd like you to give him my formal congratulations. And tell him this—don't forget, I know you've got brains—*Thirteen pear trees, ten apple trees, forty fig trees and fifty grapevines.* He made me repeat his words, then added: And tell him we haven't forgotten Polytropos. I nodded, failing to hide my puzzlement. He was a serious man, though more sober than severe. But he told me all this with a trickle of joy, with the brightness of someone regaining lost or stolen time and hoping to share it with others. And he must have noticed something, he must have seen that I wasn't enthused to have been tasked with bringing this message to my father, because he added, in a grave tone: Your father is a sage man! This last remark wasn't just directed at me. He was making this public knowledge. His words seemed to echo throughout the school, so loud that the entire student body turned to look at me, surprised to learn Feathery Feet the cripple was the son of a sage. Mr. Macías had a similar reputation. But he was a school director, and that made his sagehood self-evident. For him to say that Amaro was a sage man, in the way he'd said it, with his eyes turned skywards, seeking out the light, this placed my father on an upper rung of sageliness, one that was beyond teachings, an indefinite kind, as if, in that very moment, he was piloting one of the clouds that we could see floating by through the glass.

The image I had of my father didn't square with that of any Greek hero, nor any local hero, for that matter. To me, he was the Man Erased. Helenio Herrera, the professional soccer coach: now there was a hero, a sage too, come to think of it, who stressed the importance of air, of breathing techniques—not to mention that he always looked elegant in photos. I came to think that this view of my father, this image of him as a sage, and all that crap about calling him Polytropos, was a private joke the entire city was in on. And I wondered if all of those voices were just trying to lump me in with him, a clown with a handicapped boy to boot. Polytropos and the Limper. In any case, we were growing apart, something had cracked in Terranova, an ice floe had broken off and I was floating away—but I wasn't holding out my handkerchief to wipe away my tears as we said our farewells.

I went into Terranova. He was at the register. He always waited there for me to come home from my morning classes, so that he could close up shop and we could go upstairs for lunch. He had a tic. The moment I shut the door, he took off his glasses and held them between his fingers in such a way that it seemed as if they had their own eyes, and I felt as if I were being watched by them, his bare, castaway eyes, and by some mysterious, invisible being he carried with him. Maybe that being was the sage, the man who knew Odysseus best. While other people embellished their portraits of Amaro with new details, I'd started to take mine apart.

I was on a mission. I'd come bearing a message for him. I had spent the whole way back memorizing it like a passcode. *Thirteen pear trees, ten apple trees, forty fig trees and fifty grapevines.* And we haven't forgotten about Polytropos. Mr. Macías wanted me to tell you that.

But once I had him in front of me, I said nothing. I kept my mouth shut. I gnashed the grapevines and trees between my teeth and swallowed. They're still inside me. With all their seasons. And fruits. And birds. And gusts of wind.

He asked me if I'd had a good day at school so far. I nodded. He raised his head and breathed deep, with an ancient enjoyment:

Up we go! Smells like stew for lunch at Terranova.

The Cathedral Roof

(GALICIA, SPRING 1974)

The detective rubbed his hands together. I was disoriented and the worse for wear. He, on the other hand, had the happy expression of a man who'd just reeled in a juicy catch.

Look what we have here: could that be Amaro Fontana's son? Terranova's little runt? That's what we call him around here, Terranova. Just that. But the old chief, who's probably still off enjoying his retirement, had a nickname for him, Polytropos. Because he's wily, he said, the man of many turns. He'd never be able to pull it off if he weren't wily. He's the biggest banned book provider in all of Galicia. He must be worried sick. His student son has been arrested. What's your name again? Right, Vicenzo. But let me get this straight, his son hasn't been arrested for revolutionary activity, for protesting Franco, or graffitiing a wall with a demand for freedom? No sir, not by a longshot.

His son has been arrested for being a junkie. He got caught using drugs, and boy what drugs they were! Acid, LSD! An adventure, a trip, that's you kids call it, right? And where'd you take your *trip*? On the roof of the Santiago Cathedral! It could have ended with that. You're not the first. But why'd you do it? Let's look at your statement again. You claim that you climbed to the roof of the Cathedral, from the corner where Vía Sacra meets the Praza da Inmaculada and the Quintana dos Vivos. When asked how you managed it with your handicap, you answered that you were helped by your childhood friend, Matías Loureiro Paz, also known as Dombodán, who's also been arrested. You claimed no one dared you to do it and you had no intentions of trespassing in a sacred place or damaging a historical monument. In other words, your motives were pure. The reason, according to your statement, was that you wanted to hear the Cathedral bell toll at midnight and see the sky from the Cruz dos Farrapos. This was not, in fact, a result of the hallucinogen, because you didn't consume it until you'd climbed up to the roof. When your friend, this Dombodán character, who was wearing the backpack at the time of your arrest, was asked who it belonged to, he responded that the two of you found the backpack on the roof, beside the aforementioned Cruz dos

Farrapos, and that you decided to bring it with you thinking it was empty, completely unaware that it contained a jar with twenty-two tabs of the narcotic known as LSD, as well as approximately one hundred grams of hashish.

No, there was no revolution here; you got arrested for being a junkie, and for cursing at the arresting officers as you came down from the heavens. Most of your curses were complete gibberish, though, unless you can help me understand the meaning of things like: *Flee from death, Quiáns*!, or *Go put the horseshoes on Pegasus!*, or *Hands up, an angel's about to fall!* But the worst part for you is that we have reason to believe you're a dealer. That backpack, that magical backpack, I know it's yours, so don't jerk me around. Anyway, I guess today was your lucky day, because it turned out the backpack was in the hands of your sidekick, the bull from Bethlehem. And what did the idiot say? That he found it. That he picked it up without realizing what was in it. And then a lawyer showed up on your behalf, a lawyer sent by your illustrious father, and that's the story he's sticking to. The magic backpack. A gift that a pilgrim from Amsterdam or some godforsaken place like that left for the Apostle at the Cruz dos Farrapos. Do you have anything to add? No, you're not going to say a thing. How could you? You can still hear the bell tolling, can't you?

The bastard. He'd hit the bullseye there. The bell was still ringing in my head.

Estación del Norte

(MADRID, FALL 1975)

I called. I fell silent when I heard his voice. That day, I was on the verge of saying the unsayable. In a strange father-son pact, we'd agreed to communicate exclusively by writing. I don't know why I thought he wouldn't pick up the phone. It was an error of judgment: Sundays, when they were closed, were the days he felt most comfortable in the bookstore, cooped up in the Pinhole Chamber writing in a journal, another one, with the title of the secret book he could never seem to finish, *Mnemosyne in Hispania*, written on the front.

I was on the verge of blurting out that criminal utterance. And I hadn't taken anything. Not even Speed. The tyrant's funeral had been that morning in the Plaza de Oriente, and afterwards the funeral procession had filtered out to bury him in the shrine of shrines, the Valley of the Fallen, in the hills outside Madrid. We didn't budge from the Gnomar apartment until the time came to leave for the Estación del Norte train depot. The Atlantic Express would depart at nightfall. I should have made the call by then, but I'd been putting it off. Me, the intrepid one, the lame rebel, the so-called Feathery Feet, the bold adventurer who'd climbed into the heights to direct the symphony of tolling bells in the Santiago Cathedral; in spite of all those things, I couldn't bring myself to call. Until I was at the station with her and her indomitable smile; she had a colorful hat that crowned her head with happiness, along with a leather jacket, bell-bottom jeans, chamois boots, and not much luggage—a small suitcase and an old leather bag, like a schoolchild's, hanging from her shoulder. Most of the people on the platform wore contrite expressions that matched their clothes. Some men wore ex-combat armbands. They'd come from burying their Leader. But there were also old men in new suits looking impatient to board the train.

Finally, I dialed the number for Terranova.

And I was on the verge of making the worst joke, at the worst moment.

You're living on borrowed time, Fontana!

That sentence had cast a shadow over our lives, but we had all agreed to ignore it. Without fail, one day out of every year—we never knew which because it bore no apparent relationship to holidays or the anniversaries of fascist victories—the phone would ring, and if my father picked up, the voice would produce its favorite screed:

You're living on borrowed time, Fontana!

Every year. Like a dagger.

Because of this he rarely answered the phone at Terranova. It was usually my mother who picked up. Or me. Or Uncle Eliseo, when he wasn't off gallivanting through Europe or the Americas. Europe? The same snooping customer inquired again. Where exactly in Europe, if you don't mind me asking? The Père-Lachaise Cemetery, it has such a wonderful atmosphere, would come Comba's curt reply. But going back to the fateful call, if Amaro didn't pick up, the voice said nothing. All you would hear on the other end of the line was some scratchy noise. If every musical note has a corresponding silence, it seems to me you could say the same about every fixed phrase, especially if that phrase is a humiliating threat: the threat that spares you your life. That kind is paired with the silence of the grave. There was always a brief pause after we asked, Who is it? The leaden off-beat of silence. A dead beat. And when we repeated the question, Who is it? They would simply hang up.

And my father died a bit more with each call. Another year, another stab of the dagger.

My father? What's he doing answering the phone? This is what's known as showing your hand too soon. That's one of my weaknesses. I either keep my lips sealed or let them flap with the breeze. Because Amaro Fontana is there, at the phone, in Terranova. And I'm about to utter a series of words like a gunshot. I'm about to speak that horrid phrase. About to affect that gravelly, sinister, murderous voice, and say to my father: You're living on borrowed time, Fontana!

She's next to me, outside the phone booth at the Estación del Norte. Since the day we met, our roles had always been, and always would be, reversed. She inside, holding the earpiece the way she always did, creating a mask with her hands and hair so that no one could see her, curling her body up inside the phone booth on the street corner four blocks down, the one farthest from me, as she engaged in long spells of listening and confidential conversations I would never know anything about, and from which she would return frailer and smaller, her almond eyes gradually widening in a growing hallucination, which would make me think she didn't just use the booths to talk but also to see images, cartoons, sequences, hence her body language, using her hands as shades against the light.

She looks at me. Stares, rather. She puckers her lips. She's sending me a birdsong kiss.

She once said to me: My mother tongue was chirping.

Allô, Sanctum Regnum speaking!

I say: I'm coming back.

When?

Today. I'm about to board the Atlantic Express.

My father didn't seem surprised, neither by the fact that I was speaking to him nor my clumsy communication of the trip, with one foot already in the stirrup.

It's the best thing you could do, son. Do you remember the story of the dead man on the balcony?

I got anxious. It was the wily, talkative Polytropos on the phone. Meanwhile, she approached the glass of the phone booth and started making comic gestures, ending with a parody of a toothpaste commercial. If anyone asks you what I'm like, she had joked, tell them I have perfect teeth. My father was plowing ahead with his story, a true story, of course, about a man who died and whose mourners couldn't get him out the front door because his coffin was too big, so instead, they decided to lower him down from the balcony…

I'm with someone, I cut in.

Terranova will always be a land of asylum, he responded without a moment's thought, in the jolly tone of someone who's just signed a truce.

I was taken aback. Why had he used that expression, *a land of asylum*?

It's a girl, I said. A woman

All the better, he said. And you know what? They tried every alignment imaginable, horizontal, vertical, but they just couldn't get that coffin out the door...

Talk to you later! I'm going to miss the train.

As I left the booth, while she contentedly stretched out her arms, it hit me that Polytropos had been expecting her. It was an intuition, the vision of a traveler at the ends of the Earth. They didn't know each other. It was the first time my father had heard of her existence. Of the woman accompanying me to Terranova. I could see her, I'm seeing her now. And I could see him. Alone, returning to the desk in the Pinhole Chamber, opening his journal, and writing down, with great feeling:

She arrives tomorrow.

And the intuition that alights in my mind may have something to do with the day we first ran into each other at Café Comercial, when the Mirasol book caught her eye and she agreed to accompany me, to continue the conversation, that was how I'd put it, and come up to my apartment, to Gnomar.

It's just men, I said. There's only men living there. Little men. All gnomes. That's right, we live in a gnome cave.

But it's a feminine cave, she said after she saw it.

I must have turned as pale as a sheet when she said it. I'd heard my father elaborate a similar hypothesis about Paleolithic cave paintings. Located in nearly inaccessible crevices. Mouths that were hidden for millennia. Fissures, cracks, vulvas, he said, through which to enter the belly of the Earth. Their bodies had to be well trained. Their eyes had to be adapted to the dark, even if they had torches. Their fertile gazes impregnated the shadows with these marvelous creatures. Sublime hands. The hands of witches, of midwives, he said. And though he signed his work under a pseudonym, the usual Polytropos, even when it was published abroad, this article sparked a major controversy in the esoteric realms of art and archeology.

It was women who painted the caves, I said to her that day. That's the Fontana Theory. And I said it like that, the Fontana Theory, the way we would speak of the long-dead Darwin. Women and girls with a talent, with a rare mastery. Just look at the hands, at the size and shape of the markings. There are handprints in most of the caves. He says it was their signature. But it was a signature that meant more than just that. It's the Open Hand technique. According to him, this was the first avant-garde act. You can see the outline of the painting hand better than the hand itself. And that empty hand has mystery to it. The illusion that there's something on the other side of the wall.

She looked at her hand. At the palm of it.

Of course there's something on the other side.

I was at ease on the train with her opposite me. Within minutes I started to feel as if we'd been traveling together a long time and had finally found luck. It wouldn't be much longer.

Besides the ticket checker, a policeman would always make the rounds of the train asking to see identification. In the cozy rocking of the car, this was the only uncertainty that stole my calm.

When the plainclothes officer appeared, she handed him her passport first, with a convincing smile. These policemen would generally keep the documents and return them only as the train was reaching its destination. If they were night owls, this was plenty of time to thoroughly inspect the documents spread before them.

Are you stressed? she asked.

No, I'm fine.

You were definitely stressed in the phone booth. I could tell.

That's because they asked if you knew how to sew.

She laughed: And what did you say?

That you've been sewing since the day you were born.

She suddenly turned serious. And I was suddenly afraid that she'd stand up and walk out into the corridor, leaving me alone with the other two passengers, a married couple who wore the Dictator's funeral on their faces.

But no. I still couldn't see that she was the kind of person who never took a break from the labor of feeling, despite the image she conveyed of impenetrable tranquility, of immunity to imbalance.

It's true. I was born sewing. My mother was a seamstress, a *percalera*, as they're called in Argentina, she was from Barracas. A typographer and a seamstress, those were my parents. I know how to tie my shoes, too, if you can believe it.

My father picked up the phone, I explained. It'd been a long time since we'd spoken, she had to understand that. But he acted as if nothing had ever come between us. He was always so terse, yet that day he was ready to talk my ear off. He kept trying to tell me a story.

A story?

Yes. The story of a dead man, I whispered. A dead man whose mourners couldn't get him out of his home.

And?

And what?

And she says, whispering too, what happened to the dead man?

How should I know! I didn't let him finish. The train was about to leave and he was sitting there blabbering about how they couldn't get the coffin out the door. I had to hang up.

We had to cover our mouths with our hands for a few seconds to contain our laughter.

No, actually, I do know it.

The story?

It was a long time ago. Back when I was in the Iron Lung, my uncle Eliseo would tell me those kinds of stories. It was a form of shock therapy. Abject shock, he said. They decided to try lowering the dead man out by the balcony, but the coffin slipped out of their hands and broke to bits on the ground. There was no one inside it.

So?

There was no one in the coffin.

But *che*, what happened with the dead man?

Oh, him? He was clinging to the balcony for dear life.

Giuliana Melis?

The day was struggling to break through the rain. She went sleepless that night, on the alert. I know because every time I woke up, I'd see her reading, her almond eyes as wide as an owl's.

Io sono Giuliana! With that smattering of Italian, she grabbed her passport.

I was dumbstruck. She looked out the window at the network of waterways being traced by the drops as they slid down the glass.

Giuliana? Beatriz, Estela...You're a one-woman theater company!

The funereal couple had gotten off in Ourense. It was just the two of us, but even so she motioned for me to shut my trap.

We talked about this, she hissed.

We hadn't talked about anything of the kind.

I told you. I come from dago immigrants. And in my Italian passport I only listed the name Giuliana. Beatriz Estela Giuliana, because my mother wanted me to be named for every saint that ever lived. What's the big deal?

Don't worry, to me you'll always be Dita Parlo, the woman from *L'Atalante*, except that you don't drown in the Seine.

Lucky me! she said.

They were waiting for us at the A Coruña station. The entire Terranova embassy. Comba, Amaro, and Eliseo.

There they are! They love being alone so much they always stick together.

Finally, I had a name to introduce her by: Mamá, this is Giuliana!

And Eliseo handed her an umbrella, one of the hundred: The cubist umbrella! She stood on the tips of her toes and lifted it up like a kite about to fly free.

You know, when I was little, people used to call me Garúa.

The Thunderstone

The Pinhole Chamber, at the end of Terranova's West Wing, past the main counter, was first conceived of as an office for the bookstore, and in point of fact, this was where we kept the bookkeeping logs and ISBN catalogs, which I quickly learned to call the *Vademecum*, three yearly tomes for consultation on titles, authors, and themes. But really it was Amaro's chamber, his writing room and refuge, and sometimes even his sleeping quarters, with that maroon couch—*Chaise longue*, my boy!—which seemed to me like a sleep factory. It's the orientation! Amaro would say. And I'd feel like I was lying on a boat named, aptly enough, the *Chaise Longue*. It was the place Garúa chose as her home at Terranova, and no one objected, maybe because she fell asleep there shortly after our arrival—she'd sat down, batted her eyes, and slowly laid down her head, like someone who'd gone a year without sleep, facing the Lighthouse and the North Star—or maybe no one objected because the piano was sitting there in self-absorption, waiting for someone to notice it.

Garúa's fingers tapped artfully on the cover of the Collard & Collard, and Eliseo exclaimed: You can play!

A bit, she said. I can play a bit.

Play that bit for us, won't you?

Another day. I'll play that bit another day.

In the Pinhole Chamber, placed at varying heights, was a set of spheres, some of which were made in Terranova itself, during the early days when the bookstore doubled as a bazaar and costume shop. In a manner of speaking, the spheres orbited the room. They hung by the walls, the navigational charts, the posters for big trans-atlantic ocean liners, the lithograph prints from the *Thesaurus* of sea creatures, the compasses, and the one I'll never tire of looking at, the print of the *L'Enfant Perdu* lighthouse in Guyana. Rounding out the décor were various theater posters hidden among the shadows, which Eliseo liked to say were castaways, and they did look like castaways, in their shadowy places, like posters from the *Retablo de fantoches*, the theater troupes that worked under the Pedagogical Missions in the twentieth century. From inside, no one would ever have called the Pinhole Chamber a small room. It didn't feel like an enclosed space, a space with walls, it felt like an abstract scenography containing the kind of silence that holds onto all the things it has heard, and is waiting for an alarm, a sign to expand.

It's the same with the laughter in the photo hanging in the cabinet next to the display case that holds the Thunderstone.

This photo eclipses every other image in its vicinity. Why? Because the photo itself is laughing. That's right, you can hear the laughter. Loud laughter. No mere cackles. Laughter that isn't, so to speak, just for the camera. These laughs have fermented into the photo, transfiguring everything in it. You almost want to say that the faces are more pinched than if they were experiencing great pain.

Men of rain love the sun.

That was the handwritten caption below the photo.

And that was the title of the only book of poems Amaro Fontana ever wrote, printed in the spring of 1936 but never distributed. It became an invisible book, and he participated in that invisibility, because he never once mentioned it. He would never return to poetry. A rumor spread that he was writing a book, *The Thunderstone*—a blend of historical research and crime novel. He played up that mystery a bit, and the book really was gestating in his mind: it would be a "fall from innocence" in contemporary fiction, though it was hard to tell whether he meant this as confirmation or denial of the rumor. What was evident was that he sank all his effort and focus into the project, establishing surprising links with a research technique he called "The Prismatic Stone Path," where the stones formed a kind of footbridge that allowed one to cross a river too deep to wade through. One of the first Prismatic Stones, written in his university days, was called "The Livestock Thief," about Odysseus' maternal grandfather. The article gained attention beyond Classics circles with unexpected spotlights that illuminated the *Odyssey*. Other articles, such as "Irony in Hades," "The Lotus Flower and Retrograde Amnesia" and "The Trees of Ithaca" were treated as avant-garde texts, as a new way of excavating history by engaging with it as a remembered present—a method most of his contemporaries associated with the critical theories that had flourished in Frankfurt. By the time he published "The Cyclops and the Panoptic Eye of Power," in 1934, where he discussed the rising threat of authoritarian power in Europe, he'd already started signing his articles as Polytropos.

Featured in the photo are three smiling men, their smiles like sparks.

They're in the middle of the countryside on a sunny day. But this is no leisurely stroll. They're splayed on the ground in the middle of an excavation, as evidenced by the geometrical intentionality of the furrows behind them. Beside them, leaning up against a stone wall, are their digging tools. You'd hardly call what they're wearing work clothes. All three sport ties and pullover sweaters. Even their ankle boots, which their pant legs are stuffed into, look prim. Their clothing calls to mind a Sunday smile. A happy chore, not an obligation. The three men look like they're celebrating an extraordinary find: the simple fact of being together.

They're all young, though the man in the center appears younger than the other two. Messy curls in his untamed hair. They're all of more or less the same build, but the man in the center stands somewhat taller because he's the one responsible for forging their union. He has his arms around their shoulders. Another detail, which contributes to his youthful appearance: unlike the other two, he's not wearing glasses.

Garúa looks at the photo. It's almost impossible not to smile when you look at this picture. It's that spark. You'd have to put up a somber resistance not to fall under its spell. And she falls, she's with them. Smiling on the inside.

The man on the right, in the jacket, that's your father. It has to be. Who are the other two?

I didn't respond right away. Not because I was distracted or didn't know the answer, but because I was seeing something she couldn't, the photos behind the photo, in the same frame but invisible. There are two other photos. In one, it's just my father and the third man, a studio shot. The man is sitting with his legs crossed, while my father stands beside him with a hand on his shoulder. On the other side of the man is a pedestal with a flowerpot. It's a formal photo, a couple's photo. The date is written on the back, it was taken after the excavation, in June of 1936. The other photo is smaller but portrays a big group of men and women. A meeting of the Seminary of Galician Studies. Various miniscule symbols hang over their heads: dot, circle, cross. The stigmata of fate. Prison, exile, death.

The man on the left is Eliseo. Can you see the resemblance?

Oh, Eliseo, of course! That hair, those curls, he looks amazing! What about the other man?

I don't really know, I lied. One of their friends. Some guy named Atlas.

He's a handsome one, this Atlas.

Garúa is holding the hand-ax now. The Thunderstone.

She says the words that I'm only thinking. What I've thought every time I've looked at it. It's strange. It looks like a weapon, and it doesn't. It looks like an ax, and it doesn't. It's a bewitching piece of stone. Meant to be held the way she's holding it now.

Why do you call it the Thunderstone?

That's a question for Amaro. He's the rock expert.

No hesitation. She marched out of the Pinhole Chamber holding the hand-ax unlike I would have, solemnly, as if she were carrying something of great value and regretted having removed it from its place to begin with. Before she can ask anything, everyone's eyes, one by one, fall on the Thunderstone. Amaro, Comba,

Eliseo, the animals, the portraits in the writers' gallery, and the Republic clock—a gift sent by an exile within a packet of contraband books. They called it that, the Republic clock, because it was made to tell how much time the Dictatorship had left. Comba tries to keep it running on time, but the mechanism has always been slow.

Garúa was told the history of the Seminary of Galician studies. Born of the same impetus as the Institute of Free Teaching and the Students' Residency. To reclaim all of the time, the ages that had been robbed from freethinking. To go in search of a homeland.

To clean up the fear and ignorance rife in the country.

Who said that? My father? Yes, it was my father.

And she followed along, rapt, because my father, mother, and uncle told her the story as if it were the first time it had been told after decades of silence. And as well as I thought I knew it, the story even felt new to me. I'd heard it before, but with the distance of someone who'd found out that he'd been enlisted in a club since his childhood, unbeknownst to him, except that this triumphant club no longer existed. It had been erased. Crushed. Defeated.

I wasn't interested in the club.

I wasn't interested in the dazzling life story of Polytropos, the man who'd been erased.

I wasn't interested in becoming a slave to books. I wanted to read them, but I entertained no fantasies of working in a bookshop. I always found it odd that people would choose to smuggle books in the false backs of their luggage on their journeys to and from Galicia. I admired Captain Calzani for crossing the Atlantic with his poetic cargo, but what had captured me was the sense of the clandestine, the shipping of contraband, the lawbreaking side of things. I admired the smuggling, not the books. Always demanding attention! My thinking was that Terranova could exist without books. Comba, Amaro, Eliseo, they didn't live with books, they lived *for* books. A toy shop. A costume shop. A goods store. A window display with hog heads for Carnival. *O Porco que Voa.* The Flying Pig. A bar. Yes, our bookstore would be perfect as a sailor's bar. The Terranova Navy Bar.

Terranova could live without all these goddamn books! The day I uttered that long-masticated blasphemy, Comba and Amaro pretended they hadn't heard. They didn't even look at me. What a failure of provocation.

It was there, but invisible to our eyes. Everything was new!

Eliseo, in ecstasy, alighted on Certain Point, the place where surrealists go to talk, and gave it a quote, an image:

Like Millet's threshers! We gathered everything, all the grains that couldn't be seen. Simultaneously. Ethnography, anthropology, archeology. And we learned as we went, with our feet. The proper way.

They worked during their free time. There was one thing they never missed, whether they were excused of their obligations or not: the Santa Susana fair, on Thursdays in Santiago. They would trudge there with their notebooks. Sometimes a camera. To thresh words. Not loose words, but words bearing masks and adornments. The language of the body, of whistles. The significance of rising and falling tones. Traditional music, dialectical tensions, and peace. Haggling and coming to an agreement. Or even the exceptional backstop of the mis-agreement, a kind of right to unfulfillment. The deaf, deafening whistle of air in the market. And Amaro noting everything down, every word, every saying, every turn of phrase, refrain, anthroponym, toponym, nickname, and even every curse—the art of blasphemy, pardon my language. Everything, every single thing. Where are the journals? What became of them? They were consumed by mold and fire. Many things were stolen and destroyed. The moths glutted themselves on Amaro's phonemes.

And what was your part?

I wrote a report on *retranca*, Galician irony. *Dialectical Leanings in Popular Speech.*

This struck me as another one of Eliseo's jokes.

I started by transcribing an argument between two workers

from Baio, at the fair, after I heard one of them say: You always answer a question with another question. Don't talk to me like Cain! The direct reference fascinated me. But the other man's response fascinated me even more: What are you trying to say?

Then the calmer of the two told the story from the Bible in which we can locate the precise origins of *retranca*: "God asked Cain if he knew where Abel was, and Cain, who had just killed him, responded with that infamous line, Am I my brother's keeper?" It seemed like the conversation would end there, but no. This dialectical farmer wasn't going to give up without a fight:

Why would God ask Cain a question he already knew the answer to?

I thought that was an excellent ending, Eliseo said. I opened my report on *retranca* with this episode. A pity it was never published.

That's because you never wrote it, Amaro said.

Amaro gained quick recognition with his work on animal symbology. He'd studied classical languages at the university. His thesis had been called *The Memory of Nature in the Odyssey*, a title and topic he managed keep despite his thesis director's initial skepticism. As the project progressed, that skepticism had gradually turned into enthusiastic support. He was fast-tracked into a position as an adjunct in the faculty, and not long after that, he'd passed his examinations to be a secondary school Greek instructor. He was one of the youngest in that year's cohort. By that point, Amaro was already Polytropos, he'd already been given Odysseus' nickname by his colleagues at the university.

Amaro was a monster, Eliseo said. He was good at everything. A polymath!

The first time I read that, as praise, in a university publication, I had an anxiety attack. Was I going to be a polymath for the rest of my life? Santiago would be a perfect city if only it had a river to drown in. Romantic as it may be, the Sar isn't very deep. So, I decided to sign my articles as Polytropos, but by that point it made no difference.

You were the first to put in writing that, among his friends, Odysseus was known as "Octopus." Now that would be a good pseudonym!

Talpa occidentalis, Eliseo. The Spanish mole. That's our story. We always end up as moles.

Amaro had also written a series for the Seminary of Galician Studies that was never published. *Small Power: Bewitching Creatures*. A power with its foundation in cunning, masks, simulation, camouflage, seduction, invisibility. The power of the small is often a humoristic one, especially when it comes to self-defense. It wasn't humans who invented playing dead as a survival mechanism. Thanatopsis, or the simulated immobility of death, is a strategy many small creatures employ. Some beetles are veritable specialists. I, who'd hardly ever seen him laugh, hidden away at Terranova and gnawing on his melancholy as he combated Eliseo's nostalgic surrealism, what I most enjoyed were his stories about bewitching creatures. The firefly, the toad, the beetle, the ladybug, the spider, the snail, the butterfly, the cricket, the dragonfly, the mantis...

The praying mantis, Vicenzo, knows how to find a wolf. If you ask in French, *Où est le loup?* the mantis will point the way.

And him? Who's the third man in the photo? Garúa asked.

I'm tempted to say that the stone was now pulsating in her hands, that it was beating like a heart. Because that's how I saw it. The rest of them saw it even more vividly. The quartzite, the thunder fossil, or the *ceraunia*, as it was known in Latin. Whatever it was, it was beating. Seeing her with the hand-ax, a lyric popped into my head, with that opportunism that lyrics, songs, poems, rhymes, and rhythms tend to have—because without the opportunism of death we'd have no gravestone engravings, epitaphs, elegies, psalms, hymns, marches, blues, oaths, requiems, "bye and byes," and no drunks, like me, who go to their father's wakes, the last wake at the Big House in Chor, and build up the courage to sing, in a rasping voice, the hymn he inspires in me, I can admit it now:

Epopoi popoi popoi
You slammed hard
so hard
into the Wailing Wall.

Who?

Him, the man with you in the excavation photo.

And then, in the face of the burning silence, she added: The handsomest of the three.

My parents, in that moment, were stone. Quartzite. Eliseo moved away, almost in a single leap, towards the Penumbra. But Garúa had the ability to make human stones speak. She had an instinctual awareness of the shadowy regions that can't be talked about, and instead of whipping out words, she'd edge around things in a way that didn't frighten.

My father asked her to pass him the photo. He gazed into the eyes of the three men in it. Including his.

It was his handwriting at the bottom of the picture:

Men of rain love the sun.

He was the one who found the Thunderstone that day. It was a Sunday after Saint John's Eve. A bright day. The excavation was part of the Seminary's work. It was a joy. He wasn't an archeologist, a member, nor even a frequent collaborator. He was a friend of mine from Chor, a very dear friend. Henrique, or to us, Atlas.

He was a stonemason, and he did the work of ten men at that excavation. One of the first measures they took in Galicia after the coup was to crush the Seminary. They assassinated seventeen members; thirty-one managed to escape into exile.

My father looked at Garúa. Without glasses, his eyes were a fish out of water, beached. I didn't want him to speak. I'd waited for this moment for so long, the moment I'd hear the truth out of his mouth—where the legend began and ended. But now, as I watched him try to extract word upon word with a corkscrew, I wanted to stand up, hug him, and beg, no, implore him: Keep it, keep that secret, papá, it's your property, your shadow, your pet, your love.

That third man you're talking about was murdered, Amaro said. I think they killed him because they were supposed to kill me. But they didn't kill me. My parents paid them not to. That's the way it was. We were friends, we were happy. And in a matter of hours, minutes, he was lifeless. And I became a "mole." He found the Thunderstone, but he insisted that I be the one to watch over it. There was a legend. The Romantics thought that these stones hadn't been forged by human hands, that they had been fertilized by lightning when it penetrated the earth. That whoever held the stones in their hand would protect everyone.

Skybound Levitabism

Garúa had a wending gait. It didn't matter if she was lost in thought, on another planet, her body, her senses were never distracted. Her feet slid across the air, over the shadows. Sometimes I'd talk to her and she wouldn't respond, and in those moments I'd leave her be, because she was off in her own world, listening to other voices, impossible to know whose, or helping build a school for adults in Villa Zavaleta, on the banks of Matanza River in Buenos Aires, teaching the elderly to write their names, because once they put that name on paper, they've got a seed, they can start to build up their alphabet the way they built their shacks. And teaching them to write the names of their professions—profession? Yes, what's your profession? And they laugh nervously, the job doesn't show up on any identification documents, but it's vital to the city, this trade as a *ciruja*, a vagrant, who picks out the city's metal, glass, cardboard, rags, wrappers, uneaten food, and broken toys like a surgeon removing a tumor, cleansing the urban body, and, Víctor, one of the adult students who'd learned to write his name, wrote his profession as *Soy ciruja*, I'm a bum. And then he went on to tell the story of the mountain, a massive mountain, the biggest in the entire province, known simply as The Mountain. A geographical feature lifted out of the city's trash. An immense still life. Hundreds, maybe thousands of *cirujas* worked there. But sometimes they weren't allowed to. The police would come in guns blazing and force them out. And some would end up being plugged with lead, a *ciruja* on death's door, disappeared in the belly of The Mountain.

No, I have no way of knowing if she's in that impoverished place on the banks of the Matanza.

She seems worried.

Maybe she's meeting someone. Maybe she's headed for Bar La Paz, on Avenida Corrientes. Maybe she's thinking it isn't a good idea to go out with her friends the way she so often has, because they laugh and speak so freely that she's started to worry that maybe she shouldn't go back there at all. Is she trying to give off an impression of normality? No, that would've been a bad idea. She walks past. Glances inside. Something's off. She can smell it. She'll never go back. She'll never see those friends again.

What were you saying?

Me? Nothing. Just talking to myself.

She smiles. She's more relaxed now. Maybe the meeting was somewhere else. In Parque de Palermo. The Japanese Gardens. Or that corner they call Villa Cariño—I wonder why? Maybe she's with a lover, hoping for a bit of *Cariño*, a bit of affection, or maybe she's in one of those couples that make love inside a car.

I thread together the things she says to me and the things she doesn't. The things she tells Comba. And most of all, the things she talks to Eliseo about.

Eliseo is animated: Everyone in Buenos Aires reads. It's incredible. Parks, cafés, minibuses. Even the *malevos*, the ruffians, read, as do the *cirujas*, naturally. I once crossed paths with a *ciruja* who had a kind of portable library in his cart.

Are these for sale? I asked.

They're for reading, sir, he said.

Then I caught a cab. The cabbie asked me what I did, and I told him that I was a bookseller and had come to Buenos Aires to learn. A *ciruja* had just given me a masterclass. The cabbie liked that, of course. He started to tell me about the writers who had ridden in his back seat. And I realized that this story, the taxi driver's, was a book on the move. The journey was the book, and the taxi driver was, so to speak, writing it for me in the air. Who impressed you most? I asked. He clicked his tongue three times, and said, No question: Roberto Arlt. Want to know how I knew it was him? He paid his fare with a book. I was just starting out, I was a kid, and this guy steps into the car, well-dressed and unkempt at the same time, not to mention a head of hair with a life of its own. At first, I figured he was a musician, one of those genius composers who can turn a thunderstorm into a symphony, that's what I figured, it was summer, and the night before had been out of this world, the beams had come crashing down out of the sky of Buenos Aires, so I said to myself, this guy must have fallen from the sky too, but no.

He said: My name is Roberto Godofredo Christophersen Arlt and I was born under the conjunction of Saturn and Mercury, an astrological inheritance that has yet to be passed on to me. I'm afraid I have no money: may I pay you with a masterpiece?

And he gave me a copy of *The Seven Madmen*. It was the first novel I ever read, can you imagine? the cabbie said in satisfaction. I asked him how someone goes about writing a novel and was expecting a bunch of theoretical hogwash, but he caught me by surprise with his precision: If you want to write a novel, you have to lose thirty pounds, smoke eighty packs of cigarettes and drink three-thousand liters of coffee. He was no lunatic. He was a clock with an hour-hand that ran fast. He had me convinced with his theory of metaphysical mendacity. That's what we were talking about, right?

What?

Metaphysical mendacity, *che*!

The taxi driver took me to Avenida de Mayo. I was sleeping at the Sabbatiello Bookstore at the time. It was a popular spot, that bookstore. The first refuge for many exiles in the aftermath of the war. A place of eminent hospitality! Old Sabbatiello would always recommend me the encyclopedia corner. Those volumes will give sweet dreams to a natural son of the French Revolution!

Eliseo paused, his eyes seeking out Amaro's agreement with this story, Amaro, whose posture in that moment was that of a landbound oarsman. It was no joke. This "natural son of the French Revolution" bit wasn't some lawyer's oratorical flourish, it had an ominous effect on the lightning-speed trials of the fascist courts. There are points in history where words can weigh like lead, can kill. That's what happened here, in this city. There were no real charges. They executed the mayor and his supporters, honorable, democratic, freethinking men, all because of a metaphor.

What's metaphysical mendacity? I asked.

Imagine that lies become a creed, backed up by some supposed scientific truth. A synthesis of science and religion. Lies as the only established truth. But I think the cabbie explained it better. When we reached Avenida de Mayo, I asked him to do another loop. The man was like a professor. Every ride was an unforgettable lesson. Not everyone starts out with *The Seven Madmen*. That's like walloping ignorance with a first-round knockout. And could you imagine if, the next day, a poet named Nicolás Olivari got into the same cab and paid the driver, at his own request, with the book he had under his arm? *The Scalded Cat*, said the driver. His name was Aldo, I remember now, and by that point I was ready to throw my arms around him, to propose we set out on the greatest transatlantic editorial venture the world had ever seen. Terranova's Cabbie, or something like that.

Was it definitely Olivari? Olivari, the poet?

Yes, *che*, the one and only Olivari with a copy of *The Scalded Cat*! And the cabbie confessed: Whenever I feel like crying, and I mean really crying, not whimpering, but crying like you do in a dirty bar when you want to watch the tears carve furrows in your sooty skin, in those moments, when I want to cry like that, I listen to *La Violetta*.

And off we went to listen to *La Violetta* in some club in the Caballito neighborhood. Since no one was there to sing it, Aldo took it upon himself, his Spanish blurring with the Italian:

E La Violetta, la va, la va, la va;
la va sul campo che lei si sognaba
ch'era suo gigin que guardándola staba

I thought about invisible threads, about how the song my dago cabbie was singing, that *Canzoneta* of the far-off paycheck, of an idyllic dirty bar, was a piece of surrealist *saudade*, melancholy. We stopped to eat some pizza at Los Inmortales. And then Aldo said: We're going to pay a visit to Giribaldi's fetus! I felt that the Free Union that had united us in the poetic taxi was losing its strength. Wouldn't it be better to go to the café that Oliverio Girondo hangs around in? But it also seemed to me that his proposition was an abject dare. And so it was. We went to a place where they kept a small fetus in a jar of gin as a preservative. *It's a fetus: we put it here without disgust; it could have been born, it could have been a drunk bastard.* Aldo held Daniel Giribaldi in the highest esteem. His *Sonetos mugres,* his grimy sonnets, had made the filth of Barracas sublime. But of course Girondo wasn't in the place with the fetus. Nor was he at Café Ramos, one of the last bastions. The sun was rising. We made our way down Costanera and Aldo stopped the car outside the Casa del Pescador. We fell asleep, and I felt like I was inside the jar of gin. I continued to feel that way when I opened my eyes and the light of the Río de la Plata blew them to bits.

Do you see that in the distance, Aldo said, around the Horizon Line? Oliverio Girondo is over there. *Va solo con su solo yo que yolla y yolla y yolla*. He goes solo with his own spirit and his own spirit goes and goes solo.

I haven't read Giribaldi, said Garúa, but it was thanks to Girondo that I started reading poetry again. Words must have such a good time in his poems! *De tu trascielo mío que levitabisma.* That new word, *levitabisma*! Everything levitabismating!

I think she could tell I felt a bit on the sidelines. She came close and whispered: *And you, do you levitabismate?*

That gait of hers. She looks both ways. And sometimes, all of a sudden, she'll crane her neck backwards to look at me. When she's on a bike, she glides along as if she's riding through the air, along an invisible cable, with her head high, until she cuts a sudden turn and darts down an alley, Hey, have some mercy for the Cripple! But she disappears and waits for me around the corner, in front of the Portobello record shop.

One of the jobs she took on when she arrived was customer delivery.

There's a car following us, she says. It was lurking around here yesterday too.

If she says so, it's sure to be true. And here I was thinking she was off in some other land, while I followed her jealously through Parque del Palermo, only for it to turn out she was the one who was present, in the here and now, with her eyes on the alert.

But I said to her: Who would be following us, Garúa? Nothing ever happens here.

Borges' Clown

Borges was right there, sitting at a table by the window at that historic, exorbitantly priced café, La Biela, that looks out on Recoleta Cemetery and the Cathedral of Our Lady of the Pillar. Nearby, there's a terrace with a majestic rubber tree that may be even more historic, and even more of a cathedral, but it's still humble, approachable, with its pachyderm skin. I hung from the long branch that curls over the edge of the terrace, by my feet instead of my hands, a high-wire act on the trunk of the elephant-tree, swinging in the air with my arms open like wings: *Lulla lulla lulla-bye!* And the old man reacted like a gaucho, like someone recognizing a familiar song. He raised his eyes to the sky, using his hand as a visor, and turned panoramically, like he was tracking the flightpath of a bird. It was a tiny thing. He didn't ignore me, he placed me on high, like an omen. My gesticulating and shouting wasn't as well-received by the waiter, who watched from within the limits of his domain, with a baleful gaze that said: *Scram*. Leave. Don't bother my VIP.

Then I performed some dance steps. A twirl in, a twirl out. A cartwheel. *Et voilà!* A bow, not a ballerina's but a ballerino's, my back straight. That was when I realized he was staring straight at me. Borges, I mean. They said he was blind, or that he could hardly see. But I think he could see me through the blur, like a mirage in a dried-up sea. He whispered into the waiter's ear and the waiter nodded and stood at the ready, but motionless.

And then I left with a stick in hand as a kind of baton, doing an impression I was better at back then: walking like Chaplin, like Charlie in *The Kid*. But when I turned around to say goodbye, he was gone.

I played Chaplin, too. How old were you? Eliseo asked.

It was spring of 1973, the year everything would change. I'd just turned twenty-one. My friends were starting to get impatient waiting for me on the hill. They asked what I was doing down there, under the rubber tree, and I remember saying:

I was playing Borges' clown.

His eyes go wide. What a lucky old man he was!

And Garúa takes the cubist umbrella, dons one of Eliseo's hats, and begins to walk around Terranova like Chaplin in *The Kid*.

As I watched her, I thought: You know what, I'm really starting to like this bookstore.

How did you meet her? Comba had asked me about Garúa.

I think she was the one who found me, mamá.

From what little she's told me, Comba said, she was almost in the clutches of terror. She managed to escape Argentina just when they were going to begin hunting her down.

I know, mamá, and I don't. I know they put a bomb in her apartment. But she had a bad feeling that night and didn't sleep at home.

We have to protect her, Vicenzo. This girl is full of souls. She came to Terranova for a reason.

I showed him around here, Eliseo said, referring to Borges. When he came to Santiago. I approached him once in Buenos Aires, and he went silent when I told him I was a smuggler...of books, yes, I wanted to make it suspenseful. A Borgesian silence! The kind worth preserving in a jar. We had a close mutual friend, Ramón Martínez López, from the Seminary of Galician Studies, who lived out his exile in Austin, where he taught at the university for many years. In the summer of 1936, he had to swim by night across the River Miño, into Portugal, to avoid being killed. To think he landed in Texas! Borges was quite fond of Ramón because it was Ramón who'd sparked his interest in Nordic mythology. In a book he published just this year, *The Book of Sand*, there's a story called "The Bribe" where Ramón himself makes an appearance, shining a light on the mystery of the Icelander Eric Einarsson. In any case, one day, Piñeiro, the philosopher of *saudade*, who was also half-blind and could only see out of the corner of one of his eyes, called me up and said: Eliseo, they've set me up as Borges' guide in Santiago—the blind leading the blind. And so I found myself accompanying them as they felt their way along the Portico of Glory. Borges touched the Apostle's left foot, traced his fingers up the tree of Jesse, and knocked three times on Matthew's head. I swear. What he couldn't see or touch was the part of the Portico that I find most harrowing: Christ with the wounds of the passion on full display, with the angels carrying the Instruments of the Passion that he was executed by.

You could have described it to him, I said to Eliseo. He saw clearly through words.

You're right, but I had been rendered speechless. I'm not without my own fears. Instruments of pain terrify me. So, I focused on the things nearer to the ground. The monsters and demons. Now those, those are a pleasure to the touch.

God the Shrink

(GALICIA, WINTER 1976)

I was with Arturo Cuadrado. At a presentation Borges was involved in, by the way, at the Alberto Casares bookstore. Everyone approached Arturo to say hello. All the ladies, that is.

You see, Arturo was an erotic magnet, Eliseo told us.

He fought in the Spanish Civil War, went into exile in Buenos Aires, and while there, he headed up the publisher Botella al Mar. To think how many bottles he cast into the sea! He published a book about our captain of Planetarism, Ariel Canzani. Canzani had written the prologues to all their books, so they called it *Prólogo de prólogos*. What envy! I've never written a prologue, I'm better suited to afterwords. But I digress. We once took a trip to Tigre. We boarded the train at the Retiro Station—you know where that is, Garúa—and at one point, a nun sat down beside him. A Trinitarian, I think. She was wearing a white habit with a red and blue cross. I was reading the latest publications from Botella al Mar, with those Luís Seoane covers that would make any book seem first-rate. That day, it was the poems of Dora Melella and a peculiar butterfly, *Viaje dentro del viaje*, Journey Within the Journey, by Damián Bayón. As Bayón wrote, I, too, had been lost before I found Velintonia, the home of the Galicianist Vicente Aleixandre on the outskirts of University City in Madrid. The cold that bore down from the Guadarrama mountains out there was sharp as a knife. But all of my discomfort disappeared when I found the house, the piano master's little home, Eliseo said, when I looked into Vicente's cobalt blue eyes. So, I spent much of the ride with my mind on Velintonia, 3, until the train stopped. When we arrived at Tigre, I noted a certain strangeness, a sacred disorder, but I couldn't place it at the time. The miracle may be happening, but it doesn't make itself evident. Everything was brighter. A gleeful glimmer in the passengers' eyes. A festive gleam like lanterns hanging from the branches of trees. The joyful architecture of the wooden boats and quays. The scintillation of fleeting patterns as they slithered along the river. *Oh hermosura que excedéis a todas las hermosuras!* Oh, beauty that transcends all beauties! And so on, you know how Amancio Prada's song goes. They were holding hands. The two of them. Arturo and the nun. And they continued to hold hands for the duration of the boat ride. Like a couple. At the helm of the ship. I saw it all with my own two eyes, and they never deceive.

No. Eliseo's eyes didn't deceive. Everything he told us was happening right then. Like how he was looking at Luís and Maruxa Seoane's house in Ranelagh, thirty kilometers from Buenos Aires, after traveling on the Ferrocaril del Sud. There was a golf course. He found a ball in the grass and walked a few hundred meters to return it to the men who were playing.

I can see it! Garúa exclaimed, clutching my arm. My father did the same.

Garúa who yearns, who begs for reality. And Eliseo gives it to her. It's the only thing he has to give. A deep place in the memory where only that which you want to happen will happen.

Yes, I can see it, Garúa said again, shaking me so that I would see it too. *Che,* you know what? My father picked up a golf ball too. In his innocence, he thought they'd lost it. Because it looked like something that must have been very valuable. To a worker, to a typographer with a golf ball in his hands, it seems like an exceptional object. The spherical consistency. I remember my father saying that. The spherical consistency.

I thought, then, that it must really have been a place, a place called Deep Memory. Because Garúa, with her fist clenched, seemed to be holding that consistent sphere as she spoke. Her father had passed it to her so she could feel its perfection. The ball had arrived there by way of a poor swing, a mistake. Finding it was a coincidence. Her father's typographic gaze had a knack for noticing things that didn't jump out at the eye. But now, the place where it belonged, the place the ball itself may have sought out, was his daughter's hand.

My father was very proper, too proper, Garúa said, and he did as Eliseo had done. He walked across the course and found a group of players to return the ball to: Here you go, it was in the grass, hidden. A marvel. A spherical marvel!

Their pockets were overflowing with golf balls, and the players looked at him like a lunatic or a *linyera*, one of our words for a bum, lost in the immensity of that immaculate green.

At the time, I was sleeping at the library on Chacabuco 955, said Eliseo. At the Federation. It was a land of freedom for them in Buenos Aires—a dozen publishers that were the fruit of exile. The presses never stopped! So, Spain sent a group of thugs from the political police. Spain and Argentina always had a cozy relationship, too cozy, if you ask me. The Nazis, the fascists, and the *apes* always got along well. Your military took a great interest in Franco, isn't that so, Garúa? The war in Spain was the war of wars. Of wars past and future. And if we had your thugs here, you can be sure Franco had his thugs in your country. It wasn't so long ago that they orchestrated the bombing of the Ruedo Ibérico offices, right in the heart of Paris, on Rue de Latran! Bombs against books. I knew the place well. It was in those offices that I embraced the editor Pepe Martínez, who had done more for democracy in Spain than any single person. And yet not a soul, or only a rare few, knew of him.

When he spoke, Eliseo was like a squirrel in a walnut tree. He would leap from the trunk and proceed to hop from branch to branch as if he were never going to return to his initial story. But he always returned. Or almost always

Yes, in Argentina, there was a group of agents whose lair was located at the embassy. They infiltrated, they spied, they got their hands dirty. They were hoping to worm their way into the Federation of Galician Societies. They'd dismantled everything in Spain and couldn't stand those islands of freedom where people carried The Republic in their heads. The invisible country that traveled back and forth in people's luggage. Sometimes the luggage bore soil. Actual soil. Like the soil that was brought for Castelao's funeral rites. The burial of a diasporic prophet. He wanted to rest on Galician soil. But here, on his native ground, the murderers were in command, so we brought it with us to Buenos Aires.

Wait, were you at Castelao's funeral? I asked, feigning surprise. When was that?

They buried him in January of 1950. I remember it clearly, but no, I wasn't at the Chacarcita Cemetery.

One of my uncle's characteristic mannerisms was a series of parabolic twists of the right hand, anticipating an adagio: Death is…a *fatto* to which I pay no heed!

He liked to use that Italian word, *fatto*, instead of event or happening. And I liked to hear him say it. A *fatto*! A roar that clears the air. He spent every moment of his life combating sadness. He said he was a militant in the Laughter Party. But this time, he turned gloomier as he continued his tale: The day of Castelao's funeral, I was at an asylum called El Borda. I went to visit a poet friend of mine, Jacobo Fijman. He'd spent much of his life there. They'd tried to kill him, they shot at him, they threw him in prison. His life was a misery, one of brutal treatment and starvation, but he said that the nuthouse had saved his life. He wasn't a madman who wrote poems, he was a poet fighting madness: *God will come down to us in shrink's clothing*. He's never looked better, God has.

He waved his hand like he was turning a page, then changed his tone.

No, I wasn't at Castelao's funeral. I was, however, at the Federation on the day they attempted to occupy it. We rebuffed the fascists with lead and steel!

You've never held a weapon in your life! said Comba, with a sudden harshness. She'd been silent up to then, as if she were elsewhere. She was never short with him. In fact, she was his best listener, always tilting her head in that slight, unconditional way that tends towards rapture. But that day, something, maybe the *fatto*, had made her snap.

What would you know? he said, in the same embittered tone. You think you know everything, which parts are tall tales and which parts are true. Well you don't. I was there. I was. And I held a weapon!

Suddenly, I was afraid. Our lives at Terranova transpired in sacred disorder. And Eliseo was neither a lost island nor a solitary dolphin. He was a golden beam in that chaotic architecture. There were some shadowy areas, of course. Those hidden regions of life were part of the geography of Atlantis, 24. You could come and go without having to give explanations. Without a commotion. We were hand-axes, two-faced. All oddity was respected. Including the day that I decided—we decided?—not to speak to my father. The day I sent him a note, a cablegram, requesting that we communicate by letter from there on out:

Don't see it as an act of hostility, Polytropos, because we can be amicable and write the words that we can't, or don't know how to say aloud.

Signed, Eumaeus, the prince of swine.

The thing with Eliseo was that he spent all day opening up passageways across the limits of reality. But not like a madman. He spoke of a happy penumbra. He said that he'd heard María Zambrano talk about it when he visited her in Italy to help her pack for a move to France with her cats. She did herself that favor, gave a name to that place, that portable country where she could feel happy. The Penumbra Tocada de Alegría, the Joy-Touched Penumbra.

This encounter with the philosopher Zambrano, Eliseo said, was a kind of baptism, a second life. Italy was the trip of trips. Asked where he'd come from, he answered: from the place one is born and unborn. And that first day, in the shadows of her apartment on the Piazza del Popolo, they spoke of Spinoza's *Ethics*, of Plotinus and the universality of a religion of light. Out of discretion, she never said it, she never put it in writing, but it was Eliseo who wove the thread of García Lorca into their conversation: *I go seeking a death full of light to consume me.*

He'd been to Cuba, like her, but a few years earlier. Eliseo's trip to Havana had been financed by some relatives who owned a hardware store on Calle Mercaderes. This gave him the opportunity to attend a lecture by Lorca, who had just flown in from New York, at which Eliseo also met Lezama Lima. Lorca was happy in Cuba, Eliseo said. He'd left the United States in disgust. The only place he'd felt good was Harlem, in particular the nightclub Small's Paradise. It was the crib of jazz poetry. And it was a particular haunt of Langston Hughes, who would later spend time in Spain, defending the Republic.

All of a sudden, Eliseo vanished into the Labyrinth, careening towards the Transatlantic shelf. He came back in excitement and wonder, like someone discovering that the trout in a still life is still alive and flopping.

He declaimed:

I Wonder as I Wander, by Langston Hughes. Published as *Yo viajo por un mundo encantado*, I Travel Through a Charmed World, by Fabril Editora, in 1959!

And that trout flopped its way into Garúa's hands.

We should have stayed in Cuba, Eliseo said. He told us about the night he spent in Havana's historic center with Lorca, Guillén, Hughes, and Lezama. We're olive trees, ombú trees, Egyptian sycamores walking in the night. Who said that? Never mind, it's not important.

You were in Rome, Uncle, I reminded him. You were with María Zambrano!

Right, with María and her sister Araceli. Poor Araceli. During that trip I arranged for her books to be transported to Spain, to introduce people to her work. Ignorance was rife back then. Besides, they needed to lighten their luggage. They already had quite a bit of weight to carry around the world with them. And it was María who suggested to her sister that I could adopt one of the kittens. They already had a dozen, and that was before another litter had been born. But it was easier said than done. Her sister

Araceli spent that day and the next scrutinizing me. María felt like she was a Siamese twin. One day she said to me, I call her Antigone in my head, because she's taken no part in history but was nearly devoured by it anyway. Araceli wanted to know everything about me before she would commend one of the kittens into my care. In the end, I suppose, I passed inspection.

When I returned to Terranova, it was with the cat Antigone in tow.

That night, Comba wanted to take a walk with Garúa. Just the two of them. There was nothing noteworthy about her suggestion. They would take walks together sometimes, after dinner. A stroll around the Waterline up to Santo Antón Castle or the Abrigo Observation Dyke. On this occasion, they walked around the historic center. They sat down in the Praza das Bárbaras—Garúa had taken quite a liking to the spot. I had too. The first time we went there together, she said that there was something special about the acacias in the square, that they were backwards, their roots digging into the moon.

After her walk with Comba, she looked at me like I was a stranger.

Your mother told me about Eliseo.

Okay.

Okay? It was really difficult for her to talk about. For me, too.

If I were trying to create a wonderful human being, I'd create it in his image.

Garúa was silent for a while.

I was surprised, it was the last thing I expected us to talk about. But Comba suddenly asked me what I think of Eliseo. And I told her what I just told you, that he's a wonderful human being. And she said: Oh, I'm so glad to hear that! He's my brother. She nearly burst into tears as she said that. And I had to encourage her to talk. I said: Comba, you came out here to tell me something, and now you're all choked up. Go on, what is it?

He has a big imagination, she said.

He does.

He's a dreamer.

He is.

He's never been to the Americas.

Sure he has, he's been in Buenos Aires! Parque del Retiro, Robert Arlt and the cabbie, Alberto Casares' bookstore, Chacabuco 955, the golf ball in Ranelagh, his visit to Fijman in the nuthouse in Barracas, Giribaldi's *Grimy Sonnets*...I'd never even heard of that book before!

He's never been. Not to Argentina, not to Mexico, not to Cuba. Aside from a trip to Barcelona at the invitation of the editor Janés, he's never been farther than Portugal. Lisbon and Amarante, to be specific. Though it's true that a crow followed him all the way back from Amarante. Has he told you the story about the crow? He came back and said: Comba, there's a crow at the door. I thought it was one of his jokes, and I said: Go on then, invite it in! And he did. This crow, the Exile, could even talk a bit.

What about Ariel Canzani's ship and the book cargo, is that real?

It's all real. Everything he says is true. He just wasn't there for any of it.

I was surprised, but not as choked up about it as Comba. This made Eliseo even more wonderful than before. He'd invented Buenos Aires, and Havana, and Rome, without ever having been there! And that was when Comba told me the less sunny side of things, the side I needed to hear. That Eliseo's trips to the Americas, or elsewhere in Europe, were really time he'd spent at a mental institution. Not for insanity. She told me that he'd been caught up in the nets of the police several times for being gay. And going to these mental wards was a way to avoid prison, right?

She was asking me.

Yes, that's right, I said.

So why the silence? I've been sitting here listening to these half-baked stories as if they were true, and you just played along.

Now you know.

What were you trying to hide? That your uncle is gay?

I wasn't trying to hide anything.

Well, I guess you're not very expressive with your silence.

I wasn't trying to hide anything, I swear!

I was furious. Not at what Garúa was saying, or at Comba. I was furious at the world. I felt a metaphysical disgust towards the metaphysical mendacity of it all.

What I wanted, Garúa, was for you to get to know Eliseo as played by Eliseo. Not bound by history with all its bullshit. Not crushed by the onslaught of bigotry. Here, the violence and bigotry are in the law. Sodomites, flesh-peddlers, pimps... The legal code still refers to them that way. They lump them all together. They started with one called the "Vagrants and Miscreants" law, and then moved on to one that was far, far worse, the "Dangerous Social Elements" law. Not that long ago, people were still being sent to camps and special prisons. They came back in pieces. And the only way to avoid that was to have a doctor recommend that person be checked into a psychiatric facility before the courts got involved. Once you had the paper saying they had been checked into a facility, they would drop the case. All with the judge's understanding, of course. And a bit of money to smooth things along.

But those places are terrible too, Garúa said. The main one in Buenos Aires, El Borda, is in my neighborhood, Barracas. It's the same one where he said he visited the poet Fijman. I would avoid that street, Vieytes. That hospital was hell. And Eliseo knew it, don't you see that? That poem about God in shrink's clothing!

He didn't exactly go to a mental institution, I explained. He went, and he didn't. In Dr. Esquerdo's facility, on the outskirts of Madrid, there were the wards for the mentally ill, but there was also an area with little dormitories for people like Eliseo. People who could afford it, of course. In some ways, it was a place to convalesce. They couldn't leave, but they could go about their lives. Some reactionary doctors saw homosexuality as a disease, but there were also some who fought against that form of repression. Once when we went to visit him, he said: I'm reading a hundred books all at once! And it was true. There, with all that special company, he would hand us books that often ended up coming to rest in Terranova.

We were on our way to the Borrazás, in Orzán, a bar with a wall covered in bird cages containing canaries and goldfinches. The place was gloomy during the day, and the birds preferred to sing at night, surrounded by the neon lights. But we ended up at the inlet's Buttress instead, listening to the roar of the sea.

The foam of the waves flew over the walls, spraying salt in our faces.

We stayed firm, our hands clasped together.

The sea said everything I might have wanted to.

The Informant

His initiation into Terranova was a comical one. No one would ever have thought he was a bastard. And it was true, no one did. The general view was that he was an educated idiot.

This was mostly because of the John Deere story.

He was wild over books, there was no denying that. He came every afternoon and stayed until close. On Saturdays, he spent the entire day. He'd lose himself in the Labyrinth, the shelves in Terranova's east wing, which Amaro had named in honor of the exile Max Aub, and spend hours and hours there staring at each volume. Sometimes he bought things, but not always. The one constant was that he'd take notes in his journal about the books he saw and the books we told him about. Eliseo did most of the suggesting, after having the brilliant idea of introducing himself not just as one of the founders of the bookstore, but also an international book smuggler.

He was a teacher, he said, he worked at private schools and as a personal tutor. But his true calling, since "before he'd learned how," was to write. As proof, at his second visit to the store he showed up with a blue folder containing the manuscript of his novel, *Jalisco's Crime*, a fresh, undeniable tour-de-force, and the first serial hard-boiled novel to be set in Galicia.

He'd signed it John Deere.

The novel was based on true events. There'd been much talk about Jalisco, a shadowy character who'd murdered two women only to receive a minor sentence and disappear shortly after his release. The story went that one of the women was a CIA agent, whose file said that she worked as a secretary to (that is, she was spying on) the Galicianist Republican leader Castelao, during his exile in the United States.

It's all well and good, Eliseo would say when John Deere wasn't around, but what this man's producing isn't literature—it's tractorism!

He spent a long time trying to convince my uncle to write a preface to the first edition. The publication of *Jalisco's Crime* was imminent. An imminence that went years without being consummated. And still hasn't, to this day.

Eliseo apologized.

I'm not equipped for prologues. It would take me ages, like Genesis in the Bible. And don't ask me for an afterword either. I'm my own afterword. It's already written.

The Informant was devastated. It seemed to me as if the folder where he kept the manuscript signed "John Deere" had suddenly aged a great deal. Had become part of the family of folders bearing El Ocaso insurance's list of obituaries and the deceased.

Take my advice. Prologues are worthless. I'd even go so far as to say they're a distraction in a great work of crime fiction, a fake cadaver. A sack blocking the door that the reader has yet to open. You possess an essential quality of crime authors: your persistence, and the consistency of a writer who is what we might call a tractorist.

He heard something in the mechanics of Eliseo's reply, the subtle hiss of irony: Do you think I should change my pen name?

Absolutely not. I would kill for a name like that! It's more than worthy, it's got charisma, that name. But let me give you another piece of advice: write what you know. Why don't you tell your story?

My story? What story?

Yours, Eliseo said, suddenly serious in a way that was unlike him. You know this city's mysteries. Or you have the means to find out. Let's not play this game any longer. Do you see a point in it? You should use all of that, all the hidden histories, the things that can't be said. Shine a light on them!

Who's the protagonist?

You! The voice of the fog. A fog with a salty aftertaste.

The Informant looked out at the street. Through the display windows were visible cars in motion and cubist outlines of people. He cast his eyes to the floor. He had a proverbial comment: the best floor in the city—polymorphic, polychromatic tiles, each with its own fish. Atlantic art-nouveau. He didn't say anything this time, though. He was mulling over the salty fog. You could tell he liked the taste.

They would kill me, he said all of a sudden.

It didn't sound like a line from a movie. Or an ironic quip. He wasn't, at least I didn't think so, gifted in that art. At heart, he was simple. And exact. Exactitude, now that was an art he had a knack for. He had an exactitude that could even be finicky and disagreeable. For example, making a note of all the errors in a book, his pencil marks dirtying the margins like specks of fly shit.

We were all looking on in expectation. Even Baleia, the cats, and dead Falstaff, the parrot. Animals are very prophetic.

No, I'm sure of it. They would kill me.

Maybe he continued to slip his typed reports into the express mailbox at the post office. Maybe, somewhere, in some space masquerading as an administrative office or real estate company, some Intelligence official was still receiving his reports, which, in Eliseo's mind, composed the *Terranova File*. All our history would be in it. Things that we may not even have known about ourselves. When I found myself thinking about that, about the possibility that John Deere was still sending in his confidential reports, the feeling it provoked in me was curiosity. Though for many years, the feeling he'd provoked in me was disgust. It happened every time he cracked the door open, with that caricature of a profile, everything in him oblique—eyes, nose, speech. Because his manner of speech was oblique too. So many years of pretense had accidentally led him to appear as a caricature of his own function. Garúa picked up on this the moment she saw him. She approached me discreetly and whispered the most accurate summation I'd ever heard about an infiltrator:

That strange fish is a snake.

We all knew that John Deere was informing on us. Within the bounds of Terranova, we treated him like a government official, a consul, or something along those lines. The Informant. The astonishing thing was that Garúa saw it the moment he walked in the door. And Goa, who had come to our house as a cook after escaping from a brothel in the Praza Campo da Artillaría, had sussed him out by his smell. One day, with all the naturalness in the world, she said:

That cock-eye in the raincoat is a liar. Teacher my ass, pardon the expression.

How can you tell?

He doesn't smell like a teacher.

The Informant was changed. He came wearing a beard. Not a long one. Like a first beard. A blonde-streaked fuzz, shadowing an old face which the needles of time had stopped trying to prick into nobility or wickedness, aiming instead for shock or dignity as his face continued to droop. The gaze that always seemed to me alternately dopey or malicious now seemed more aware of the tragedy, at the same time as it disagreed with it. He hadn't come to Terranova much in recent months. And his drop-ins were furtive. He'd say hello to my father, but not strike up a conversation. Even his greetings were different. They were missing their hypocritical flattery, though his lips and hands still had that foppish looseness. Eliseo, who interacted with him on an absurd plane of language, which seemed to amuse and divert him, said that he was probably growing distant out of a sense of guilt.

Or a sense of absurdity! My father would say. History opened itself up like an abyss before his eyes. And it's the grunts like him who experience the stupor of it most directly. He was an ant carrying information to eternity. And all of a sudden he discovered that this eternity was a heap of rotting meat.

Fine, fine, Amaro. Abysmal history! But from here on out, put on the Cambalache tango, the junkshop tango, for him.

This time, it was clear he hadn't come to spy, because the visit fell outside of his usual routines. He had a mission. To order books.

He already had the titles written down. Poetry. Just poetry. How strange.

There were two notes.

One: *La realidad y el deseo*, Reality and Desire, by Luis Cernuda.

The other note he handed me left me speechless:

Poemas: The End.

The music of *The End* echoed from some place in my own Hidden Land, a bell that reverberated through the entirety of my hippocampus. He interpreted my silence as ignorance. It was a collection published by Visor. An event unto itself. I had read it.

It's an anthology of poems by a North American woman. My daughter has assured me it exists.

I was sitting on my kneading trough, a restored table that had been brought from Chor, where it was formerly used to store flour, dough, and cheese, and which wielded the same kind of enchantment over me as a lock whose key I was in sole possession of. I got up without looking at him, without responding. My voice refused to speak. The decision was made by my phonatory-articulatory systems. I'd never exchanged a word with him. Nor had I wanted to. I'd never hidden my disdain, and I didn't feel that way because he was a snitch, or not solely for that reason, but because of the slimy appearance he gave off as an intellectual. It bothered me that he touched the books, I felt bad for them, as if they were in the hands of a pederast, and it infuriated me when he brought them to the counter after having touched, and annotated, and underlined them all over. He'd try to spark controversies around dusk when the Thelema people came to the store, at least that's what Eliseo called them—they were the devotees of Gargantua's abbey, they lived by the creed "Do what thou wilt" and, at the least, brought an atmosphere of "Say what thou wilt" to Terranova's twilight hours. The Informant would walk right up, introduce himself, and chat. Sometimes he didn't even react to Eliseo's remarks: Would you look at that, Nothingness has come covered in spelling mistakes! And he would reply: Oh, there's Don Eliseo with his insinuations again. It enraged me to think of him wandering in the Magic Labyrinth, in the various regions of Mobilis in Mobili, or around the Transatlantic shelves and the Penumbra. He sniffed and sniffed, always on the hunt for the Hidden Land. But he wasn't there to sweep the place. In the end, he was hidden too. There were sweeps, and quite a few of them, but these were performed by members of the "Social," Franco's henchmen. On multiple occasions, I entertained the thought of following him and hitting him over the head with the Thunderstone. I can't believe it, what a horrible accident. A Bible fell from the top shelf and hit him in the head.

I went off to look for *Poemas: The End*, the Emily Dickinson anthology. I had an urge to tell him that we didn't have it, that it had run out of stock, that it was a much-awaited translation and we had none, because, he had to understand, not much had been translated into Spanish, in Spain, since the times of Juan Ramón Jiménez. It was amazing, the poet's shrewdness, not trusting anyone prior to his exile, militantly allergic, prophylactically cordoning himself off. And what courage it must have taken to write a book like *Platero y yo*, Platero and I. He was one of the few who knew of Dickinson. Because Juan Ramón Jiménez was, it must be said, a kind of Emily too. People can be divided into two categories: the ones who feel too much and the ones who feel too little. And then there are the ones who feel everything. Some of them sit beside each other in the Penumbra. I see them as interlinked bodies. *In den Wohnungen des Todes*, In the Houses of Death; *España, aparta de mi ese cáliz,* Spain, Get that Chalice Away from Me; *Cahier d'un retour au pays natal*, Notebook of a Return to My Native Land; *Sombra de aire na herba*, Shadow of Air on the Grass; *Poeta en Nueva York*, Poet in New York; *Mundo de siete pozos*, World of Seven Wells…They're all bodies that have to be kept safe from predatory hands. Like those that come in the name of a recipient who hasn't requested them, who knew nothing about them—meanwhile you, when you see the book, know exactly who it's for, who's going to open it, and who, in turn, is going to be opened up by it. You can see it in the way he turns the pages as if he's afraid of damaging them, or of the brittle sheaves falling out and being carried up by the kind of gust of wind always lying in wait on the corner of Rúa Atlantis and Rúa Far. The case with Emily's book and The Informant's daughter must have been something along those lines.

I was tempted to tell him no. It pained me to think of selling the book to this bilabial voiceless plosive of a man. I looked at the book, and I looked at him. You seem so comfortable there, Emily, dressed up and bathing in light in your Pinhole Chamber, in your room in the house in Amherst, writing poems that overflow with love for your sister-in-law, your secret love. Don't move an inch. I'll protect you. You'll stay there until they call us.

But then I heard my mother speaking to The Informant. Ever the diplomat, my mother. Always so generous that she'd even let him in on jokes about her age: I'm like Agatha Christie, I married Fontana for his archeological affections—that way, his interest in me will only grow as the years go by. But not today. There's no joking today. They both speak in an almost complicit, pained tone of voice. Complicit. Pained.

She's not doing well, says The Informant. They're telling us not to hold out any hope.

We always have to hold out hope, she enjoins, placing her hand on his shoulder, an unprecedented gesture, as if she's trying to provide him a transfusion of that immaterial substance.

I only have one hope left at this point, he says, dispirited: That it happens quickly. Without pain.

And the book leapt from the shelf into my hands.

The book knew what I later found out from Comba. This is no fantasy. Some books know when they're needed.

The Informant looked up and squinted at me in perplexity, like someone being confronted with their name after going ages without hearing it.

Before he left, he went to see Comba. She always had more to give. Time, that is. She indiscriminately offered her ears. Limitlessly. Why don't you set up a confessional? my father said. They couldn't have been more different, but in this particular art, she reminded me of Expectación, from Chor. Expectación might be walking around with a hundred-pound pile of clothes or a mountain of grass on her head, but that still wouldn't keep her from stopping to chat without a thought for the time. Meanwhile, you would try your best to follow along, as her lips shaped essential information in rising and falling tones, always with flair, her hands acting things out and creating subtitles, and you couldn't help but think how awful all that weight must be, how much she must be suffering. And yet it was Expectación who'd worry about the other person: What's wrong, are you congested? No, no. Have you eaten? Yes, yes. Well, you must have stitches in your gut to eat and not put on weight. And she'd mutter as she went on her way: They don't know what hunger is up in the Big House. My father was the opposite. He moved through the day like someone with wax in his ears. He had to take an extreme interest in something to listen. Even still, he'd grumble: I've just wasted five centuries of my life speaking five whole minutes with that *illustrious* man. A blast from the past, from Eliseo: when we were young, you could hardly get Amaro to shut up. The war took that joy from him. Somewhere along the line, he transfused that quality to Eliseo.

Can I get you a coffee? Or a glass of Campari? There must be some whisky around here too, Amaro is a whisky man. And thus, The Informant, now that the Dictatorship was on its way out, finally entered the sanctuary. Our Pinhole Chamber. He'd spent so many years searching for it, and now he was being invited in by the woman of the Listening Ears and the cat Antigone in her rocking chair. Comba shut the door.

A long time passed. We began to exchange intrigued expressions. What if The Informant had been hiding a bitter criminal under that pained mask? If he was watching his world fall apart, was it possible he wanted to rip out Terranova's heart? Some had already tried. The Guerrilleros de Cristo Rey, Warriors of Christ the King, had twice thrown Molotov cocktails through the window. He expressed disgust about those episodes. He even went so far as to say he felt like a part of Terranova. I appreciated Amaro's interpretation, when it was just us again, for bringing back the levity:

We should consider The Informant as part of Terranova's historical patrimony.

When they finally emerged, The Informant rushed out, obliquely, giving a farewell with an invisible intention.

After we closed the store, Comba invited us into the Pinhole Chamber.

A Campari, really? I said, but no one laughed at my sarcasm.

His daughter has cancer, Comba said. And the treatment has had the opposite of the intended effect. It left her defenseless.

She paused. A moment for grief. *The End.*

He also told me something very serious, something to do with us. There's an agent in the city from the Argentine Anti-Communist Alliance, the Triple A. He's dangerous, this assassin. He goes by Almirón, and apparently he has contacts in the Spanish police. They're coming for her, for Garúa. He heard it first-hand.

The Six Lights

It was raining for us. For those of us peering out through the windows. A lazy rain, its drops more inclined to slide down umbrellas, heads, and shoulders than fall to the ground. A drizzle that slowed as the day passed. And all the movement in the street. And the green car, a Seat 1430, that was parked right in front of Terranova.

I motion for Comba to send the elevator down with the agreed-upon book. A Mirasol title. A sign, a sigh.

My father picked up the phone. I know who he was calling: Verdelet. It had cost him fettle and flour, as the saying goes. He spun the dial for each number so quickly it looked like an orbit. It's not just for her, Comba had convinced him, it's for all of us. They'll put an end to Terranova!

I was pretending to shelve books. With my back to the door. Three people came in. Leading the charge, in a raincoat, was

Pedrés, the Secret Police inspector, followed by an equally corpulent stranger with a trimmed mustache and beard, in a gray suit and black tie with a tie-clip that shone like a medal. Standing guard at the door was Cotón, Pedrés' partner. Concave and Convex, Amaro liked to call them.

It was Pedrés and Cotón who performed the sweeps here. Sometimes on a whim, to intimidate us. Other times, they came looking for something specific. Their most common prey in years prior had been the Ruedo Ibérico books and notebooks printed in Paris. But those were also Terranova's most well-guarded guests.

And one of their protectors was Pitts.

Do we have any copies of Pitts left?

That is, Robert Franklin Pitts' book, *Physiology of the Kidney and Body Fluids*. We'd received a box full of the Mexican edition. It was in high demand from doctors, even those in other cities. What few we'd gotten had come by coincidence, to conceal the true cargo. Our "Mexican" classics were by León Felipe, Max Aub, and Luis Cernuda. My father also displayed, as a holy trinity from Mexico, Antonio Machado's *Collected Works*, a leather-bound edition of the complete works of San Juan de la Cruz, and William Blake's *The Marriage of Heaven and Hell*. Here's Whitman translated by León Felipe! The last suitcase with León Felipe's work had been brought by Alexandre Finisterre. A poet and editor, Finisterre spent much of his life seeking recognition for his patent as the inventor of table soccer, which he'd dreamed up during his convalescence at a wartime hospital in Catalonia. Why didn't León Felipe come back? He asked my father. It was supposed to be a sure thing. He himself had expressed an intent to return, and he'd gotten as far as the airport, but two hours before take-off, he stood up and exclaimed: I'm staying! If it had been a few days later, his funeral committee might have crossed paths with the desperate families searching for their children, university students who were killed or disappeared by the military at the Tlatelolco massacre. I thought, in that moment, that León Felipe was one of them, one of the massacred students, and that his body was whispering an obsessive idea: They've always got us located.

Eliseo held Finisterre in high esteem: His life is even more surrealist than his poems, and it's not so much that I believe in him as in his fantasy. He said he grew up with so many siblings that he subsisted on light as a child. Light gulped down with the isotonic of the sea. And the truth of it was in his eyes. Comba would say: That's his only possession, his gaze.

The Pitts book, with its kidneys and bodily fluids, acted as a false cover to protect these clandestine creatures. Some even had the covers of books by Francoist ministers, like *El crepúsculo de las ideologías*, The Twilight of Ideologies, by Fernández de la Mora, and *Horizonte español*, Spanish Horizon, by Fraga Iribarne, re-bound in our friend Helena's workshop to conceal Ruedo Ibérico books. Are there any twilights left? Another horizon is on its way out!

Once, sometime around 1966, they took Amaro to the station for an interrogation.

Pedrés, with a well-known reputation as a torturer, liked his catch phrases: You can't make an omelet without breaking a few eggs. They didn't want to break any eggs, they just wanted to know the true identities of the men behind the pseudonyms Santiago Fernández and Máximo Brocos, who'd coordinated a report with Ruedo Ibérico called *Galicia Hoy*, a critical pamphlet that had infuriated the Minister of Information so greatly that he'd break as many eggs as it took to find them.

Amaro said it didn't matter what they did to him, he had no idea. He knew, he told them, that a powerful man in a rage was capable of killing someone over a line of poetry. He cited the example of Stalin, who had ordered the assassination of Osip Mandelstam for that very reason, a poem.

A poem?

A single line.

Christ...

He knew that could happen to him, too, but he had to apologize, because he had no idea of the men's true identities.

When he came back, he said he spent the entire interrogation trying to focus on Pitts. He should get around to reading that book sometime. No, he *would* read it, he had to.

Neither Pedrés nor the man with him seem to be in any hurry about their incursion into Terranova. They look at the portraits in the gallery of writers. There are also framed quotes hanging on the wall, some of them anonymous and others with the author's name cited. But one of the frames contains a quote that's not like the others. It's longer, typewritten. The unfamiliar man moves closer in order to read it. It seems to capture his interest. As soon as he's done reading, he laughs and calls over Pedrés. No, he hasn't read that one. He moves closer.

Man requires a certain quantity of calories in order to survive. What is that quantity? The figure seems to be a rough 3,000 calories per diem. From this we can infer that a healthy adult male who undertakes consistent physical activity expends some 3,000 calories in a twenty-four-hour period. But here lies a curious fact: intellectual activities require very little energy expenditure. It has been said, and rightly so, that it costs one less energy to read and comprehend a book than it does to simply hold said book in one's hands. Energy expenditure, of course, being understood in terms of proteins, fats, and carbohydrates.

Domingo García Sabell

Notes for an Anthropology of the Galician Man, 1966

The quote was there because Amaro thought it was a magnificent way of exalting books by using them as an object of irony. A Prismatic Stone of the finest quality. During his last visit, he and Eliseo had convinced Captain Calzani that it should be added as an appendix to the avant-garde manifesto of Planetarism. The quote put him in a good mood. It made him laugh.

But now he watches, impassive, as Pedrés and the bearded giant are the ones to laugh. They make a few jokes. Then they whirl around, their expressions shift, and their faces regain their character. Pedrés gestures to Cotón, who's still at the door. In the blink of an eye, uniformed officers have appeared on the sidewalk outside. The Greys. Cotón gives them some signal, and they arrange themselves outside such that they're blocking the exit.

What's the meaning of this, inspector? Comba asks.

This establishment is closed for the time being, ma'am. We're going to perform a search.

What country are we in? You can't close a bookstore!

We most certainly can if we have reason to believe that bookstore is housing a terrorist.

There's a hidden peephole in one of the ceiling lamps. A secret eye for Garúa to watch through. Big enough for photographs to be taken, should the need arise. The room she's occupying on the second floor with Goa has been barred. And Eliseo? No one knows where Eliseo is. He can't stomach brutality. Neither physical brutality, nor the brutality of language. One day, he encountered a rat on his way up the attic stairs, one of those little rats nibbling away, as Comba says, on the botany books, and Eliseo screamed in surprise. The rat dropped dead from the fright. Eliseo stared at it in the hopes that it was playing dead, using cataplexy as a survival mechanism, or had maybe nibbled on a bit of that stupefying Menéndez Pelayo, but no. He poked it with the umbrella handle and saw that it had gone stiff for good. This was a traumatic episode for Eliseo. He came downstairs and sat down in front of us, pale as a sheet, petrified, his shirt hovering away from his body, as if he had taken on the air of the dead. What's wrong, Eliseo? Comba asked. I took a life with a scream!

A terrorist? A terrorist at Terranova?

Amaro glanced at the wall clock and then his wristwatch. Several times, slowly. A gradual action, but an action nonetheless, and one which caught Pedrés and his colleague's attention. Timepieces often have some greater significance in situations like this.

Comba's eyes are steeled by all the years she has spent cleaning up fear. She faces up to them:

Many years ago, and it's been raining ever since, Pedrés, when I was a young woman, two thugs like you and this man showed up on the street with the old synagogue where I lived with my family, where my widowed mother sewed to earn a living, and you turned our home upside down. Why? Because you were looking for two dangerous fugitives, that's what you told us. One of those was Amaro, my husband. And the other was my brother. You've met Eliseo, haven't you, Inspector?

Stubborn and tenacious, Comba put her question to him without batting an eye, but Pedrés's golden rule was no-questions-allowed. Another of his factory-made phrases, famous among those he'd interrogated, was: The only one doing the asking right now is me.

So, his response was to ignore Comba and shout:

We have the area surrounded, don't get any cute ideas about trying for the rooftops!

The stranger remained silent and impassive. He was born on a moonless night, Comba thought. She had an inkling of who he was. The hunter. Unspeaking, unblinking, he only watched. He was growing from within. Looking bigger and bigger. His only sign of impatience was to bring his thumb to the tie-clip and give it a polish.

No more questions about the search warrant, said Pedrés. We have permission to take action when we suspect a dangerous element might escape. And that's what we're looking at here.

Looking at what?

Hand me those photos, Rodolfo.

Still wordless, the stranger sticks his hand into his pocket and hands him a few pictures.

And you, come here. This was directed at me.

They were photos of Garúa. In various places, with various haircuts.

Do you know this woman? And without waiting: Don't be stupid and try to deny it. We know she's been to Terranova. No, we know she lives here. It'll be best for everyone if she turns herself in.

Turns herself in to who? For what?

This time, the inspector allows the sliver of a question to breach his defenses.

There are some things we need to verify. She's travelling on a false passport.

He shook off the moment of doubt with an angry reminder:

Enough with the questions. Tell her to turn herself in!

What would a terrorist be doing in a bookstore, Pedrés?

Eliseo emerged from the Penumbra. Holding a revolver. With aplomb, I'm even tempted to say like a professional. He aimed it at the stranger. It seemed like he was aiming straight at the tie clip.

I suddenly felt like I was observing the scene as the clock on the wall. Every one of their faces was a distinct historical representation of shock in the face of the inexplicable.

This is a real Six Lights – I know you can tell, you ape. Hands up!

The unfamiliar man must have been quite familiar with the revolver's quality, as Eliseo said, because he immediately obeyed. It was an impressive moment, seeing all of them with their hands halfway in the air.

You're sick, Eliseo, said Pedrés.

That's not a good tactic, inspector, my uncle responded. I wasn't sure he knew how to use a gun, but I had total faith in his dialectical capabilities.

It's not a good tactic, Eliseo said, to treat a healthy person as if they're sick.

You know perfectly well what I'm talking about, said Pedrés.

It's you who doesn't know what he's talking about. You've never had a clue. You're a demented torturer. And you have the gall to come in here, tossing aside the law, at the beck and call of a criminal. Let's not beat around the bush, we all know who he really is. Tell us, Rodolfo, what are you doing in Spain? Why are you here? Could they not keep up with all the coffins they'd built at the cadaver factory back home? Have you given the inspector all the gritty details about how the business of death works? I think they sent you abroad, along with the Necromancer, because the cadaver production was out of control. Am I wrong?

I'd never seen Pedrés nervous; crude and agitated, sure, but not like this, he was in a daze, he was almost shaking.

You're sick, Eliseo. I mean no disrespect, it's for your own good.

Let's leave things as they are. We'll talk about that gun another day. Don't do anything you might regret.

I've got plenty of lead to do my regretting for me, Eliseo said.

I heard the poetic inflection in his voice. That's when I realized the Six Lights was empty.

Pedrés never dropped into Terranova again. The hunter disappeared. Garúa was certain it was Rodolfo Almirón, a corrupt cop with a gruesome record, one of the organizers of the Triple A, which had opened the way to the Argentinian Dictatorship during the Dirty War, not to mention taking on mercenary work in Spain for terrorist acts like the one in Montejurra, in the spring of 1976. My father was sure that Verdelet had placed a call to the governor, but the governor had taken an eternity to intervene.

Not long after this, Eliseo went before the judge, accompanied by my parents. He revealed the origins of the gun. He'd bought the Six Lights six years ago from a man who was emigrating from Chor, without bullets. But why? He was thinking of collaborating with a group of Portuguese surrealists, in what they called Operação Papagaio, Operation Parrot.

Operation Parrot?

Yes, it's an unknown episode in the recent history of the Iberian Peninsula. But it's entirely real, your honor. The surrealist group at Café Gelo, friends of mine, decided to take action and put an end to Salazar's Dictatorship. This was in the spring of 1962. There had never been a surrealist revolution before, but that was about to change. The operation consisted of commandeering the broadcasting system at Rádio Clube Portugués, playing the national anthem, and calling for soldiers to desert from in the colonial war, then inviting people to gather in the Baixa neighborhood in Lisbon. They weren't able to go through with it because someone talked. The PIDE, the Portuguese political police, detained the core group of surrealist poets. But no one ever heard about it. The strange thing, your honor, is that the revolution on April 25th, 1974, only two years ago, employed the same *modus operandi*, if you will, as Operation Parrot. It began with a song, with the broadcast of "Grândola, Vila Morena," at the very same radio station and at the very same time. And in that revolution, at least at the beginning, there was but a single death. The death of a poet. The death of a surrealist, of the founder of abjectionism, the man who, seeking to reach that avant-garde of total renunciation, declared: What can a desperate man do, when the air is vomit, and we are abject creatures? You see, that man, Pedro Oom, who owned nothing more than a plastic flower, died celebrating a toast to the 25th of April, Portugal's carnation revolution. It was a revolutionary death. He died of joy.

Eliseo "took a trip." That was the agreement they had reached. Things were trickier this time because of the confrontation with the police. It was going to be a long trip. One he would never return from.

So in the end, it was true that you had a weapon! Comba said, her eyes red with the emotion that conveys a person's determination not to cry.

Yes, darling, but it had no lights.

It seems I'm going to see a doctor, in Madrid, while I'm visiting, said Eliseo. I like that expression. What brings you here, Señor Ponte? A doctor's visit! And tell me, how do you feel? Optimal, unhappily optimal! I remember a conversation with Jacobo Muchnick in his office at Fabril Editora. He wasn't upset. In the span of two years, he'd created the best book nursery in the world. That's no exaggeration. But there were capitalists in the Compañía General that ran the place, capitalists rotted inside by worms, and they censored a truly innocent book, *El porvenir de la incredulidad*, The Imminence of Incredulity, just to slight him. Muchnik was in low spirits, but he still had his spark. He said to me and Pellegrini: The important thing is to commend yourself into the hands of a doctor with whom you can die happy. Pellegrini put together an excellent anthology of surrealist poetry, but the most surrealist of the three of us was Don Jacobo.

He entered the Pinhole Chamber and walked over to the cabinet. There's a piece here, a *miniature*, he calls it, that Eugenio

Granell sent me from New York. He was born here, in this city, but hardly anyone remembers that. Retrograde amnesia. Somewhere in the Penumbra, we've got a copy of *El hombe verde,* The Green Man, which he wrote and published in exile. I'm a green man too. Here it is, here it is. The letter with the sheet music to "Lullaby for a Mechanical Baby." Go on, Garúa, play it for us, that piano has spent its whole life quiet!

He and Amaro headed to the train station. Amaro carried his luggage. Eliseo had his arm hooked in Amaro's, and with his free hand, he lifted one of the hundred umbrellas in farewell.

The melodies of the "Lullaby for a Mechanical Baby" continued to ring out in Terranova.

Expectación

(GALICIA, SUMMER OF 1977)

As a child, I always hung around in the caretakers' home. With Expectación and Dombodán. I only ever remember the two of them being in that house. Never an adult male. Whenever we went to Chor for the weekend, or during a vacation, the first thing I would do was go see them. Expectación was cooking for the Big House in those days, but without fail I would find myself seated at the table in her humble home, the white oilcloth spread over the table providing the only gleam in that smoke-blackened home. I ate my meals there. I slurped up her collard-green stew with the zeal of Oom's rabbit. In the Iron Lung, when Eliseo told the story, I would imagine the smell that wafted through Expectación's house. When I was left alone, I understood *saudade*, the concept Amaro and Eliseo argued over so frequently. Arguing. As a child, it upset me deeply, it threw me into anguish when they raised their voices like that, until I discovered that an argument was a play. And that, like actors, they always embraced at the end. Meanwhile I remained on the sidelines, an audience member. But man, did they rile me up!

Saudade is an animal feeling! my father would boom. We all have it; all animals have it, I mean. Give a dog a bone and take it away. There's *saudade* for you. It's in their bones! This was my father's thesis, and he would run through all the fauna and their respective *saudades*. And then he would fly into a diatribe against Teixeira de Pascoaes: The prophet of *saudade*! As if we didn't have enough of them already, now we have to deal with the religion of *saudade*. Stick to Buddhism!

Who was this Teixeira? His name was never spoken on the radio or the TV. I only ever heard it spoken by the two of them, and it brought out their worst instincts.

And then Eliseo would play his cards: Cosmos, Fiat, the Word, the Soul of the World, the fusion of Spirit and Matter, Desire and Memory, Life and Death. These are the things I'm talking about. And you? You're too busy grinding your teeth over a missing bone.

And what I was longing for was Expectación's stew.

She told Garúa what I'd learned by hearsay. That Dombodán had been born out of the blue.

Out of the blue?

She appeared one day with one hand on her stomach and the other motioning that she was about to give birth. Edmundo had died, but Grandma Balbina was still alive. And there were more people around the Big House back then. But no one noticed, or no one bothered to. Expectación always wore heaps of skirts and sashes. Like geological layers, my mother said. Comba had gone to spend some time there, wrapped up in her own worries, that is, me. On what was inside her. With an eye to the moons. To the stars, every single one. But it turned out the universe had its eye on Expectación. That day she couldn't keep quiet anymore, the baby was practically coming out of her mouth. She came early, at the aurora—she used that word, *aurora*, which tickled the neo-Grecian Amaro, who exclaimed, with patriotic zeal: She must be the one person in this corner of the earth who calls the sunrise the *aurora*, as it's meant to be. It's because I get up very early, sir, Expectación said. Anyway, she came early that day, at the aurora and with milk in hand, because she'd just milked the most generous of the cows, the one that still had a name, Elektra, and it all seemed to have come in the same pitcher, the vivid animal light, the sliver of white, and the scent that allowed Expectación to guess which field the cow had been grazing in. What Amaro called a genesiac sense of smell.

But that day she came at the aurora with the milk in hand,

with the oily milk and its bestial shimmer. She set down the bucket all of a sudden, or tried to set it down, she dropped it in her agitation, in view of the awakening of the slumbering milk, the mill-dust, the foam, even in her mouth, the lactose of words, the foam of saliva.

What's wrong, Expectación?

It's coming!

What's coming?

Husqvarna. That had to have been it. After an entire week up in the mountains, he came down itching to tear something down, even if that something was a person. He took another swig of the tumbadiós they served at Bar Bonanza. You could hear his engine starting to rev, the rudimentary gears of his neurons starting to turn.

You gotta go to the livestock fair and ask the salesman about that miracle with Dombodán.

Husqvarna handed off to Mambís:

Yeah, how'd he get Expectación pregnant without fucking? What kind of tool's he got?

Sunday morning. Pleasant weather. Church bells ringing for the noon mass.

Dombodán could work himself into a state with espresso. Piping hot, lots of sugar. A fresh espresso and some sea urchins.

Sea urchins he'd caught himself. Eight-year-old urchins. A cosmic number. Creatures from outer space, spit out by a spell and hiding underwater with their Aristotle's lanterns, grouped in intersex colonies, male and female alike, a far more advanced species than we are. That's all a person needs to be immortal.

He's not my father, the salesman with the hat. My father is an oiler in the Merchant Marines.

We'd occasionally climb up a hill called the *Man de Deus*, the Hand of God, each of us sitting on one of its divine fingers, our feet dangling over the abyss. It was the best view of that slice of the Horizon Line, with the busiest cargo ship and oil tanker traffic, all of the ships coming or going from the ports in the north. Every so often, we'd have the joy of seeing a big sailboat that opposed the rigid trajectories of the rest of the ships, one that seemed to be out purely for the sake of sailing.

I'll bet he's on that sailboat, I said, allowing myself some hope that it were true.

Dombodán was more realistic, even in his dreams.

No, he's an oiler-oiler.

And he said it with his gaze intent on the merchant ships. These boats looked like the kind where no one came up on deck purely for the sake of it, to wave at the people on the coastline. No, these were no-distractions boats. And Dombodán put such intensity into his gaze that it seemed as if he were trying to pierce the hull and travel into the heart of the machine room so that he could see his father there, drenched in sweat and grease, untiring. He couldn't come up. He couldn't leave the boat. He couldn't come back. And suddenly, I understood what Dombodán's eyes were saying when he stared at the Horizon Line. The boat was trapped on that line. It couldn't follow any other route. And the oiler, his father, was its only crew member.

Husqvarna and Mambís were making jokes at his expense. The mood had struck them. It was their day off, they had a break from slicing through massive trees, and they'd come down from the mountain looking for something that would offer a bit of resistance. Something firm. The chainsaws had stopped, and all the horsepower was in their arms. Dombodán was powerful in his own way, though. As lean and sturdy as rebar.

My father is an oiler. He can't leave the ship. Just once, he stopped in Antofagasta.

He what?

Stopped in Antofagasta. Here's the letter.

And it was true. He always carried this letter in his back pocket, still plastic-wrapped in its air-mail envelope.

Look here: *Antofagasta, Atacama, Chile.*

I'll be damned! So, what's the letter say?

A drop of water fell right onto the spot where he was writing it. The first drop in forty years. Can you imagine? You can still see the spot where the ink ran. He said they needed to fix the roof.

Expectación doesn't know how to read, said Mambís. Plus, what would there be to read if the ink ran?

Shut up, said Husqvarna. All of them, Husqvarna, Mambís, and the rest of the clientele, huddled around the letter. Around the drop, the place where the drop had splattered, the discolored circle of the eyes. Their heads rising in search of a roof. The roof covering the most miserable house.

My old man, Garúa told Expectación, told me about this Galician priest, a really special guy. My father had met him through work, because the priest had come to ask how much it cost to print a book. He never ended up writing one, but the man himself was a book. His last name was Tréllez. Wait, was it Tréllez? Anyway, he was very generous. He apparently died dancing at a club. People said his family back here in Galicia was very rich. That they owned the most famous health resort in the region, A Toxa.

I've seen it from the outside, said Expectación. I don't think I'd like to bathe there. The casino, sure. I'd love to see how cards are played. But the baths there don't sound so great to me. Because I like to keep to myself, you know? They say that's how rich people are, that they like to keep to themselves, well I like to keep to myself too. I've never been much of one for social mixing. I see the things they do, the way they live, but I don't want them to see me. That's my heritage. Not letting them see everything I do, what I eat, whether I've slept or not. But I know plenty about them. I wash their clothes, empty their chamber pots, and that's a lot to know. I don't know every last detail, but I know plenty about the people in the Big House in Chor, the Big House in Reitoral, and that dentist who built himself a mansion—you wouldn't believe how much money you can make from teeth—anyway, I know plenty. I can say all this to you because you're not rich, Garúa. Or are you? No, no, you're not rich. This one's half-rich, she said about me. He's like a son to me. She laughed: Or half a son! He suckled on one side while Dombodán suckled on the other.

I was scared Expectación would tell her about us getting arrested for climbing to the roof of the cathedral. And about what had happened at the police station, with Dombodán taking the charge for the backpack. Expectación and I exchanged a glance. And I saw that she wouldn't. That neither of them would ever have done something like that. I was disgusted with myself. For entertaining the thought. For not trusting them.

The best day of my life was the first time we all went to the beach together, Expectación said, everyone from the village all crowded onto the back of a tractor. We're real close to the sea. But we weren't going to get all caught up in those waves, no sir. The young people do it now, but all the women my age would walk along the shore or at the most, dip our feet with our clothes still on. Mrs. Comba had given me a bathing suit, but it was a long time before I put it on. And I certainly wasn't going to put it on for lying in the sun. No sir. At the beach, around other people…I'd sooner drop dead. I like to swim when no one else is around. But the sun, I can't resist the sun! The sun drives me wild.

And she burst into that laugh of hers, a laugh that was like a thousand years of laughter.

I'm so sweet on the sun I worry I'll get pregnant again!

We went into the little chapel, Cabano do Santo, which is on the property of Big House, with Expectación and Dombodán. At the time, there were three highly venerated icons in the area. The most eye-catching of the three, and the one that gave the chapel its name, was an icon of Saint Anton with a baby pig at his feet. Animals make frequent appearances in holy houses. And song lyrics. When there was an animal in the mix, no matter what kind, it immediately grabbed people's attention. Did you know that Saint Anton, the patron saint of animals, is also my guardian, the patron saint of cripples? When I said it, I exaggerated my limp, spinning around in what I call the "Bacon Style," but nobody laughed at my routine. A tragedy. Then we stood in front of Christ on the crucifix. The one in Chor is extremely realistic. The art of embellishing suffering is one of the great merits of Catholicism.

Without much conviction, I said: He was like that before I got here, I swear! Garúa was the only one to take the bait. What do you mean? On the cross! It wasn't us. You jackass, she hissed, gesturing for me to shut my trap because we'd moved on and were standing in front of the jewel of Chor, an icon that ferments in the shadows, the most lifelike of them all, and Expectación said: It's made of living wood! A Virgin of Good Hope, a Virgin of O. To people in Chor, she's the Pregnant Mary. To my father Amaro, she's the Annunciated Virgin of Chor, because during his time in the Seminary, he wrote a piece on this unique icon. She's so expressive in this rendering that she has a reputation, according to diocese's guide to religious iconography, for being "not made by human hands." In his study, Polytropos made an ironic inversion of that hypothesis. If the carpenter Geppetto said of Pinocchio that he was made from the best wood known to man, what could we say about this Madonna Annunziata? Because this image, carved out of humble wood by honest hands and fertile eyes, is the most human of offerings. Something along those lines. Apparently, my grandparents from Chor, Edmundo and Balbina, hadn't been too enthused about his comparison of their Mary to the doll from the legend, but Amaro made up for it by drawing great similarities between the image in Chor and that of the Lady of the O, our Lady of the Expectation, stored in the museum at the Santiago Cathedral. He estimated that they both dated back to the fourteenth century, rather than the sixteenth, as the experts had decreed.

Her left hand was on her stomach, and her right was raised as if to warn that the child was getting ready to come into the world.

He wants to say something, there's something he finds funny, Garúa said.

It must be me! I said. After I got out of the Iron Lung, Comba told me to come pray to her one day. I came by myself, and she whispered: *Che*, you're not so ugly after all!

Finally, a smile from the group. Another miracle from the Pregnant Mary.

She's in a funny mood today, said Expectación.

Today? I always remember her being like this.

Well, she has her days, Expectación said. Yes, she has her days, Dombodán echoed. And then she said, as if in a trance: Our Lady here still has plenty to give!

And then, in her second voice, which was a low, grave tone that came, in a manner of speaking, from deep within: Do you want to have a wedding?

It wasn't a joke. The look in her eyes was a dare. I, who had spent the whole time joking, was at a loss for words.

I can't read, but I know the missal by heart.

I took the opportunity to make a joke: So, it'll be in Latin?

Of course. That was our "going to the movies."

Garúa stood between Dombodán and I. She was playing along, she was excited. I laughed, but it was the nervous kind. I was afraid. And I know now that Dombodán was too.

Can the three of us get married? asked Garúa.

And Expectactión, already assuming a vicar's voice, said:

I'll marry anyone who wants to be married! There's only one condition: you have to love each other.

Dombodán

I'm not built to die.

I didn't come up with that, I'm not trying to brag.

It was the doctor.

Here's what he said:

This boy isn't built to die.

And my mother, Expectación, nodded in respectful silence. Because the doctor's words were the Gospel to her. He's earned a reputation for being good at soothing people's nerves. I'm sure he knows what he's talking about.

The first thing he asked me was:

Do you want to die?

I like questions like that, you know, calling a spade a spade, but my tongue got all tied. That happens to me sometimes. Especially when people ask me good questions.

No, no, I don't. I don't want to die.

There's a gravestone in the cemetery at Chor with words engraved into it that sound like the stone itself is lisping: *Here lies someone who did not wish to die.*

And the doctor kept going but took a different tack.

Are you trying to hurt yourself intentionally?

No.

Then why do you raise your hand against yourself?

This took me a long time to understand.

Expectación looked at my hands in disapproval. I did the same. My hands were there, on their own, covering each other, trying to disappear. I shoved them between my thighs.

The doctor stared at me hard, but not out of a desire to crush me. There are two ways of looking at something that moves. One is to distract yourself, the other is to find something in it. I'm pretty good at telling those two ways apart, it was one of the first things I ever learned to do. Being able to tell when someone's coming for you. When someone's going to hunt you. Knowing which leg a chicken is limping on, you know. I think his stare was a stare of distraction. He stopped writing in his notebook at one point. He listened. Asked the occasional question. Here was another good one:

Let's be frank, Dombodán. Have you ever contemplated suicide?

Why was he asking? Because of the falls? I'd fall from roofs, bridges, trees, horses, bicycles, my motorcycle. I'd ride on the carousel at the fair, and once it really got going, when it was spinning as fast as it could, I'd let go of the chains. I can fall from any height. But nothing ever happens. It's an impulse. An art.

You've seen it, Garúa. You saw us fall from the alder tree into the river, and nothing happened. What could have gone wrong? Rivers are made for falling into.

I'm not hurting anyone with these falls, not even myself. You know that better than anyone, Vicenzo. I've been falling my whole life. Falling feet down. And what I know better than anyone is how much some people like to make a big fuss and spew toads and serpents over any little thing. The ones who will grind an axe down to nothing. Some people are just looking for an excuse to feel envious, even if that means they envy the act of falling.

Everyone went around town saying:

Expectación's boy is touched in the head.

He's got his wires crossed, the landlady's boy.

Little Dombo, God bless his mother, is a drug addict.

I don't know why they had to bring my mother into the falls. Or the drugs. I was sober when I did my falling. I think they stuck their noses in my business because I didn't have a father. But I know I have a father. At every fair, every funeral, people would gossip: That one, the one with the salesman's hat, that's Dombo's father. Nope. I'd know my father when I saw him. Right away, at first sight. My father is an oiler, I know it. I shut their traps with the letter from Antofagasta.

This falling business, that was something Mr. Amaro understood. Even though it was a fall without falling, when I was up on a ladder trimming the vines. I fell and landed on my feet. And he said: Nice fall, my boy! And then he said something brilliant. What was it, Vicenzo? What was it he said?

You're a classic, Dombodán. That's what he said.

Right, a classic. I really liked that.

I didn't like that the doctor had used that word, suicide. Some words are better left unsaid. My mother knows that better than most. That's why she calls the Devil the Artist. And whenever anyone asks about her son—sometimes with me standing right there, can you imagine?—she always stays her course, she prays, but she never lets go of the rudder:

Well as far as bad things go, he's doing pretty well.

Hah! Go dig around in your own shit. But that doesn't satisfy them, of course. What they wanted to hear was: Catastrophe, cataclysm, bloodbath. I've got lots of words like that. Whenever I'm not so hot, I take them like golden pills. And man do they taste good!

How are you doing, Dombo?

Optimal. *Unhappily optimal.*

Those were good lyrics, Vicenzo. And *Epopoi, epopoi*, that was good too. And "The Wailing Wall." Your guy is great with songs, Garúa. It's too bad The Urchins went to shit. How long did you all last, Vicenzo?

About a year. No, less.

You can't get anywhere like that. Look at the Rolling Stones. They've been around almost as long as Os Satélites, in Coruña. That's how you build a fanbase. Suicide, hmph. Expectación never brings it up, but I can always hear the grumbling in her silence. The inward muttering. I don't think she's ever talked to herself out loud, not once in her life! When I was little, I used to think her stews tasted so good because of how much she talked around the pot. That talking was a way of giving the stew substance, constantly stirring around those incorporeal spices. Radon. Mr. Amaro talked about radon once, about the radiation of stones, and how it produces *saudade*. The scientific nature of *saudade*. My mother chewing on radon. The smoke from the fireplace. The black shadow. The plankton hanging in the damp air. And words like nettles. I could hear her now, chewing in disgust on that rash-inducing word, suicide. I was sitting in an armchair. The doctor's office didn't even have one of those chaise longues. My body had nowhere to fall.

Finally, because he was no idiot, the doctor decided to ask the question in a roundabout way:

Have you ever thought of leaving life behind?

I felt one of the spines in Christ's crown dig into me. They're always hanging around, scattered all over—it seems like there's thousands all over the world.

I said:

Have I ever contemplated suicide? I don't know. As for leaving life behind, no.

The doctor smiled. He told my mother that I had an intelligence in the rough, which I liked. And then, with this tone of scientific certainty, he declared:

This boy isn't built to die.

I was seeing this doctor because of Mrs. Comba. She'd gotten them to let me out of prison so long as I agreed to undergo treatment. And I did. I locked myself in the attic closet in the Big House, hidden behind the wall of leather-bound and bundled newspapers, which no one had been in since we'd gone there to look at what your father was filming for us, Vicenzo. You can still see some of our amazing falls into the river. We looked like cartoons. Anyway, that's where I shut myself away. I locked myself in and left the key on the outside. I was by myself, alone with the daguerreotypes, the photos, and the old Super-Eight projector. Expectación was the only other person who knew I was there. She had the key and she wasn't going to open the door no matter how loud I howled. Everything creaked. It was a capsized boat, and I, strapped to the bed and clawing and gnawing at my own skin, was a castaway desperate for a pocket of air. An air that turned out to have a deceptive smell, a freshness that would quickly turn into a smell of decay. I found out afterwards that it was Expectación; she would crack the door open at night to spray a Floral Harmony air freshener into the closet. My salvation. Nine days and nights battling against that scent, against that plague of *Golden Bouquet* freshness.

It was true. I wasn't built to die.

The things she must have heard. The things she must have had to bear. How much she must have cried on the other side of the door. Resisting even her heart's command: Open that door, Expectación, or I'll tear out my eyes. Her hand in pain, calloused, from clutching the key in the lock but never turning it.

Not once did she open it for me. That's a mother.

Cleaning Up Fear

I couldn't clean up my fear, so I left, Dombodán said.

Clean up your fear? asked Garúa. She was asking both him and the air. After all, it was fear that had brought us to Chor. We were going to spend a while outside the city, in a hidden land, because sinister forces had breached Terranova.

Dombodán was telling us about his time working on a farm. An industrial farm. The Chicken Hatchery. He was in charge of "social order." That's what the owner had told him when he started, that it was very important to maintain "social order."

Social order?

Yeah, he has quite a few businesses, this guy, and he's spent a lot of time thinking about the whole thing. The biggest problem a hatchery can run into is fearful hens.

I would think the bigger problem would be the fearsome ones, I said.

Well, it's the fearful ones that end up dying. That's the problem. Basically, social order is about putting the feeding troughs in strategic places. Otherwise, the chickens will get scared and start to crowd, because the smartest ones know it's in their interest take up as much space as they can. But a moment will come when the fearful ones start to crush each other. All because of fear. They litter entire spaces with it. And it's hard to clean all that fear up afterwards.

Hard how? Asked Garúa.

Well, because the fear stays behind in their spaces.

We were all silent for a while. The only sound was that of me wobbling on my platform shoes. I had a harder time walking when I was overrun by unease. And that image of a space littered with fear had sent it surging through me. Nowadays, Dombodán was working in a fireworks factory, in some far-flung place on top of a hill called Mar de Ovellas, Sea of Sheep. It was for safety reasons that it had to be so far away, he explained. Factories like that couldn't be in close proximity to residential areas.

I've heard, I said, that they never turn off the lights in those kinds of farms.

Never. They keep them on day and night.

Why'd you quit?

Because of the music.

The music?

Yeah, the music. There always had to be music playing. And I like music. But the owner wouldn't let me change it. He said it had to be that music, exactly that fucking music.

And what music was it?

I don't know. I can't remember.

All the insomniac anguish of those birds seemed to fill Dombodán's eyes. The anguish of creatures that aren't permitted sleep.

And you're not afraid? asked Garúa. It's dangerous, isn't it, with all the gunpowder around?

No, I'm not afraid. We make happy things. You have to picture a festival. That's the image you need to have. The sky at night. Total darkness. And all of a sudden, there's a palm tree of light! A glittering snake! A rain of stars! That's what you have in your hands. And it does wonders for cleaning up your fear.

He took a few steps forward and turned to face her, the epitome of a happy man:

I'll have to make a Pinwheel Firework for you!

We'd only gone for a few weeks to get out of our fearful space, but Garúa was starting to feel more and more at home in Chor. You'll be safe there, Amaro had told her. Of course, Comba had added, only the people in Chor know that Chor exists. The smell of autumn was hanging in the summer air. Garúa was fascinated by

Expectación, by her way of being, by her body, with that astral corpulence, an incessant orbit that created its own time. And by her manner of expression, by the words that came to her mouth, by the punctuation of her laughter. And she liked Dombodán. I was surprised. But I liked that she liked Dombodán. And I liked watching them fall together. Because Dombodán quickly initiated her in his art. During our free moments on the weekend, they would ride bicycles down the grassy marshlands and fall into the puddles. They would speed down the hills and angle themselves like clumsy birds as they fell into the maize fields. Or they would fall on the dunes and roll down. But most of all, they would fall into the river. From the bridge. From the branches of the alder trees.

Film us, Vicenzo, film us! And I would mime the act with an invisible camera.

They would help each other up, sopping wet, caked in mud and dirt and covered in blades of grass. They would embrace, and I would film them. It was my way of returning the embrace.

We went looking for him in the afternoon, but took a different path around the hill, one that would give us a view of the sea from the Man de Deus overlook. He brought his lunches from home and ate with his coworkers in a shed. On our way, at the crossroads before the turn for the workshop, was an abandoned house.

Or rather, a boarded-up house. Because it didn't show signs of abandonment, it was neither crumbling nor in ruins. Some hidden hand maintained it. Its walls were made of stone and the wooden parts—the doors and window frames—were painted indigo.

It's a beautiful house, said Garúa. Too bad there's no one in it.

I knew who used to live in the indigo house.

One afternoon, as we passed by, an old man was there splitting wood. He worked methodically, but also with the calm of someone who prized a symmetrical cut. One of the entry doors led out to the storage shed where they kept the wood. It was a single door, with its upper leaf open, revealing a lamp with an old lightbulb hanging from a braided cable on the inside. The bulb didn't so much illuminate the darkness as it took the form of a luminous bubble that the shadows left to its own devices.

I knew who this man was too.

He returned our greeting and dug the blade into the tree stump, a sign that he was in the mood to talk. I think it must have been the novelty of Garúa that animated him.

Garúa, this is Mr. Miguel.

What? I won't have any of that Mr. Miguel nonsense! He said in amusement. No one uses church names around here. You must have meant O Croto, The Tramp!

The Tramp? Now it was Garúa's turn to be amused. Why The Tramp?

Because I'm The Tramp's son. His youngest. My brothers are called Os Golondrinas, The Swallows. My father emigrated. At first, he'd send the occasional message, but soon enough he stopped sending any signs of life at all. One day one of the locals who had emigrated came back and said: Your father's off working as a swallow. And then he said: If he comes back at all, he certainly won't be coming back rich! I guess "swallows" were some kind of nomadic day-laborers. People thought it was a funny nickname. And that's how we got stuck with the name The Swallows. A few years later, another local came back, a man who owned a pizzeria next to the Constitución train station, on the other side of the pond, and he handed me a bundle and said: Here's your father's legacy. He was a good man. He knew no master but himself, and he kept his own counsel.

But he was a swallow, wasn't he? My older brother asked.

Sure, but what your father really was, was a tramp!

A tramp? What's a tramp?

Someone who doesn't have a cent to his name but doesn't owe a cent either. Poor, but free. He lived in a train car on a dead-end track. If he wanted to travel, he would ride on the tops of the cars. That's who your father was.

In the bundle were a bandoneon, some old newspapers—*La Protesta* and *La Antorcha*—a book—*Martín Fierro*—and a Six Lights wrapped in a poncho. That's what the neighbor called the revolver. All it's missing are bullets, he said. This gun has never been fired.

How do you know?

Because it was mine.

My brothers, who were already getting ready to leave, decided the best person to look after his legacy was me, the baby of the family. And that's how I inherited his name. The Tramp. The tricky part is that they also left me with the house. And I was the only one here to take care of our mother. And the livestock. It should have been me who left. Every time I see the sea, the Horizon Line, I think about her.

Who? asked Garúa.

Sabela, the girl who lived in this house. She said to me one day: I'm leaving. What will you do? And I said: Hold on, I need to see how my mother is doing. And I couldn't go back. Not that day or the next. When I was finally able to make it, her father said:

Sabela left for Argentina, she went off to Vigo and took the boat. She spent the whole night before she left chopping wood. I said to her: Daughter, that's enough, you need to rest. But she didn't even hear me. All night she was out here chopping wood, all night.

Her parents were already very old by then, The Tramp told us. I don't think they could bear to burn even a single one of those blocks of wood. It's all still sitting right there, where you see it.

He looked at me: You know this story, don't you?

I nodded.

Sabela was Henrique's sister, Atlas's sister, he said. And Atlas, the stonemason, was good friends with your father, Fontana, wasn't he?

I nodded.

When the war broke out, a group of Falangists came to kill Fontana, at the Big House. But they couldn't find him, so they came here instead and killed Atlas. He was a good kid, that Atlas! He's buried right over the hill, outside the cemetery. They wouldn't even bury him on hallowed ground. Sabela said she couldn't stand this miserable, grief-ridden place any longer. Every day, she said that. And she said how, if she could, she would board the boat with her house, her family, her wood, and her brother's bones in tow. All of it.

I glanced sidelong at the bulb. A moth was trying to penetrate that bubble of light.

The Tramp, I said to Garúa, knows *Martín Fierro* by heart.

That's amazing, she said. I only know the part about the solitary bird that consoles itself with its song. That's as far as I can make it.

I couldn't tell you why, but when I read it, it all stuck with me in a single sitting, like my mind had already made up a place for it. Every so often, I take a swig of moonshine to refresh my memory.

He tapped his head: But it's all right here.

What The Tramp does is very important, I said, though he protested with a wave of his hand. It is, it's very important. Whenever there's a wake, people can't wait for the priest to finish so that The Tramp can stand by the deceased and recite *Martín Fierro*.

Garúa smiled, but it was a smile that couldn't hide her incredulity. Which is what made Dombodán's arrival so opportune.

Did you know, Garúa, that The Tramp goes to all the wakes in Chor dressed as a *gaucho*?

I should have been over there, riding on the tops of train cars. I'm full of nostalgia for things I've never experienced. But I come here every day to chop wood, in case Sabela returns.

And the Six Lights? Garúa suddenly asked.

I gave the revolver to a good man, to Eliseo, the uncle to little Fontana Jr. over here. He said he loved it for its culture.

It's raining.

There are leaks in the Big House. Not just in the attic, but also in the sitting room, where rain falls through the gaps in the hinges of the skylights.

At Expectación's instruction, we set out pots, tubs, and some chipped casserole dishes. With the varying heights of the drops, and the different sizes and materials of the vessels, the house turns into the stage of a percussion concert, into a massive instrument in and of itself.

I notice Garúa moving up the stairs to the balustrade in rapture, then standing on her tiptoes and grabbing a zinc basin, an iron pot, and a copper casserole dish. Listening. Outside, on the roof and windows, the rain taps with a thousand fingers, but the sound that rings out inside is the laborious perforation of whichever raindrops manage to sneak through. They have to have a certain weight in order to fall, and each one of them achieves a different note.

Expectación finds Garúa's rapture amusing.

This is starting to feel like a *requiem aeternam*, she says. I'd prefer the sun to come out and play its paso doble.

No rain gets through in Expectación's house. We eat her stew with such zeal that our slurping turns into a piece of music. A hymn of thanksgiving.

Expectación says it rained much more than this when she was a girl. Two, maybe three times more. It would start raining on the 15th of August and not stop until the end of May. Even the frogs would drown. They had a saying that famine had to wade its way into Galicia.

There's no way it could have rained that much, says Garúa.

Oh, you don't think so? When we were at mass, one of people's favorite times was when the priest would tell the story of the Great Flood. How furious God was with his creation, how well he instructed Noah to build the Ark with all the carpentry measurements, how he'd brought on all the pairs of animals—that was all great. But the part everyone was always most eager to hear was the part about the rain. Father said that it had to rain for forty days and nights without end for the water to cover the Earth. And all of us in our pews would exchange glances, until someone murmured: That's not so bad, sounds like a drizzle to me! And then Father, who had his sense of irony, would say that it had rained an entire year. Or two. And with that he made it a happy Easter, as the saying goes.

Garúa was very upset with us, with the Fontana family, when Expectación told her that she didn't know how to read or write. All those years in the Big House, from the time she was a young woman, and no one had bothered to teach her.

She never wanted to, I said in our defense. My father tried and she ran away. They couldn't even intimidate her into learning.

Is that true, Expectación?

When I was a girl, in my parish, Uz, all the letters that came were either to tell you someone was going to war or that someone had died. Always. You opened a letter and a dead person popped out. And I would think to myself: What do I want with this reading and writing business? No one's going to spring a dead person or a call to war on me, or, for that matter, a fine for collecting wood on the mountainside.

But you can read other things now, Garúa said, teasing. There are love letters—you could read or write those!

But that's even sadder!

Look, I know how to write my name. That much I know.

And she wrote it out, slowly, singing each syllable as she went:

Ex-pec-ta-ción

And when she saw it, when she saw her name, she burst into laughter. The laughter of a thousand years.

A Lump in the Night

(GALICIA, SPRING OF 1978)

The doll amazes me. There it is, sitting in the window of the Noah's Ark toy shop. One of the shops I yearned to go into when I walked down Rúa Atlantis on my way to Terranova. They've always had good toys, but I could never have imagined something so avant-garde. A doll with crutches. Marybela. The most elegant of them all. Her wavy hair like a mermaid's. I have the same bemused feeling of surprise as when Eliseo gave me a magazine whose cover featured a young Marilyn Monroe standing up on crutches, set against a snowy background. The little limping Monroe put on such a nice smile for Canada's Rocky Mountains!

There's a backstory on the box, in English, to explain: *I broke my leg riding Pony too fast.*

You go, Marybela! It's a magnificent explanation, like a

universal law of human behavior. I should walk around with a sign around my neck: *I was riding Pony too fast!*

I can't decide if I should buy it and bring it to Garúa as a gift. Come to think of it, I've never gotten her a gift before. Except for those cherries. A cone of cherries. And chestnuts. A cone of chestnuts so hot they burned your hands and covered them with ash.

But no, I'm not going to show up with Marybela under the crook of my arm.

It would be better to bring her cherries.

Ever since she came, Terranova has changed.

What would you like to do? Amaro had asked her.

I'd like to repair books, she said. I know a bit about it. My father had bookbinding friends who also worked as occasional book repairmen.

It's settled then, Amaro said, you are hereby named Terranova's book physician. You can set up a field hospital on the second floor. With the way things are up there…Those wretched souls are going to welcome you into their arms like Evita!

The first thing she did was buy work overalls from El Barato Mercantil. Every so often she'd come down for a *mateada*, a máte session. She brought that custom with her to Terranova. There was a pair of Uruguayan exiles in Monte Alto, a man and woman, who never missed Garúa's *mateadas*. The woman always came in high spirits, with emerald eyes that never hinted at any deep wells of suffering. And yet, one day she told us that she'd had a part of her tongue cut off. You what? It was me, I did it with my teeth, she said. I was being tortured. I swore I wouldn't talk, and I bit my tongue so hard that part of it came clean off.

She sipped her máte. She said: I'm sorry, I shouldn't have told you that story.

Why shouldn't you have? The world needs to know these things, said Garúa. It's too full of navel-gazing snobs as it is.

She spent mornings curing books up in her field hospital and afternoons with us on the shop floor. And whenever we received an order she'd go out on her bike to deliver it. No one asked her to, she'd simply offered. She said it was the best way to get to know the city. But she stopped for a while after the visit from the goon squad. And she didn't pick up her delivery route again until we'd come back from cleaning up our fear in Chor.

I also felt like I was cleaning up my fears surrounding her. As far as I was concerned, if bewitchment wasn't unsettling it was no bewitchment at all. Everyone thought we were together, and I certainly wasn't going to be the one to whip out a megaphone and set the record straight. I liked that other people thought that. And I liked to entertain the thought myself.

One day, Garúa didn't come back. From her deliveries, that is. She called to say she'd be back late and that we shouldn't worry. This was enough to pacify my parents. We had dinner. They went to bed. I said I was going to down to the Pinhole Chamber to read for a while.

And down I went, traversing mountain ranges and bottomless depths in the sea charts.

I went outside. I headed down Rúa Atlantis. I decided to make my way to the Lighthouse, to let the sea hit me with a cross to the jaw.

It was on my way back that I saw the bike with its unmistakable saddlebags chained up to a lamppost near the Mercado de Santo Agostiño. The bike was next to the entrance to a club, Xornes, which we'd been to once before. The dance floor was in the basement. You could hear the music from outside, "Killing Me Softly with Her Song" or some shit like that, because all the music in the world seemed like shit to me in that moment. I was going to go down, but the White Duke came back from oblivion and said to me: Get out of here, Starman, don't go down there! I backed off but didn't go far. I sat waiting on the top step of the market's stairs. Until she came out.

She left with him. It didn't matter whether I had suspected it or not, but she came out with him. With Cecilio. The journalist. A regular at Terranova. My father thought he was a great writer in the making: He's wasted on journalism! He's a real nice guy. An alternative type. Shows his solidarity. A real catch.

She unlocked the bike and held onto it by the bars as she walked alongside him, totally spellbound, or so it seemed, by the journalist. Thanks, Uncle Eliseo, for the quote from Eustasio Rivera: Don't backtalk, you quarrelsome half-breed!

I didn't make a peep. I was little more than a sullen lump.

He lived nearby, in the Praza dos Anxos. I sat down on a bench in the next square over, Praza María Pita. At least I had the company of the clock here, as it tolled the hours and quarter hours. It's hard to believe how long a quarter of an hour can last. I felt like a swallow, a bum, a tramp. I felt good. Better and better. The songwriter in me had smoke pouring out of his ears. My mind wouldn't stop turning as it churned out immortal songs of heartbreak.

Sunrise. Someone shook me awake, and it wasn't the municipal clock.

What are you doing here, *pibe*?

I came to listen to the time, I said.

We started walking. Slowly. Like someone carrying daybreak on the handlbars of their bike.

When we reached Rúa de Panadeiras, she climbed onto the seat.

Get on, she said. Right up here.

And I sat down on the handlebars.

We rode down Panadeiras. She wrapped her arms around me. She was strong, for all her scrawniness. It had been a long time since I felt so safe.

Blue Fingers

Do you want to see them?

I'd have preferred to listen to her play. Her hesitations, her mistakes, her blue fingers and fingernails like stray dogs testing out the notes that imitate a dog's trot. The hydrocephalic girl hammered on the keys. The dogs barked with the fortissimo notes. She started to ease up. She smiled. Very good, I said. Great job with the *Canine canticle*, and with your blue fingers, and thank you for the smile.

Do you want to see them?

Zita, a teacher at the Conservatory, had asked if I would be interested in giving lessons to a girl who needed special attention. Zita was a friend of the girl's mother, and had been her previous teacher, but she'd had to give it up for other work. The girl had been born with the condition, but they'd managed to save her life through intensive care, and her health improved so much that she could live an almost normal life. What she couldn't do, except in special circumstances, was to leave her house, to go beyond the bubble.

They'll pay you well. Her parents have money. She comes from a fancy house in Bella Vista, like me, but she's also sharp, like me! Her mother works in the San Martín Palace, in Exteriores. And her father is a frigate captain. The kind who stays on land, you know. There's always a servant in the house. You won't have to worry about anything but the music. And the girl is a sweetheart.

Do you want to see them?

They're all there together.

Who?

Them. The Men.

She took me by the hand. She pushed aside some books on a shelf. There was a peephole, a glass eye that gave a wide-angle view of the sitting room.

We could see them, but they couldn't see us. We could hear them, but they couldn't hear us.

They were dressed in civilian clothes, but they all addressed each other by their rank. Their speech was inflected with the marks of hierarchy, but there were no exhortations or furious speeches. That said, the entire tone of the conversation was resolute, determined. This was an Intelligence job. There was a risk of death. Actions and eliminated elements. One of the men gave a speech that set my terror gland on fire. He used the term "strategic maneuver" to refer to the police's use of live ammunition as a way to disperse the crowds that had gathered for the funeral of Representative Ortega, or, as he said, not bothering to hide his mirth, *ex-Representative* Ortega: We have to make them realize that we won't even allow them death. Soon afterwards, Gloria's father stood up and we immediately went back to our piano lessons. Shall we play Chopin's second Nocturne? It's easy, right? said Gloria. For you, maybe, but not for me. I liked to tease her like that. And I hugged her. We embraced so tightly that I was afraid she'd shatter into pieces in my arms. If the heart has a history, Gloria's was one of the bodies it chose to live it in. On the surface, she seemed aloof. Closed off. She was a fourteen-year-old girl with a second age. In a body that concealed another body. This all happened on a December day in 1974. When I left the house through the service entrance, I turned back. I had such an urge to go to my neighborhood and call up Gabriela, to see if she wanted to grab a coffee at La Flor de Barracas or a bite of pizza at Los Campeones. Or to find Mónica at night, on her way out of the *El Descamisado* newsroom, so that we could grab a drink and chat at La Paz de Corrientes or La Perla de Once. Or to go to the British Bar in Parque Lezama, it was one of my favorite spots. Forget about all that, I said to myself. I had to create someone, a separate person who'd live inside me and protect me, who'd always keep an eye out, always be on the alert, never letting me call phones that might be tapped, go to marked spots, or be seen with risky people. I turned back. In that very house were people from the Triple A, the Argentine Anticommunist Alliance, a far-right death squad with that operational efficiency of rank: vice-admiral, commodore, colonel, brigadier, and so on. Except for one man, who they called El Caudillo. Not out of deference, despite the title, but more as a sign of respect to a guest. He was one of the youngest in the group, and he brought out that particular revulsion you get from refined people with vulgar speech. We're going to keep on bagging game. Not just macaques, I'm talking big game. He was addressing military men, and maybe that was why he was trying so hard to use firm adjectives, because his soft voice was out of sync with his message: Words are female, he declared; deeds are male.

I knew exactly who this fascist was, he was infamous. He was the director of a magazine with the same name, *El Caudillo*, which was really a wayfinder for the criminals in the Triple A. They marked objectives in its pages. Its writers weren't journalists, they were *batidores*, scouts. They didn't provide information, they offered denunciations. Anyone who they singled out for criticism—whether over an article, book, or play—was mobbed, murdered, kidnapped, or tortured within a matter of days. Or bombs were planted in their homes. They did the same with the uncorrupt unionists and anyone else with a prosocial outlook, like the slum priests. For example, Carlos Mugica, who witnesses say was murdered by Almirón, the same ape who visited Terranova and got set loose in Spain.

That's where I got my start, in the *villas miserias,* the squalor villages that were gathered on the banks of the Riachuelo creek in Barracas. We had a school for children and adults; age wasn't a factor, and really, it was their life stories that taught us the real lessons. There was a little old man there who always came to school in a straw hat, and he was whip smart, he had this astonishing trick where he could memorize anything on the first go-round, and he was skinny, super skinny, like a vertical line. I asked him what he lived on: On hunger, beautiful! It wasn't a complaint, he was trying to be funny. I like all the words you use, he told me, especially the ones with lots of syllables, *hecatomb*, *catastrophic*, *protocol*, things like that. They give me lots to munch on!

I'd worked on a publication called *Cristianismo y Revolución*, Christianity and Revolution, which operated in the shadows. Mass fear production had started a long time ago by then, since the dictatorships of Onganía, Levingston, and Lanusse, and we were always in fear of the Triple A. There was already a Special Subversive Chamber, which people called *El Camarón.* The people who printed the magazine for us, who we also learned a lot from, were some old exiled Spanish anarchists who'd set up a printing press in the Liners neighborhood. They were real jokesters. They had covered the walls in calendars of gorgeous women. And the oldest of them, lifting one of the pages of the calendars, said: Look, *che*, we spend all day picking up chicks!

The mouthpieces of the dictatorship talked about instituting a Reich that would last decades. The combination of the Nazi Reich and Franco's "Crusades" was a cocktail that intoxicated the Argentinian military's higher-ups, but they weren't alone in that. When Lanusse stepped down in 1973, we took to the streets and gathered in front of the Devoto prison, singing: Lanusse, Lanusse, we gave him the vamoose! These were entire days, months of pure joy in the streets. There was a lot of talk about *la juventud maravillosa*, the marvelous youth. And of joining forces with the Chilean socialists: Allende in Chile, Perón in Argentina, Get the Yankees out of América Latina! The Yankees were never truly gone, but we couldn't see it at the time. Pinochet enacted his coup, Allende's government fell, and he was killed. But in Argentina, those who seemed to have been thrust out of power were still there. Meanwhile, with the mirage of Perón's return, we dreamt of an Argentinian revolution. There was this one graffiti that really made me uncomfortable. Bastard or corrupt, Perón's the man for us! It was hard to tell the irony and bad jokes from fanaticism.

Whenever you voiced a doubt, and you had a lot more doubts than you voiced, the more veteran comrades would tell you that, when faced with a dilemma, Perón would always elect to follow popular feeling. That's when I took the step. I didn't want to engage in politics like a nun in the Church, but I did want to be a part of that *juventud marabillos*a, to participate in the play that was being put on by the people, like a theater of life.

The mirage was shattered at Ezeiza. The messiah Perón was awaited by one of the biggest crowds in living memory in Argentina, but he never even landed his plane. What happened there, with the fascists storming the gallery, the *juventud marabillosa* receiving a beating, the first torture room set up in the airport hotel, was all part of a different play: old powers putting on a show to tell us who was really in control, the inevitable rise of cannibalism.

There was a worm in the apple. It didn't just rot. The worm devoured it from the inside. At a meeting, one of the fascists who'd put the worm there in the first place, said to us, pointing at the abyss off the table: All of you, you're out there, in the Etcetera.

On our way to Ezeiza we were people, *the* people, a marvelous apple, full of hope, but by the time we got back we were no longer humans, we were just the Etcetera. They'd knocked in our teeth. The teeth you see when a person smiles.

We didn't want to be the Etcetera. So we decided to fight.

Perón's widow, Isabelita, stood in as president, but everyone knew that the one pulling the strings was the "Necromancer," López Rega. That was the real shattered mirage: the Minister of Wellness directing the Triple A's terrorism. Meanwhile, the Minister of Education and Culture accepted his position with an insane speech decrying avant-garde artistic expression, in the name of God and Country, where he said that all such works were visual, intellectual, and moral aberrations. Some people poked fun. Nazi language about "degenerate" art had returned. But those kinds of statements held great meaning. They were symptoms. A new landscape had taken hold, an Argentinian spring. And we were right back to the dirty look. Everything started to change. But this wasn't one regression among many, a *chirinada*, a blow, we were used to that kind of setback. The issue was that people stopped looking, stopped listening, stopped speaking, because when the Triple A first began committing their atrocities, a particular person would die and it was a horror. Then another. And another. And the dead, at first, had a name, they were from a place, had a family, a job, an eye color, long or short hair, were wearing a yellow poncho or a green windbreaker. But they soon became the Etcetera. Deaths could no longer be counted on fingers. They couldn't be counted at all.

Then came the act of chance that shook up my entire life. That music class with the blue-fingered girl. I'll never know if it was a coincidence or not. I never spoke to her mother, never even saw her. Sometimes I think the coincidence was the girl herself. I don't know.

No, I was going to stick around for the time being. I'd found The Men. I had to wait for the right time to contact Diana, a link, one of The Eternaut's daughters. That was our name for Héctor Oesterheld: we took it from his own work, he wrote a comic we all devoured. This comic book turned out to be prophetic, depicting the occupation of Buenos Aires by a regime of terror unlike anything ever seen before. There's a copy in the Penumbra at Terranova. It's the first edition, from '57. It must have come in one of those suitcases. Isn't that great? The Eternaut arriving in an emigrant's luggage. I tried to read it again. I opened it. But I couldn't get past the first page. The story told in its strips is what's happening now in Buenos Aires. Oesterheld himself was disappeared. In my last phonebooth call, they told me he'd gone missing too. The old Eternaut.

I had to learn more. And I did. A month later, during a break between the Nocturnes, Gloria took me by the hand again to watch and listen to The Men. The Caudillo wasn't there this time. The guests weren't the same. I even recognized one of the faces there. It was *Joe* Martínez de la Hoz, one of the men responsible for taking Argentinian oligarchy from theory to practice. His presence, along with the so-called Admiral Zero, seemed to have changed the atmosphere in the meeting. They were past hypotheses and speculations. Their speeches were more decisive, spoken in victorious tones. They were already talking about staging a coup and taking power, but as a rule, they avoided those "outdated" terms. What they were going to do was install a new regime that would change the course of the country's history, what they called the Process of National Reorganization. The first step was to root out subversion. My horror gland was on fire again. I'm not a good spy, I thought to myself. I would have crumbled right there if it hadn't been for the blue-fingered girl. She squeezed my hand. She held me up.

The one they called Admiral Zero was General Mola, the brains behind the military coup in Spain. He read out loud the secret instructions he'd written for the Spanish military takeover. And he read as though he was stabbing each syllable into the air, like he had written it for Spain, but also Argentina, where they could reapply it forty years later. He said: "We must create an atmosphere of terror, we must sow a feeling of domination through the unreserved, unscrupulous elimination of all those who do not think as we do..."

However, Admiral Zero continued, this instruction refers to firing squads. We would do well to avoid that tactic here. What operations have been carried out thus far, such as those of the Triple A, have played their part: not only did they clear out the Peronist zoo, they also made death visible. But now it's time to take death off the main stage, to make it invisible.

He read again: the unreserved, unscrupulous elimination of all those who do not think as we do…

There will be no deaths, he said. But he didn't say it like he was trying to create intrigue. He said it as if he were elaborating a completely natural new dimension of death. Death without any dead people.

There will be no tribunals. There will be no funerals. There will be no prisons, trials, or habeas corpus. No bells will toll. In other words, there will be no problems. There will be no labor strikes. There will be no protests. There will be no agitators.

In the absence of death, no one will be believed if they cry out about the dead.

Because, what's more, the world will support us. The world that matters. The Christian world, the West. The civilized world.

You know too much.

You're never going back to that house, not even to that neighborhood.

You're never going back to the University.

You're never going back to your parents' house.

Diana says all this to me in the Botanical Gardens. I've always been perplexed by how few people visit them. A source of comfort and discomfort. Who could the few other visitors be? There's a woman, a young woman, who won't stop staring at us.

We end up at a minibus stop in the Plaza de Italia. The girl from the gardens approaches us. She and Diana greet each other as friends. I do the same. My name is Hilda, she says. Diana gets onto the first minibus. Hilda tells me we're going to take the 60 to Tigre. One of her contacts will be waiting for us with a boat. They'll take us to one of the islands.

We float through the channel, surrounded by insurgent nature, until we reach our destination. So close to the city, it feels like we are penetrating into a protective forest, into a land that conceals itself. They introduce me to an elderly man, frail but still spry, wearing a pair of glasses that seem like they exist more to contain the boundless curiosity in his gaze than to help him see better. He introduces himself as Francisco Freire. He stands before me, listening to my story, the story about the blue-fingered girl whom I taught to play the *Chanson canine*, by Erik Satie, and how she got up and took me to a place where I could spy into a meeting of the head honchos. And when I ask him if he believes the unbelievable story I've just told him, he replies: I believed it from the start, from the moment you mentioned Satie's *Chanson canine*. Precision, precision.

He's thoughtful for a moment, mulling over the new information. He says:

Sounds like we've got an oligarchy with murderous tendencies on our hands.

Freire tells me about an organization similar to ours, the Montoneros, that needs to develop an intelligence network. What he doesn't say is that the network already exists. He assigns me a few tasks. And I end up joining. That's what I was doing until I had to flee to Europe.

Do you know who the photos I was developing in Madrid were of? Around the time of Franco's funeral, there was a meeting of various heads of intelligence agencies and Latin American police forces, along with CIA agents and members of the Fascist International, like the Italian Stefano Delle Chiaie. This is when they planned Operation Condor. Hunting for fugitives and exiles and handing them back over to their respective repressive regimes. Franco's police force helped too. There are torturers back in my country who took courses in Spain. Torture courses. Can you imagine that? What are you off for this time, honey? Oh, nothing too extravagant, just a little torture course.

I knew what Garúa went through in the phone booth. News of an extermination. Fall after fall. One friend after another. They gave hardly any information, no more than a name, first Beatriz, then Diana, then Marina, then Estela. Yes, Estela too. The four Oesterheld sisters. She had a baby boy. Her baby is alive. Apparently a friend poured water on his horror gland and took the boy to the old Eternaut, to the pacifier of the Sheraton Hotel.. So that he could say goodbye. And then they took him to live with his grandmother. An exception. Children are disappeared too. All our friends are disappearing, Garúa. But that's not the worst part. The worst part is that our society is disappearing with them.

I generally went with her to the phone booth at Monte Alto, near the water. Sometimes we went by bike. Slowly, so that I could keep up with her. But on our way back, when she came out with her lost gaze, she would pick up her bicycle without a word and hurtle forward without waiting for me.

When we first came from Madrid, she asked if I would be willing to open a P.O. box for her in my name. And to let people send mail to the box in my name. But she would have the only key.

And that was fine with me.

I liked the idea that letters would arrive for Vicenzo Fontana but be opened, read, and subsequently destroyed by someone else, without me ever learning what was in them.

She finally let me read a few lines the other day.

It was Rodolfo Walsh's farewell to his daughter María Victoria, Vicki. Her *nom de guerre* was Hilda. The day before her death on September 28th, 1976, was her twenty-sixth birthday. She was asleep in bed with her daughter that night. She was woken by the blaring megaphones of the army at seven in the morning. She died on the terrace, riddled with bullets as she faced a...helicopter. I had never read a letter like it. From a father to a daughter, to a woman killed in action. As Amaro says about certain books, it's a Biblical graft.

It read: *I won't be able to say goodbye, you know why. We die in persecution, in obscurity. Memory is the true graveyard. It's there that I keep you, that I hold you, that I celebrate you, and maybe even envy you, my beloved daughter.*

We also have an edition of Walsh's *Operación Masacre* at Terranova. I opened it and couldn't put it down. A cross to the jaw. How could you put down a book in which the writer starts out by saying that he has no interest in revolutions or other political nonsense, but that he was drinking a beer when someone approached him and said: An executed civilian is alive.

And Garúa said:

Everything you heard was a monologue. I was talking to myself. No one was there. And you didn't hear a thing. Not a thing. Understood?

Understood. I didn't hear a thing.

Whatever it may have been, I imagined that something was happening. That the steamroller of History was rolling ahead and that sticking a crutch into its gears wouldn't be enough to sabotage it.

What are you going to do now, Garúa?

Now? Now, I'm going to clean up the fear in this room!

She put on a comical smile, stretching her mouth with her fingers. And then she did the same to me. It was a smile to be shared.

Let me cut your hair, she said.

Come again?

I've only cut a man's hair once. He asked me to. He couldn't go outside with his long hair. It was dangerous. One of those Ford Falcons could drive by at any second and disappear him just for that. For having long hair.

There was a story in what she was telling me, pulled from her penumbra, and that was enough for me to agree. For me to want to agree.

I joked:

You can cut whatever you like.

Curls and locks fell in sheafs, drawing a circle of animal texture on the floor of the Pinhole Chamber. I never thought my head could hold so much. A rug woven from hair and time. She shaved my head. My thoughts were on display.

And Garúa's hands gently rocked my memory.

The Horizontal Malady

She was in the phone booth for much longer than usual. The call came late. A young soldier, a draftee, stopped in front of the booth, waiting to make a call. She turned her back to him and pretended to hold a conversation. The uniform probably put her on edge, even if he was, as she said, a poor *colimba*, a kid doing his compulsory stint. The draftee was counting out coins in his hand. He was growing impatient. At first, he paced back and forth in a small radius, never more than a few feet in either direction, in a militaristic fashion. Then he fidgeted like he was dancing to a Caribbean *son*, the coins in his hands like maracas. I was afraid he'd make an advance: a young woman alone in the corner of the neighborhood, in a phone booth, might be seen as prey. And I was afraid of her being afraid. Of her situation in the phone booth, anxious over the lost time, hogging a line that was rarely occupied, but clinging to the phone so that the soldier wouldn't enter. God knows who he was trying to call. Maracas. He had a ton of coins in his hand. He was starving for conversation. Someone was waiting for him somewhere, in a neighborhood in Madrid, in Extremadura, in the Canary Islands, it was impossible to know. These draftees sometimes stopped into the bookstore. Military service was compulsory. One day, one of these kids had come in, and was staring at the portraits when he asked me, in his Andalusian accent: Who's this? My grandfather. Was he a writer? No, he's our patron saint. My answer didn't throw him for a loop. The kid was sharp. And the one next to him—not Hemingway, the other one, the one with the pipe? That's Manuel Antonio. A poet. A sailor. He died young. Did they kill him? The soldier asked. The question was no surprise, it's a normal thing to ask in this country. I said: They would have, but he died before they had the chance. I thought: they would have killed the hell out of Valle-Inclán, too, but he also kicked the bucket before they could get around to him; he beat them by a few months, so instead they killed a dog and buried it in Boisaca Cemetery in Santiago, at dusk on the day before the writer was to be buried. Manuel Antonio only ever wrote this book, I said as I handed it to him: *De catro a catro*, From Four to Four. He opened to a random page and read, in a low voice: Roubáranos o vento aquel veleiro, That ship took the wind from our sails. It was beautiful to hear Galician spoken in an Andalusian accent. It was a new language, born on an invisible island. What did he die of? The soldier asked. I was going to say tuberculosis, but I remembered something the poet had written: He got sick from the horizon. He came down with the horizontal malady. I'm from Cádiz, he said, and the horizon has made me sick too. And he walked out with the book. It was his. I got out of military service because of the horizontal malady. My body tumbled from that line. My body is insubordinate. My body is a hostile idea. It's in the lyrics to an Urchins song, hidden in a scratched record. My body is a deserter, a maimed angel from the Tenth Legion. Epopoi popoi popoi. I was about to move from my corner and wait in line for the phone booth so she wouldn't feel alone. But the draftee turned around and walked away.

Garúa picked up the phone. Waited. Hung up. When the Lighthouse light swung around and shone onto the phone booth, it looked like an aquatic realm. And, as she restlessly put down and picked up the earpiece, as the earpiece picked her up, she reminded me of Mandrake the Magician in the issue where he's trapped inside a glass box filled with water all the way up to his head. And handcuffed. He has to find the keys to the handcuffs and then retrieve them with his teeth. All those terrible contortions. Feeling like it's time itself that's drowning. Hoping for it to burst and for him to escape from this negation of time.

I see Garúa glued to the earpiece with its spiraling aluminum cord. Her head hanging. Her body sloshing this way and that. She crouches. She goes on listening but bites the knuckles of her free hand. A Dos Caballos roars down the dark street, headed in the direction of the Lighthouse. It stops not far from the phone booth. It's a couple. A woman with long, curly hair exits from the driver's side door. In the darkness, her long skirt seems like a prolongation of her hair. She glances cautiously into the phone booth without opening the door. Garúa springs up. Wipes the tears from her eyes. Shakes her head. Smiles. Gestures with her hand. The woman goes back and starts the car.

The long lights. The flashes from the Lighthouse.

This time, Garúa comes down the corner of Verea da Torre. She's not angry at me for spying. She hugs me. So thin, so strong. She hugs me. She bites me so hard that it draws blood. In this moment, I know she's saying goodbye.

The Pinwheel Firework

(GALICIA, WINTER 1979)

I can't believe what I'm seeing. Dombodán is crying. The dam broke in his eyes. It hasn't burst in mine yet. Whatever gland it is that controls that function, mine's not normal. My tear ducts face inwards. They clog my neurons. They leave my eyes dry.

I should hug him. Kiss him. Lick up his tears, and with their salt in my throat, say something. No clichés. Something historic. He always looks at me like he's expecting a historic statement. His look isn't one of devotion or submission. It's that of someone expecting you to fulfill your duty.

She's going to war, Dombodán.

How's that for historic. It threw a wrench in the gears of his sobbing. He went rigid. All the springs in his face tensed.

I went further. I told him what I was too scared to tell to myself:

It's entirely possible that she'll die. She will die. And we can't do a thing.

He didn't agree with me. I didn't agree with me either. He knew what needed to be done. What I needed to do. But no one was going to do anything. History, the wretch of History, had been set in motion.

Garúa had said to me:

I don't want to leave from Terranova. I don't want to say goodbye there. Please, let's go to Chor. I'll have them pick me up there.

There were two. They showed up in a red Morris Mini with a white roof. The driver, bearded, got out, gave a quick wave, and went back into the car to grab a coat from within, then proceeded to wrap himself in the coat, take a few steps, stretch his arms, light a cigarette, and turn around and lean up against the car, looking out at the road they'd come from. He stayed in that position until it came time to leave. The other man, skinnier, in a jacket, a V-neck sweater, and bell-bottom jeans, gave a nod of his head and murmured, Hey, how's it going? There was less gel in his black hair, but I'm sure it was the very same Tero, the photographer who'd been to my apartment in Madrid. But neither he nor Garúa gave any indication that we might know each other. The pair of them went walking down the pathway beside the Big House, which passed the oak tree and led all the way to the river. Dombodán and I went into the house, but only so that we could sneak through the backdoor into the garden and out through the gate, which led onto the shortcut behind the pigeon loft.

They were on the riverbank, near the prismatic-stone footbridge. The gabbling of the water covered over their conversation. At one point they were arguing furiously, leaving the forest in a daze, unaccustomed as it was to raised voices. We couldn't hear them clearly, but I knew what they were talking about. Whether to go back or not. The rift between those who wanted to engage in politics and those who wanted to go in guns blazing. Those who saw a suicide where others saw a victory. The Counter-Offensive.

They came back along the pathway, which acted like a voice amplifier. Hidden behind a boulder, we heard:

I'm sorry, Mika. I'm not a fortune-teller, I'm just doing my job.

She fought back a sob. She put her hands in her face, shook her head, and said: Let's go, Tero! We have a long road ahead of us.

And she added, in a different tone: I learned braille so that I could read in the dark. It's the only thing I'm taking with me from the bookstore. The *Odyssey* in braille. A parting gift from the old man. Apparently it came from Argentina a few years ago.

Te quiero, país tirado a la vereda, I love you, country tossed by the wayside, he said. And they took off running.

Dombodán ran ahead, hoping to arrive in time for a miracle, but I didn't want to go any faster.

We looked out at the road like two snubbed bums. The Morris Mini was fading into the distance without special effects, flanked by the fields of upright, uniform maize, but the sparrows flitting in and around the tops of the stalks dispelled any image of a military operation in the fields.

Expectación ran up to us, huffing.

Where's the girl?

She looked at Dombodán: What are you crying about?

She's going to war, mamá! And this bastard let her go.

I knew, from the way he said it, that this was one thing he would never forgive me.

That night, the chain of explosions rang out through the entire valley of Chor. People peeked out their houses in terror. Every night, folks in Chor would go to bed with an aperitif of Apocalypse flashing on their television screens. Every home was a fear-filled space. But what they found upon peering outside was the most spectacular fireworks show they'd ever seen. And at ground level, a Pinwheel Firework spinning in endless circles.

Ambulances, police cars, fire trucks, and civil service vans all raced to the scene, though they were cautious in case of any devices that had yet to detonate. The factory owner came too. In general, no one worked at that hour of the night, unless there was some urgent order to fill. But he said that Dombodán had asked him for extra hours that night in exchange for the day off. He'd had no reason to say no.

After that night, everyone assumed Dombodán was dead.

They pictured his pulverized remains on the mountainside, like dust from a shooting star.

But the next morning, Dombodán was sitting on the Man de Deus. By himself, looking out at the Horizon Line.

Thirteen Pear Trees, Ten Apple Trees, Forty Fig Trees

(GALICIA, FALL OF 1990)

As far as I'm concerned, suicide isn't the right word, I don't care what they say. He died because he wanted to. He chose what he called, in one of his diaries, "The Good Death." He, along with his friend Fermín Bouza Brey, another sage from the Seminary, was one of the few to write about this taboo topic. He made an ironic note in his diary: "Euthanasia in the Galician tradition is an anti-traditional tradition. In folk poetry from Galicia and the north of Portugal, we can find references to an abetted farewell for folks with irreversible illnesses, such as the case of a terminally ill woman in Guimaraes who is given teas of 'a smoky and perfumed nature to ease her into death.' There are also tales of select places, such as the so-called Picoto do Pai, Father's Hill, where elderly folks on their deathbeds were laid down for their final rest with a bedsheet and a piece of cornbread."

My father didn't trek to a hilltop with cornbread in hand, though he did bring a sheet. He also brought the Thunderstone. So that he could return the hand-ax to the man who had found it. That summer night, Amaro visited the spot outside the cemetery where his friend Atlas was buried. And he laid down. He buried the Thunderstone. Then injected himself with insulin. Double the recommended dose. He covered himself with the sheet. Went to sleep. And never woke again.

You should cry, Comba said.

I'd been out by the Lighthouse. For hours. Praying to the sea. Begging it to sweep me up. To help me reach the Horizon Line.

Setting out to sea is its own form of hope, don't you think?

A negative hope, Comba said. The only place you need to set out to is that couch, the way he did when he wanted one of his three-hundred-year sleeps. Do you remember that? He would wake up and say: Boy, does it feel good to sleep for three hundred years!

I laid down in the Pinhole Chamber and let eons pass me by. Has it been three hundred years yet? I asked when I woke up.

Comba looked old and frail to me as she smoked her Gauloises. She only smoked occasionally, on festive or disastrous occasions. I marveled at the control she had over her movements, that theatrical flourish, a pause that allowed her to take the initiative in the face of a problem. Comba Bacall, Comba Signoret, Comba Magnana, Comba Ponte. That carefree puff. But this time, she let the nimbus of smoke wrap itself around her graying hair.

She said:

Three hundred and one. You slept a year too long!

It was my grief. In every sense. I remember how, at first, I came down with a fever and started arguing with him. Every so often Comba would press a warm rag to my forehead to soak up the sweat. And I started to calm down. Him too.

I asked him: By the way, what do you know about Odysseus that the rest of us don't?

The most important thing to know about Odysseus, he said, is that he has a password. A code that gives meaning to the entire *Odyssey*.

Is that something you can share with me?

Of course! You should know. Always remember: Thirteen pear trees, ten apple trees, forty fig trees, and fifty rows of grapevines. Those were the trees in Ithaca's garden. And ultimately the key to his being recognized. Because when Laertes, his blind father, hears him list off these trees, he realizes that the man speaking isn't the impostor he'd previously thought. It's the unmistakable mouth of the earth that speaks in the end. It's what Laertes taught him as a boy when it was just the two of them in the garden. Odysseus, the castaway who the sea spits onto the sand, is recognized by the dog, the swineherd, the wetnurse—by humble folk, because everyone else is too wrapped up in their own concerns. But it's the recognition of his blind father that proves decisive, and the key to that is his memory of the trees. The entire plot of the *Odyssey* can be boiled down to a series of subplots that act as devices to rob Odysseus of his memory. To rob him of the key. Think about it. Most of his crewmen imbibe the lotus flower because they want its sweet relief, even though they know it will wipe their memories so thoroughly that they'll be unable to recall their own names. While Odysseus sleeps, his crewmen kill the Oxen of the Sun that are grazing by the ship. They know they're violating every rite of sacrifice, but they proceed anyway, picking out the fattest oxen in their zeal for a feast. But the Oxen of the Sun are immortal, and they remain alive, albeit in a horrifying fashion: their skin writhes around on the ground and their innards gurgle, filling the island with an incessant, terrible moaning. And the Sun demands justice. If they pay no heed, if the crime goes unpunished, they will leave the earth and go off to illuminate the darkness of death. A bolt of lightning sinks the ship, the crewmen die. Clinging to the mast, Odysseus is the sole survivor, and he finds himself on an island where time doesn't exist. There, he'll be offered immortality, but he'll reject it. That's an extraordinary thing to do, as much in his time as ours. Imagine that, refusing immortality! And his reason? He wants to go home. He doesn't want to be a god or a demi-god. That would mean renouncing his human memory. Losing the key of the trees.

I can hear him, hear Amaro, in his notebooks. That minor inkling is all that it takes. And it makes me feel so good. Writing must have been created, among other things, so that we can put words to things we aren't able to say aloud.

Why this passion for the *Odyssey*? Because it flips the script. Odysseus is a conqueror, a victor of the Trojan War, the war of all wars, and suddenly we find him lost, missing. What does that storm mean? Now, he has to fight with himself, he has to journey within, shed his heroic trappings, and reconstruct the man. That's why he fights so fiercely: to protect the core of his memory. The secret of his name and the number and names of the trees in Ithaca. Think about his encounter with Achilles, when Odysseus decides to travel to the land of the dead, to Hades. It's one of the best dialogues literature has ever produced. Odysseus sings the praises of the hero's countless glories in life, but tells him, in so many words, that he now stands atop the highest pedestal in the kingdom of the dead.

Think, then, Achilles: you need not be so pained by death.

What a conversation! You wouldn't hear repartee that good even if Hades had a tavern stocked with Avia wine! His response is pure *retranca*, a genius turn of irony that we'd never expect from the vainglorious warrior who could make a man tremble with a mere gob of spit. There's a rivalry between them; there always has been. And the Greeks like their ample vocabularies, they like to invoke the gods, to wax poetic about great deeds and the fine fettle of arrows that hit their mark, but here we can see that they favor, ever so slightly more, the slight prick of the needle, the humorous barb. Among all the dazzling techniques employed by this Homer, the "second" Homer, who might have been a woman, the granddaughter who guided him around taverns by the hand, is the one that turns the sublime hero into a sardonic dead man. Think about it, that's exactly how Achilles handles wily Ulysses, he chastises him for his empty words:

"Let me hear no smooth talk of death from you, Odysseus, light of councils. Better, I say, to break sod as a farmhand for some poor country man, on iron rations, than lord it over the exhausted dead."

Thirteen pear trees, ten apple trees, forty fig trees...

You've started talking to yourself, said Comba. You're like your grandmother Nina. If she ran out of thread, she'd sew with her words.

I was reading, ma.

Terranova, October 1st, 1957

We went to see Vicenzo at the Sanatorium today.

A disaster on my part.

I might as well have been the man who walked into a wake, looked at the dead man in his coffin, and cried: "I've got it worse!"

I know I should go, but my body fights this thought, and my heart and mind aren't on good terms. The one doesn't send orders, and the other doesn't pump enough blood. It isn't lost on me that my crisis of will, my collapse, foretells a loss of intellect.

He's immobilized, face-up, with his body slotted into the machine. All he can do is look into that mirror. Vicenzo notices my bitterness. My disconsolation. What am I expecting? For him to console me? His reaction is understandable. He's doing me a favor. He's giving me a jolt. An electro-shock. Activating my mind. Setting my heart beating.

He says: I never asked to be born.

It's as if it's the first time he's spoken.

Comba tries to hold fast, she goes to the window, but the sobbing breaches her defenses. After tossing away his life in a few words like that, it seems to me the boy deserves a few tears. I wish I could offer him some. I wish I could gather them in the palms of my hands and offer them up for him to drink.

What a magnificent remark, Vicenzo! I say to him with sarcastic solemnity. Comba orders me to be quiet, to leave, with a furious glance. It's my own fault.

Back at Terranova, I started writing yet another article denouncing the situation. I knew that it was impossible for it to see the light in Spain. Anything related to the polio epidemic is either manipulated or censored. As the case numbers have grown—thousands of people, mostly children—the news stories have diminished. Criminal negligence on the part of the regime. They refuse to so much as open an official registry of the cases because the figures would wreak havoc on their code of silence. In the United States and other nations, the cases have fallen to insignificant levels after they undertook mass vaccination programs a couple years ago. Meanwhile, here in Spain, the numbers are skyrocketing.

What's going on? This can't possibly be intentional, it can't possibly be another form of punishment against the people, such brutality would be inconceivable, but it may as well be intentional for the way they're letting the disease run rampant. I did some digging, went to the official organizations and health sites, but all I've received are evasive answers. Out of complicity, servility, or fear. I managed to get in touch with Verdelet in Madrid and tell him of my suspicions; he said he was very sorry to hear about

Vicenzo and would find out what he could. He returned my call far more quickly than usual, and this time it wasn't to tell me to quit being paranoid. He was stunned, I could tell. Something was wrong. It couldn't have been clearer. He had to come to A Coruña, had to see me in person. The story he told me when he arrived was one of abject horror. The nationwide vaccination program was deadlocked due to a tug-of-war between rival factions of the Regime. There were two types of vaccine, each from a different foreign company, and a vicious battle had ensued to secure the contract. It was a power struggle, bribes and all, between the Falange and the upper echelons of the military, waged via their respective patsies in the ministries of Labor and Governance.

What about the health concerns, what about the children? What's going to happen? This is a crime against the people. I suspect there's a similar historical negligence at play with the hunchbacked girls. From what little I've been able to ascertain, their condition is a kind of undiagnosed spinal tuberculosis that hadn't been treated in time with a shot of penicillin. Now the authorities have invented the fiction that the girls' deformity was caused by some physical trauma and have chosen to treat them by trying to straighten them out! Do they plan to keep them strapped to their beds ad aeternum?

For once, Verdelet didn't ply me with liberal ironies as a springboard to conservative conclusions. He wasn't in the mood for word games, and words were in no mood to play. I met him during my time in the Seminary. He'd always tease us when we went out to conduct field work: The lot of you are always off chewing cud like a herd of cattle! He declared himself the first ultraist poet in Galicia. And when he said it, he lorded over the rest of us by reciting a boxing poem that he paired with pugilistic theatricality. He was well-liked, and the articles he penned rang out like mortar blasts. They were magnetic. He yearned to make the tiger's leap over to Madrid, and he did. On his way, he shed his leftist's fur and took on the sheen of a top-tier swordsman for the right-wing press, and he did so without sacrificing any of his style. It was his most productive era. He always complained about that: I did my best writing against the Republic, I'm a shadow of my former self now. A well-paid, well-placed shadow in the upper echelons of the government, to be fair. What I am not, and will never be, Amaro, is a criminal. Those were his words upon our first meeting after the war, in a room in the Prado, in front of a Goya painting. I come at least once a week, he said, so that I don't lose my vision.

The polio story had left him at a loss for words.

Maybe you could write something about it, I said.

They've castrated me, Fontana. I've got no balls left. But I'll keep you in the loop.

Eliseo's just coming in from the Sanatorium. He prefers to go at dusk and tell the boy stories before bedtime.

I ask how Vicenzo is doing and he says they spent two hours laughing at ghost stories.

I ask him to tell me one, too. To frighten me into laughter.

Henri-Frederic Amiel in his Journal Intime, said: Every day, we leave a bit of ourselves behind.

I'm not sure how much of myself I left behind today. But it was a lot. Almost everything.

Everything.

I turn off the light. I lie down facing the Lighthouse and the North Star. Goodnight, Polytropos.

The Reign of Emptiness

(GALICIA, WINTER OF 2014)

Viana, the clandestine girl, gave birth to her daughter today. The first Terranova native. It happened in the Pinhole Chamber. With the help of Expectación and Goa. If I had to be born again, I'd put myself in their care. I think my uselessness ended up being helpful. I was standing there with the spheres, all of us astonished by life, and suddenly Expectación came and placed this contraband in my arms.

Her name is Estela. Estela Marina. Do you like it?

I love it. Look her over, I'm sure she was born with the name tattooed on her somewhere.

I was surprised at how small she was. I was sure she'd be bigger than her mother. That she'd envelop the bookstore. That the spheres would break. That the Bibles would creak. Everything's calmer now. The cats, Baleia, they're all watchful, overcome with a sense of responsibility. I even forgot my Syndrome, or my Syndrome gave me a break. That afternoon, we brought the two, mother and daughter, up to a big bed on the second floor. And not one but three doctors came. Women doctors. Begoña, Amparo, and Lola, of the Terranova tribe.

Lola asked about the father.

The father is an immortal, I said, with a wink at Viana.

You can already see it in her, said Amparo. She came out knowing how to laugh. Most babies take forty days to learn that. Aristotle said so.

Well then Aristotle was a dope! exclaimed Expectación. My boy laughed on his first day, the moment he saw his mother. Yours truly.

Zoroaster was born with laughter on his lips, said Begoña. They say that's where his astral wisdom came from.

Then he's like mine, said Expectación. My boy's off at sea now, following the stars.

She'd come to Terranova from Chor when Adelaida and the Aviator put the Big House on the market. She had no respect for them: They're always acting all holier-than-thou, but their virgin is the Virgin of the Fist! After the explosion at the fireworks factory, whose official cause was put down as an electrical failure, Dombodán finally managed to embark on a ship, not a Merchant

Marine ship, but a cruise ship, as a caretaker in the cabin reserved for pets. That's life for you, said Expectación. There's no livestock left to tend in the countryside because we killed them all, so now he's taking care of animals on the *Queen Mary*. He won't stop until he gets to Antofagasta.

Expectación had called to tell me she needed a roof to sleep under.

I told her she was welcome here, of course—a wetnurse would be a big help.

Sure, she said, when you were a baby you suckled like a full-grown adult.

I didn't want to explain the bookstore's situation to her. Terranova's days were numbered. In fact, after we shared a laugh over my mammary passions as a baby, I told her I could really use her help, that she'd become a good bookseller in time. In time, yes, in time she'd make for a top-notch funeral, she joked. But I insisted, and as I spoke, I began to believe the words coming out of my mouth.

Ever since the Argentinian girl taught me to read, she said, meaning Garúa, I've only read one book. I liked it so much that I said to myself: What would I want to read another one for? I'm going to read this one for the rest of my life. I must have read it ten, fifteen times by now. *Pedro Páramo*. It was written in yeast. You leave it for a night and it ferments, it fills up with new things.

By now, you're probably the world's foremost expert on *Pedro Páramo*.

Oh, I'm sure.

Just you watch. We'll set up an event for the friends of the bookstore: "Expectación and *Pedro Páramo*." The day will come, and professors will show up and everything.

Whatever you say, boss.

It was a lucky thing that Expectación was there when the clandestine girl went into labor.

In my helpful uselessness, I'd spent the entire night before talking to Viana.

Neither of us could sleep. She was close to giving birth. She could feel the baby squirming around. Clearing a path. I couldn't fall asleep and had been in owl-mode for several nights because of the ultimatum. I was afraid they'd try a surprise eviction. It was happening all over the place. It didn't matter how old the renter was, how badly he needed a roof over his head, or whether he had a disability. Who was I to care, though? What did it matter if one bookstore closed, when so many other shops were closing too? A hole, an empty space, another hole. Emptiness grows, but due to its nature no one notices its reign until they find themselves trapped inside it. The eviction of souls, the cheapening of the imagination, the loss of oxygen. Bookstores that act as nurseries, workshops that buzz and sing, insurgent art magazines, these are the antibodies of a free culture, antibodies that enrage emptiness. We're the targets of an undeclared war; where's my Iron Lung? This is how I see things. This is how I talk when I'm alone. Broadcasting short-wave frequencies into the *Terranova Night*. No, I'm not going to bother Viana with my sob stories. She's fighting back against emptiness. She's an antibody of fulfillment.

What made you think to come here, Viana?

I thought it would be the safest place. I talked to Crash and we both agreed. What could be safer than a bookstore? It's the first time I've ever been in one. Boca di Fumo would never expect to find me in a bookstore. It would never occur to him to look for me here.

Where have you two been living?

In a prison. The old prison. That was a safe place, too. And it's in a beautiful spot. Who's going to come looking for you in an abandoned prison? That's where we hid the day with the helicopter, do you remember that? No one could figure out where we'd gone. Well, there's this tunnel, a little passageway under the cliffs. But it's not safe anymore. A traitor, O Bate, went off and told Fumo about it. We had to run away. Too bad. We'd done the place up nicely, with a crib and everything. And all the prison visits we could have ever dreamed of. At night, we'd go out onto the patio and look at the Lighthouse and listen to the sea. It was one of the best spots in the city. This bookstore's not bad either, Mr. Fontana.

What's Boca di Fumo after? You said he was on the hunt for Crash.

He's after the two of us. He wants Crash to be a replacement in prison again, but the real kind this time, the maximum-security kind. They want him to take the heat for one of the Master's captains. He could get ten years. They've already figured it all out, the story, the false evidence. People used to do this back in the day, didn't they? Like with the war in Morocco. The poor would go as replacements for the rich.

Yes, that's true. But what do they want with you?

At first, when I was getting paid for the prison visits with Crash, Boca never looked at me twice. I was an errand girl. Until one day, he told me: You're my girl, my favorite, my little slut. But he *really* started to want me when he noticed me looking forward to my visits with Crash. He saw that I'd put on makeup, brush my hair, dress up. And that I was feeling good. One day Crash told me: You're my Hemoglobin. I thought that was such a pretty thing to say, for him to call me his Hemoglobin. He wanted to get away from them as soon as he got out. And they never even bought him that guitar they'd promised! We got by on the sea and the battles. He played the part of a Viking during the festivals in Catoira, and of a Roman in the Esquecemento festival, you know that one? The one where the imperial soldiers didn't want to cross the Limia River because there was a legend that said it would wipe away your memories? Anyway, he went up front, right behind the President of the Deputation, who was playing Pontius. And they gave him a bonus for lending a hand, because the president was really short and couldn't cross on his own. He also did the one with the Moors and Christians in Astorga. He went as a Moor one day and as a Christian the next. He was surprised when they paid him as much to be a Christian as a Moor. Lately he's been preparing for the Battle of Elviña, for the anniversary. He's going to be an assistant to the English general, Sir John Moore. He's going to be the one who carries the general's body after they kill him. He's learning curses to shout at the French. Not in English. In French. So that they'll understand him. *Va t'enmerde.* Go to hell. Something like that, but a bit cooler.

Boca di Fumo was a nobody, Viana told me. He'd gotten that nickname because he'd smoked as a kid to look more manly. Even back then he was already hanging around outside schools to sell spliffs. Then one day, by total coincidence, he had a stroke of luck. He catered a party at some rich person's house. A friend who worked at the catering company was sick, and just like that, there he was. Boca was a good-looking guy, and was always trying to move up in the world. He has a knack for chitchat. He makes a connection. He's a snake charmer. He can do high and low. He can be a thug, a buddy, or a salesman, whatever you need him to be. And he tells good jokes. That's how he found the Master. His jokes. He poured the Master a glass and made a joke. And everyone laughed, so the Master said: Do you know any more? Luckily he'd come with plenty. He had an entire routine ready. That's how he caught the Master's eye, the eye of God the Father, the All Powerful. Boca would sell out his own mother before he ever bit the boss' hand. That's what I'm counting on. That he's afraid of making too much noise. That he won't do anything so big that it ends up in the papers.

The Master cloaked himself in mystery, Viana told me. She couldn't say for certain whether she'd ever seen him before. Sometimes she thinks there are a half dozen Masters. About him, Boca di Fumo hardly says a word, not even to brag. His connection with the Master is a precious commodity that he has no intention of sharing. I pissed him off so much one day, she said, that he let a bit spill. He'd started a diet, so I asked him what it was. Big shot that he is, he said it was the same one the Master was on. The Master was a guy you had to respect. He'd gone to Barcelona specifically to see this super expensive doctor, who was the one that told him about it. I laughed at Boca, thinking this shared diet thing was funny: So, what, the boss is a vegetarian now? He flipped his lid and started cursing me up and down, all over a little joke. To him, the Master isn't just a boss, he's like a guru.

You know, Viana told me, the Master used to be a lawyer, and he knows so much about laws that he can break whichever ones he feels like. I was having a hard time believing that this massive dirtbag, this guy who doesn't care whether he's stealing from earth or heaven, was a champion of a healthy lifestyle. An exercise fanatic. A nature lover. And a Buick lover too. He collected fancy cars. Then Boca told me the story about the cigarette butt. It was like something out of a movie. They were staying at a vacation house, and the Master was having dessert with his family while the two of them, Boca and O Bate, were at another table, the table for the help. At one point, Bate smoked a cigarette and tossed the butt onto the lawn when he was finished. A Lucky butt. The Master didn't call anyone over, he got up himself and grabbed Bate's attention. Here's what you're going to do: you're going to pick up the butt you just tossed onto the grass, you're going to shove it in your pants, stub it out on your balls, and then you're going to grab a towel from the pool and fan out the garden until there's not even a fucking memory of smoke left here. Boca burst out laughing when he told me this, like it was something out of a history book. He was so fired up he started singing the Master's praises. How he didn't waste his money on stupid crap. How he traveled the world. How I just had to hear the way he talked about landscapes, architecture, film, and art. Art most of all. He was a big art collector. Old and modern. He was crazy for art. And the body was an art too. He was a culture fanatic. Just like me, said Boca. Since when have you cared about art? I asked. He flew off the handle again. I don't know a thing about it, but I'm not Crash, babe. I'm not going to end up as some bum who carries around a guitar with no strings.

Maybe not, but that's art, I said. Doing whatever you want.

Well, I guess we'll just see what you end up wanting to do, won't we?

Master, Master, Master. I hadn't been able to get that strange name out of my head since the moment I'd heard it from Nicolás, Old Nick's son. And Viana's story stirred my abject memory. Though I didn't totally disagree about the butt in the grass. I needed to know who he really was, to uncover the identity of the shark that was about to snap Terranova in its jaws.

I called Cecilio, the journalist. He'd had surgery on his larynx a year ago and was forced to learn to speak again. He didn't want to, but he did. Now he speaks with a raspy gusto.

What bad news have you got for me today, Fontana?

No bad news, just a riddle I was hoping you could help me solve. A rich man, very rich, a former lawyer with his hands in real estate and probably some other "magical" activities, big into culture, a major collector of art and antiques and Buicks. Goes by the Master in some circles.

Cecilio perks up, I can tell. His finger covers the stoma in his throat, and his chest forces out the air. He overcomes the emptiness and speaks.

No shit! You've just painted a perfect picture of a dirtbag named Fernando Lamarella.

I need a contact, Cecilio. It's urgent.

No can do. I've got no in.

There wasn't much time. I had to find the key to this lock, speak to him personally, convince him to instate a moratorium. Just like with whale hunting, Mr. Lamarella. If he had money, and he clearly did, if he was interested in art, we could make Terranova into an art space too. Literature, art, healthy food. We could talk. What was he planning to do with the property, build apartments? The city was full of empty apartments.

Ah. I'd forgotten about emptiness, its reign.

I tracked down some phone numbers. A central office. I'm afraid we can't put you though to Mr. Lamarella. But you could request an appointment to speak to one of his representatives. What's that? A personal matter, a deeply personal matter? Alright, you can leave a message with me.

Tell him I'm calling about Terranova.

Terranova? The secretary asks, with professional stupor.

Yes, Terranova.

That's all?

That's all.

They hang up. I shouldn't have said anything.

I call Old Nick. They can't put me through. He's in a meeting. What about his son? He's in a meeting as well. Until when? We aren't quite sure.

It's urgent!

There's no answer. The secretary knows my voice. She clearly has instructions.

Please, Rebeca!

The mention of her name nearly breaks her. She's not used to this hermeticism, it feels violent to her. But she hangs up.

I can't escape the feeling that the die is cast. Not because it's too late; because it always was. Rental law is written for landlords. Any contract signed by an individual, even if it comes with co-signers, can be nullified at the owner's request. That was their approach with me. I refused to leave. The case was fast-tracked through the courts and they signed an eviction order. Ten days to clear out. I took down the sign and sent an appeal to the judge. A lawyer friend told me: You have no chance, and you'll have to foot the bill, too. But I hope you do it anyway. I hope you write that appeal. I'd love to read it. And more than anything, I'd love to be there when the judge reads it.

I wrote:

Your Honor, seventy years ago, my maternal grandfather, Antón Ponte, was pricking his fingertips with a needle in the seas of Nova Scotia and Newfoundland, or Terranova, so that the warmth of the blood would keep his hands from freezing. That man had a dream. I live in that dream. I'm writing to you from inside it. But it's about to be frozen to death by an indifferent, implacable cold: the expansion of emptiness, the reign of injustice...

The reign of injustice? Don't you think that'll only piss him off?

I don't know, but somebody's got to say it!

I can't remember how many days it's been since I sent that Writ of Opposition. I call my lawyer friend. The procedure has been fast-tracked, but they still haven't set a date for the hearing. It should be any day now. But the judge has the owners' lawyer foaming at the mouth. Sooner or later, they're going to file an injunction.

And the judge?

He said to me the other day, cool as can be: I'm going to read that swan song one more time.

Night falls. Ramiro, also known as Sibelius, comes back from combating emptiness. He can play Bach beautifully on a Yamaha keyboard—almost a child's toy. If only the traffic were to stop. If only the city were to go silent for one second, they would hear Bach ringing out from these little keys.

Goa goes to welcome him. She brings a mug of tea to warm up his hands and his spirits. That's how she puts it. And he responds: I'd rather warm up my body.

Goa devours books. She sniffs them. Dances with them. Cries over them. Kisses them. Gets angry with them. Shouts at them.

Oh to hell with you!

Why don't you go see which way the wind blows!

She reads multiple books at a time and uses coffee spoons, bay leaves, or cigars with their red heads peeking out as bookmarks.

They seem to love each other deeply, Sibelius and Goa. They understand each other without words.

Sibelius came to Terranova for her. She told me: There's a man, he's very proper…

You can bring him in, Goa, you don't have to explain anything to me.

It's not bringing him in I'm worried about! She exclaimed, a bit nervously. There was always a certain suspiciousness in her. Scars of the past. He was going to be a guest, he would pay for his stay.

He's not a bum. He used to be a priest.

A priest?

Yes, and a parish priest, too!

We stood staring at each other. One of those moments when another person's life makes you reflect on your own. She broke into laughter first.

I've been wanting to talk for a long time. And I'm on edge today. I need company.

Have a glass, Sibelius!

No thank you, I already had some tea. I quit alcohol a long time ago. The altar was my pub.

That was Christ's blood, I said. This is Campari.

It was before I came to Christ that I drank the most.

Sounds like you didn't end on good terms with Him, did you, Sibelius?

With Christ, yes, at least in part. But not with Him, no.

He wet his lips on a bit of Campari.

I couldn't get past this idea of God's mood swings. After all the work he's put into creation, he decides to bring down the Great Flood in a fit of anger. Like some pagan tyrant! Honestly, when I reached that point in the story during my Bible study lessons, I had to repress my rage. Sometimes I skipped over it. And took a drink. People thought it was water, but it was Fockink gin, excuse my language. Or the story about Job—it ran my patience through. And I would take another swig of gin.

I disagree, Sibelius. I had so much faith in that moody God, who seemed to proclaim: The future is over! My uncle Eliseo saw him as one of the great characters of abjectionist literature. The moment in which the creator comes to revile his own creation and tries to destroy it. I experienced that in the Iron Lung...I felt like I was a part of the story.

I came here as a young boy, said Sibelius. I remember how they used to sell hand-made spheres and those famous globes.

That was one of my mother's arts, making globes. With wires and colorful paper. She would even add color. I can see her painting the Polynesian islands, one by one, and they're no easy thing to paint. After that, it felt so vast to watch her paintbrush stride zinc white across the snows of Siberia. They were lined with linen, and they all had something inside them. A walnut, a chestnut, a cherry pit, Comba things.

Terranova was the best memory I had prior to the Minor Seminary in Santiago, Sibelius told me. We came the day before I left for the Seminary. I bought one of those globes. And a copy of *Robinson Crusoe*. It was my first year. They confiscated both the book and the globe. I'd already been told they wouldn't let me keep things like the book, but I never understood why they took the globe.

It must have been because it spun.

I thought he was going to smile, but I saw that the pain of the episode hadn't faded with time. That it bore a spherical unease. Every so often, he would complain about his ulcer. A terrestrial emptiness.

It was past midnight. I was absorbed in my reading of Amaro's journals for *Mnemnosyne in Hispania*, where he talked about the expulsion of the Jews from Spain in 1492, in a section titled: "Operation Holy Child of La Guardia." He'd documented the case of a repressive, propagandistic operation with its basis in a fabricated crime. There was no such child, and no such crime ever took place, Amaro wrote. The yearly celebration at the altar dedicated to him is nothing but the celebration of a horrible lie. The entire false sequence of events was the handiwork of the office of the Spanish Inquisition, one of the most powerful and efficient secret services in the history of the world. Because of their means and the particular results of the operation—which included the immediate expulsion of the Spanish Jews and the confiscation of all their worldly goods—Amaro saw this scenario as the original precedent for the criminal actions of twentieth-century totalitarian states. The case of the false martyr proved so popular that people continued to re-purpose the fabrication, and even famous figures got involved, such as Lope de Vega, with his play, *El niño inocente de la Guardia*, The Innocent Child of La Guardia, in which he forged a patriotic myth: "Thousand times fortunate Spain, to have been blessed with such a martyr, and the father of your fatherland!"

Amaro goes on to talk about the great religious, historical, and cultural controversy occupying the minds of the grand figures of the seventeenth century: to whom should the patronage of Spain fall, Saint Teresa of Ávila or the Saint James the Apostle? Francisco de Quevedo's involvement was decisive on this point, with his rejection of the reasonable possibility of a co-patronage, in his exhortation *Su espada por Santiago*, Thy Sword for Santiago…

Look at that. A conspiracy to stop me reading.

Who's there?

It's too late for anyone to still be roaming about. For anyone to be knocking on the door to the Pinhole Chamber.

It's Expectación. She has the look of someone who's just come from fighting with a host of deities in bed.

I'm sorry, she says. I know it's late, but it's my conscience.

It's never too late for conscience. It's a muse!

Whatever you say. All it does for me is keep me awake at night. I don't have the same luck as other people, like those dopes who show up on the TV quacking about how they can sleep with a clear conscience. Who can sleep with a clear conscience in this day and age?

Not me.

Me neither, she said. She went quiet.

What's wrong, Expectación?

We have the Virgin.

I didn't understand her at first. But she hit me with a cross to the jaw.

We have the Pregnant Virgin, the Annunciated Mary, Our Lady of Chor, here with us, the one that Mr. Amaro said was a treasure.

It was stolen, I said. My aunt Adelaida and the Aviator reported the theft, but they never turned up any leads. There are whole gangs dedicated to it. Icon thieves. Professionals. They swapped it out, and for years...

Expectación let me go on talking. Her face, at those hours, looked to me not like that of the woman who had been my wet-nurse, but a wood-hewn Indian idol.

I know all that already, she said finally. But the Virgin is with me.

What do you mean?

She was wearing a robe over her nightgown. I was still in the seventeenth century and hadn't paid any attention to Expectación's waist. She opened the robe and took out a bundle of rags, which she delicately unwrapped until there it was, tiny, beautiful, and with those watchful, ancient eyes: the Annunciated Mary.

What's this doing here? It's not ours!

I was nervous, confused. Irritated.

But Expectación shrieked louder than me.

What do you mean it's not ours? Then who does it belong to? Your stupid aunt and uncle? Those gangs you just talked about? If it weren't for me and Dombodán, there wouldn't be any Virgin at all. It was us who put out the other carving. The Tramp made it for us, and he did an excellent job, by the way, they looked identical. We did it to protect her. Lord knows where the real one would be right now if it weren't for us!

Never let go of her, Expectación!

She sleeps in bed with me every night.

The Origin of the World

Baleia was barking.

In her old age, Baleia never barked. And now she had started barking in surprise at her own barks.

Of course, I had no memory of the sound, and her barks startled me out of my reading in the solitude of the night, I thought that's where they were coming from, these barks, from the margins of the page, from the lanes and weeds of the white spaces.

It was a historic, telegraphic bark, trying to transmit some fundamental information.

I stumbled out of the Pinhole Chamber and was blinded by a flashlight.

What do we do now? A voice called out.

What we came to do!

I felt a hard blow to my neck and didn't hear or see a thing for a good while.

I had a hard time regaining consciousness. Because of the pain from the blow to the neck, my dizziness and uncertainty, and the humiliation of feeling impotent on the floor, not to mention all the effort I was making just to understand the vertiginous action unfolding in Terranova. The air thick was with smoke and cries for help.

In the Penumbra, Crash, Expectación, and Goa were spraying a fire extinguisher and flapping sheets in the air to try to put out the fire climbing up from the floor to the shelves. The assailants must have poured gasoline. Luckily, the floor was tile and Terranova's defenses seemed to be proceeding without issue. Meanwhile, Sibelius was standing on the staircase with a rifle trained on the two assailants, leaving them frozen in place. I thought his words were a surrealist verse, until I realized he meant them: It's for killing elephants! It's for killing elephants!

And those familiar with such things must have known it was a serious weapon because the miscreants stood stock still, paralyzed, with their hands in the air.

For the love of God, don't shoot!

There's no God here! Shouted Sibelius. Coming from him in particular, and with that rifle in his hands, the words were quite convincing.

Please, Father!

Father? How do you know that? Sibelius asked, unsettled.

I know everything about Terranova!

Crash came in from the background, covered in soot and panting from the effort of putting out the fire.

Don't listen to this snake. Boca di Fumo always has his eyes on the boss, right? He loses a tooth every time he tells the truth, and look at that, he's not missing a single one. But let's not forget about his buddy Bate over here. He'll eat anything, but bone marrow is his favorite.

The smoke pouring out of Terranova had unleashed a panic on Rúa Atlantis. Voices. People peeking out of windows. The wailing of a siren.

Who sent you?

It was pointless to ask, but somebody had to. So I did.

Their response was to make a run for it. They headed for the door but stopped in their tracks when they heard the blast of Sibelius' rifle. They were as stunned as we were. But the most stunned of us all was Sibelius. He had shot straight into the wall clock.

I killed time! He cried out.

It stopped ages ago, I said.

On our way to the police station to give our statements, Sibelius told me how the rifle had come into his possession. Back when he still practiced—and did so with faith—he'd gone to the home of an elderly parishioner, a rich banker, to take his confession.

It turned out to be his last, Sibelius told me, what they called "giving someone their spurs." But the old man was lucid in his own way. After I'd absolved him of his sins, I told him to pray an Our Father, in penitence. An Our Father? That's all? he asked. I told him it was plenty. He must have been pleased to hear that. He was a stingy man. That was when he asked if I had a gun. Me, a gun? What do I need a gun for when I've got the cross! Sure, but where can you go with a cross that a gun wouldn't be more helpful? He said confidently. And he told me about harquebusier angels. Images of these blonde, gun-toting angels intimidating indigenous people. What's a man without a gun? A blunderbuss, an harquebus, a rifle...Anything will do! History proves me right. I'm a priest, a man of God! I said in irritation. He clicked his tongue as if he hadn't heard and said: I have something for you, Father. He struggled out of bed, opened up a closet, and came back.

Take it, he said. It's a big-game-hunting rifle. For killing elephants.

Hold on a minute, have you killed elephants?

I already said the Our Father. Goodnight.

He rang a bell. The housekeeper wrapped the rifle in a sheet and showed me to the door with a smile.

What happened at Terranova wasn't an act of hostility, like in the past, nor even a reprisal. The operation had one clear motive, and the subinspector who took our statement seemed to agree about that much, at least. The goal had been to create a blaze that would lead to the immediate vacating of the premises and the condemnation of the building. Not only would they clear me out of the space, they'd destroy the very architecture they were trying to preserve. It would be cheaper to rebuild anyway. Cheapening as a tactic. The cheapening of lives, of matter.

You're right about the cheapening, murmured the sub-inspector after listening to my rant.

That's exactly what it is, the officer said. The most serious aspect of this case is that there were lives at stake.

And what have they said? The arsonists, I mean.

The two little buffoons are saying they came in to put *out* the fire, not set it. And that they were almost shot dead by a big-game rifle.

The only thing I shot dead was a clock, Sibelius said. The poor clock of the Republic.

Daybreak was beautiful in the bay. I looked for the spot where the starlings would have been swirling in the sky. I imagined that the flocks had returned and were tracing elephants. We stopped for a coffee at the Atalaia, in the Recheo gardens, right in front of the

Police Headquarters. A woman approached our table. She wanted to have a word with me. She introduced herself as inspector Ana Montés. Do you mind if I sit down? Well, seeing as you've already taken your seat... She smiled. But it wasn't a sense of carelessness she was conveying, it was action. Her expression and her posture, the calmness of her sustained gaze, reminded me of the way that the light introduced itself on the other side of the bay in the mornings.

No, no coffee for me. I'll take a black tea, and then, not beating around the bush, she said:

I head up a group that investigates the theft of religious icons in Galicia. So that we can return them to their rightful place, of course.

How interesting! I said.

She smiled again. Her gaze had advanced, testing a possible gap in my cerebral cortex.

Icons, Sibelius said somberly, that's the only beautiful and authentic thing left in the Church now.

However, they don't belong just to the Church, the inspector said. They're a part of our national heritage, they're an artistic treasure that should be shared with believers and nonbelievers alike. Do you know how many valuable pieces—gold and silver chalices, crosses, baptismal founts, and gargoyles—disappear every year? It's a plague. There's lots of money in it, and entire gangs, not to mention influential people, involved. Because these thefts would never happen if there weren't people willing to spend fortunes on the items.

It's the Reign of the Emptiness, I said.

Yes, that's a good way of putting it, Mr. Fontana. They're sending irreproducible work into the void, into emptiness.

It's a lot like what's happening to bookstores, though there are obviously some differences, I put forth. But I got the sense that Ana Montés hadn't come for idle chitchat.

She looked straight at me. She hadn't touched her tea.

Mr. Fontana. I know it's not your style, or mine, for that matter, we both like to take things slow, but there's no time to lose.

No time at all.

You have something highly valuable at Terranova, something that doesn't belong there.

I don't know what you're talking about.

Don't play games with me.

Ana Montés' gaze had cut straight through to my cortex. It was absurd to try to keep up this facade.

We didn't steal the Annunciated Mary, I said. We're keeping it safe.

You and everyone else, she snapped. Everyone starts with good intentions. But many of these icons never return to their rightful place.

I snapped back.

What would you have done, inspector? Abandon the Pregnant Virgin, let her fall into the hands of some dirtbags who'd sell her as soon as they got their paws on her? The Virgin is going to return to Chor. Or to a museum. Wherever you and your team say.

No, she said. She brushed her coppery blond out of her face. She said: We'll do you one better. We're going to perform a miracle: we're going to bring down one of the biggest players in the business. One of the biggest in other "magical" businesses too. You know who I'm talking about. We wouldn't be having this conversation if the thugs he sent been successful last night. We'd have lost the Annunciated Mary. And we'd have lost Terranova with it.

What could we possibly do to bring down Lamarella? He's untouchable. You've probably spent years trying to find something to pin on him.

Ana Montés stood up and waited for us to get up from our seats as well.

Let's go to my office. It's right across the street in the Headquarters. Something major has changed. We have the hook, the line and the sinker now.

She'd brightened up again. On our way there, she made a confession: Did you know I stole a book from Terranova when I was a teenager?

Yes. It was *Hymns to the Night*, by Novalis. A lot of rain has fallen since then, but I remembered you the moment I saw you. A shame that teenager didn't come back to steal more.

She was shocked. The color drained from her face. I thought the copper in her hair would turn white.

It's been with me all these years, that book. Even now, it's sitting right on my nightstand. I should give it back to you.

Keep it. It's in a good home.

Fernando Lamarella, the Master, always turned to the same expert in sacred art when he required consultation in his treasure hunting endeavors. He had other collaborators, but this man, a retired professor, a churchgoer with a respectable public image and an austere life, was Lamarella's most trusted confidant when it came to evaluating valuable pieces and deciding whether to acquire them or send them to the black market. Why did he do it? Ana Montés told me that it wasn't exactly for money, though he got his share, of course. For him, the greatest satisfaction came from being able to touch the art, to possess it even if only temporarily, and most of all, to be able to put a price on it. Imagine that, putting a price on a Virgin, or a Christ!

He had a weakness that he mistook for a strength. His vanity. Among the documents they had recovered from a group of religious art thieves, they found a report on various sculptures in the Deza parish, a report that was a work of art all on its own. It had the precision you'd expect from an expert in religious icons, but also a unique perspective that set it apart from other similar reports, which were usually hastily cribbed together reproductions taken from books, catalogs, or newspapers, or copies printed from the internet. The report Ana Montés was talking about wasn't attributed to the professor, of course, but when she compared it to his other writings on sacred art, she was sure she'd found her man. But it was vanity that struck the final blow, and it was vanity that led him to confess without even realizing it.

The history of culture is like a detective show, I muttered.

But the important thing is the detail, Inspector Montés said. That's what tilts the balance—the detail. A scruple. And I found it in this man. It wasn't easy, but I found it.

Expectación wasn't hard to convince. She got along famously with Ana Montés. Each after their own fashion, they were both enchantresses. Lamarella wasn't hard to convince either. The Annunciated Mary was a unique virgin, one of the icons donated by Saint Elizabeth of Portugal during her pilgrimage to Santiago in the fourteenth century. In the version the expert told the Master, he'd stumbled almost by miracle upon the icon. An elderly woman had secretly switched the original for a copy and kept the original herself. At first, her intention was to ensure it stayed in good condition and protect it from theft, a growing problem in her parish. But now, after so many years, in her desperation, she'd decided to sell it. And because part of this was true, he spoke with genuine passion. The woman was no fool, but she didn't know how much it was truly worth. The Master could get it for a bargain and sell it at an exponential profit on the black market. But the woman, Expectación, had one condition. She didn't want to go through a middleman. She wanted to look in the eyes of the person to whom she was entrusting the Pregnant Virgin.

And that's how the Annunciated Mary found her way into the Master's home, swaddled in a sheet and nestled in the crook of Expectación's neck like a baby girl.

And there she lingered, equipped with a well-hidden tracking chip.

Fernando Lamarella was in the news, but this time, it wasn't a story about what a model businessman he was. The papers published a photo after his arrest, in which he appeared with a baleful scowl on his face, his eyes turned away from the Pregnant Mary.

They found lots more. A small religious icon, a pregnant virgin, had brought about the fall of the Master's empire. As Ana Montés put it, it was a vast geology of dirty money covered up with artificial grass.

Among the implicated businesses was the old Hadal real estate company. With that, the Terranova eviction proceedings were put on hold.

The journalist Cecilio called. Struggling to make his voice heard, his finger on the opening on his throat, his entire body engaged in the effort.

I'm glad to hear Terranova won't be closing. I want to be buried there! Got anything hard-boiled you can recommend me? Sure, I'm sick, but don't try to foist any sleepers on me. I want to read something that wakes me up.

The link between a person's life and what they like to read is unpredictable. According to the saying, we are what we read. But it could just as easily be said that we are what we don't read.

Someone will come into Terranova and say: My husband's left me. He ran off with another woman, finally. I encouraged him to do it, I was tired of pretending. I told him: It would be better for everyone if you stayed with her. We're all real civilized, all real fucked-up, aren't we? Well, now I want something heady. Something erotic, and I mean really erotic. No subtlety or indirectness. Something that will make me want to put the book up my snatch. Ah, that'll be the *Song of Songs*, I said, look no further than the Bible. Then there was the customer who came in yesterday. I knew his wife had died recently. I knew they belonged to the Opus Dei. He whispered: I'm looking for *Senos*, Breasts, by Gómez de la Serna. He said it like it was the most libertine book known to man.

Just a moment, I said. We have a marvelous illustrated edition published in Buenos Aires, from back in the days when it was banned here.

I once saw the spine of that book in a cabinet under lock and key, he said. Anytime I cracked open another book, it was that one I was thinking of. And the key to the cabinet. The key especially.

Cecilio tells me he needs something really hard-boiled. Something dangerous. Far from light.

Read *Ferdydurke*. It might do you good to go back down the path to immaturity.

Every time I open that book by Gombrowicz, my uncle Eliseo pops out of me to talk about how he translated a portion of it. Me and Eba, all in one go, he'd boast. That's right, we finished it in a day and a night. Eba was a genius! Gombrowicz had named the Cuban translator Virgilio Piñera as president *in pectore* of the Translation Committee. There were fifty of us translating from the French to the Spanish, and the rest took their time, but Eba and I finished our part in a single sitting. The passage that reads: And so for the Mature, I was mature, but for the Immature, I was immature…

Eba was the intimate, feminine name Eliseo used for Eduardo Blanco Amor. A few years later, in Buenos Aires, Eba wrote his masterwork, *A esmorga*, On a Bender. The manuscript came to Galicia in the luggage of Isaac Díaz Pardo. It could be its own novel, the history of that suitcase! My uncle would exclaim in the Enigma. Now that was a true Noah's Ark. They tried to publish *A esmorga* here, but the censors treated it as filth. They wrote it off in three or four lines. The censor wrote, more or less, that it was a tale of drunkards and whores. *Not to receive authorization*. It was published in Buenos Aires, in 1959, in Galician. And a year later in Spanish, under the title *La parranda*, The Binge, by Fabril Editora. In Terranova, somewhere in Terra Escondita, we have a box of *benders* and *binges* that crossed the waters in 1961 with Captain Calzani. The box was discovered by Garúa many years later. She was moved. In her reddened eyes, you could see the final image of a broom sweeping up the bits and pieces of the narrator's head after his death by torture. *Unos cachitos de cosa blanca, así como materia*, some white stuff, yes, like matter. The truest cross to the jaw there is!

I've already gnawed on the *Ferdydurke* bone, Cecilio says. I need some other relief.

I gather that he wants to talk, but not about books. I hear his breath, the sound of a diver who's descended too far.

I'm living on borrowed time, Fontana!

You're not built to die, I tell him. Come spend some the summer at Terranova. Expectación has made a little garden on the attic terrace. You should see the foxglove all over the roof!

There were many terracotta roofs in Galicia where plants and flowers grew thanks to the rains, a cultivation of wind and the beaks of birds. But the roof of Terranova, in summer, was a celestial field, thick with foxgloves. The building quivered in delight at its own body: the final achievement of an architecture whose materials dreamt of a second nature, a pink-candle meadow. Whoever it was that designed Terranova had envisioned foxgloves, and ultimately, that's what we got. The first time the blooms sprouted I couldn't believe my eyes. I was so excited that I rang up Old Nick to tell him the news. Foxglove? Yes, it's a herbaceous plant, *Digitalis purpurea*. This was at a time when the invasion was close at hand. He was irritable. I don't need you to tell me what foxglove is, Fontana! And then he said something that definitively awoke my suspicions: I don't want you touching that roof. I don't want you touching anything! I thought his words would bother me, but they were actually a source of joy. Expectación started a small garden on the terrace. Besides the foxglove, I also remember an art-nouveau garden with Padrón peppers and tomatoes. Speaking of Padrón peppers, I told her I'd read a book that mentioned a historic epigraph in a cemetery in Padrón, which read: *They say some are nice, and some have bite. That last one sure did bite.*

Well, prepare yourself, because every single one of these will have bite, Expectación said. They've got the sea in them!

I should take a photo to send the world over as a postcard: *Field of Foxglove on the Terranova Bookstore*. I've hung the photos of bookstores that Uncle Eliseo sent to us over the years on the walls in the Pinhole Chamber. I can finally understand his admiration for Bugs Bunny, the hero of the Chicago Surrealist School. In his view, every bookstore was one of thousands of entrances in a universal burrow. He could travel to and from any of the tunnels, even the underwater ones, and if one were ever sealed, he could pop out of another. No ill-tempered powerful figure, no Elmer Fudd, could ever catch him. Most of the photos, of course, were from Buenos Aires and Montevideo. But he also sent pictures from places as distinct as Porto and Istanbul. I glance over them every morning, and I exclaim, *aurerra, endavant*, up with the hearts, *allons, enfants!* There he is, The Melancholic Ruffian, in San Telmo. Let's see it, Ruffian!

At first, Eliseo would send these jarringly formal letters. Letters you couldn't help but find funny if you knew him: *I am pleased to inform you that I am doing well for the time being, thank God, and I am thinking fondly of you all, including all the animals in the house.* Things like that. It made us laugh, but Amaro said: He's not doing well. All these clichés sound like a cry for help. My father called the sanatorium out of concern but received only mollifying answers. Mr. Eliseo Ponte is responding favorably to treatment. What treatment? The treatment befitting his problem. His conduct, they added, has been exemplary. Could Amaro please speak with him? Why, of course he could, but he'd have to call at the proper time of day. He'd have to call the central office during patient phone booth hours.

But it was only ever the central office that communicated.

Maybe there are too many of us calling, Amaro said to soothe Comba's worries. But he was just as disconcerted as she was, if not more so: They couldn't be subjecting him to electroshock or anything like that, could they?

My parents went to visit him around that time, in the late seventies. Though he seemed well enough, he wasn't the same Eliseo. He'd turned serious and taciturn, even enigmatic.

One day, sometime around the spring of 1980, the clinic called. They wanted to inform my parents that the patient-internee Eliseo Ponte had exited the premises without permission during the forest strolling hour. He'd apparently escaped with the help of another person, who'd been waiting for him in an automobile. No, they couldn't provide any further information. No, the police hadn't been contacted. He wasn't dangerous. And whether or not to report him missing was up to the family to decide.

We went months without any word of him. By this point, the only one who didn't seem anxious was Amaro. It was as if there was an invisible thread connecting the two. Eventually, a folder arrived with a postcard inside it. It's there right now, on the wall, the photo of the staircase in Porto's famous Lello & Irmão bookstore. And the postcards kept coming, one per season, like stamps in a passport.

But they all came without a return address and bore stamps from Paris. In the brief handwritten notes, he never discussed feelings or states of mind. He gave only basic information, photo captions written in the royal "we," such as: We went to London to see the National Gallery, and fell to our knees in front of Rembrandt's *Self-Portrait at the Age of* sixty-three. In one of the postcards, as if he were talking about a mutual acquaintance that needed no introduction, he mentioned "my friend, Pierre." From this, we understood the "we" not to be royal but real.

Fewer postcards arrived as the eighties came to a close. The last one was from the spring of 1989. A vintage postcard, from the thirties, picturing La Moderna Poesía in Havana. And that was it. That is, until May of the following year, when we received a package the size of a suitcase containing…a suitcase. The return address was in Paris, but not in Eliseo's name. All it said was: *Maison de Retraite Tiers Temps,* 24-26, *rue Rémy-Dumoncel,* 75014, *Paris, France.* The package was accompanied by a note from the asylum directors in which they informed us of Eliseo Ponte's death, with a medical certificate attached. In accordance with his wishes, Eliseo's body had been cremated and the ashes sent to people he trusted, so that they could be spread in *un certain point de l'esprit*, that was the literal expression. A certain point. The leather suitcase, with a world travel motif lining the inside, felt empty, but when I opened it I found Pedro Oom's plastic flower and a poem signed by Samuel Beckett: *Comment dire*.

What is the word.

I'm not sure exactly what went on in the privacy of his mind, but I think Amaro interpreted all this as a message. He was silent for days as he prepared his farewell. He was the last of the Men of Rain who Love the Sun. His prediction that the Thunderstone would protect whoever held it had come true. He never could have imagined that a fabrication would hurt him so deeply.

In July, 1980, one of the founders of the Argentinian Mothers of the Plaza de Mayo was found dead in Madrid. I saw it in the papers, a brief article from the inside pages. They identified her as Mrs. De Molfino. Her body had been found by the maids, who'd noticed a putrid smell coming from her room. Noemí Gianotti de Molfino had landed in Barajas Airport on July 18th, in the company of two men who it was later divulged were a part of the dictatorship's commando unit. Back then, there was hardly any information about the case. The judge sealed it without an investigation. It hadn't been long, only a few months, since Garúa had left for a lost war. I decided to go to Madrid, for no particular reason except that I was being urged by a rebellious pain. The woman's body had been found in an apartment-hotel room on

Calle Tutor. I met with Antonio Novalis, a foreign news correspondent and friend of Cecilio's, at Café Oliver. From there I made my way towards the Prado, where I would find Verdelet, Amaro's old friend and now a high-level functionary, in the Goya room. My father privately referred to Verdelet as The Oracle. But I never made it to my consultation.

On my way to the museum, on Calle Marqués de Cuba, I was suddenly surrounded, sandwiched may be a better way to put it, by two thugs who shoved me up against a wall and got straight to the point.

What are you doing, what do you want?

What are you trying to find out, cripple?

Find out about what? I came to Madrid to see the art…

Well, the sightseeing's over for you. The Argentinian's case is closed. She killed herself.

I was going to try to say something, but the other man opened his mouth first:

If she didn't kill herself, she was killed. So what? Whoever did it has probably gotten out of Dodge by now. They went off to dance the tango. Nothing happened here. And nothing else will happen, for now. What the fuck are you doing going around asking about other deaths? Who the fuck do you think you are, some crippled Columbo?

I tried to slip their grasp. The street was nearly deserted. My body was emitting clear signs of emergency. My teeth wouldn't stop chattering. An involuntary percussion that reverberated throughout my skeleton. It was burning hot in Madrid. I was cold at the same time as I was sweating bullets.

The thug directly in front of me grabbed my hand without looking, as if in distraction. I heard a finger break. My finger. I was so terrified in that moment that I didn't feel the pain. I felt it afterwards, though. It was all-consuming. The pain of History channeled into my pinky.

Don't even think of filing a report. We're cops. We'll be there, at whatever station you try. That's right, we're cops. You're Spanish too, aren't you? Well, we're trying to do you a favor here, Spaniard to Spaniard. Get out of town. Today. I don't care if you hop on a train or a plane but go back to your fucking bookstore *today*. Got it?

I didn't know a thing back then. I thought that I knew, and that I could rage against the world. That I had come out unscathed from the Iron Lung, the cylinder I'd been locked in as a child. But within a matter of seconds reality had started to revolve solely around my broken pinky.

Despite the apparent calm, Madrid was a fire-spewing cauldron.

It wasn't long afterwards that the February 23rd coup attempt took place in Argentina. Two years later, the dictatorship was toppled. But just like in Spain, they tried to seal away the past, they tried to legislate impunity through the Full Stop law.

It wasn't easy to move towards the truth.

There were more people trying to cover things up than there were trying to uncover them.

One of the people I asked about Garúa's fate back then, at the twilight of the Dictatorship, told me that it wasn't clear whether she'd managed to enter Argentina or had fallen at the border, which was the norm in this return-turned-fatal-trap. From Madrid, the logical route would have been to travel through Lima, though she may also have tried to go through Cuba.

But who was it that brought her from Galicia to Madrid? Who was it that picked her up? I described the characters to him, told him about the reappearance of the man who'd developed photos in my Madrid apartment, photos of the neofascists at Franco's funeral. The man with the jet-black hair. She'd called him Tero. And Negro.

Negro Tero? Any one of us could be a Negro Tero at some point. Even you.

He confessed that the entire Counter-Offensive had been a delusion on the part of the higher-ups, and that the organization had fractured. The dream of the *juventud marabillosa* had come to an end.

He promised he'd let me know if he found out anything more. I never heard from him again.

The same as ever. Every morning when I go into the Pinhole Chamber, I think she's going to be there. I crack open the door. I see her. And she's there for the time it takes a lamp filament to burn out.

After much deliberation, I decided to set up a computer in the Pinhole Chamber. I only use it to explore. To see where she's been. To visit pages dedicated to Erik Satie and read the comments. I've searched all her names. The ones I heard. The ones Tero called her: Tana, Chinita; on the day she left he called her Mika. That alias brought me to Mika Feldman, an Argentinian rebel who had been a captain in the army of the Spanish Republic. Then I tried the name on her Italian passport: Giuliana Melis. Only one hit. A girl who worked on a Pasolini film. A coincidence or a case of identity theft. It's not her, but I like to envision her in the film, in *Salò*, the way that I like to envision her on the edge of her seat beside me as we watch *L'Atalante*.

But what I always, always end up watching is the video of the starling flocks, *Stormo di storni!*, in the Rome sky: *Questa è la scena che si presenta nei cieli di Roma, ogni sera al tramonto!* This is the scene that appears in the sky over Rome every day at dusk!

Al tramonto! At dusk. There are days when someone will come into the bookstore: I'll know because of the bell at the door, but I won't get up, because I'm busy or occupied with something, and all of a sudden my heart will skip a beat, because when I look up, I'll see someone with their back to me, in a colorful wool hat, fur coat, hippy skirt or flight pants, and I won't say a word, I'll watch their every movement, as they stand up on tiptoes, outstretch their arm, and pull out one of the Libros del Mirasol relics. Yes, yes. Precisely that one, *El cazador oculto*, The Hidden Hunter, the last copy.

This is the same as *El guardián entre el centeno*, right? *Catcher in the Rye*?

Yes, that's the literal translation of the title, I'll say. It's the same book, by the same author, but *The Hidden Hunter* is a better book than *The Catcher in the Rye*.

Pity, they don't laugh. Garúa would say: *Che*, was that supposed to be a joke or a kick in the pants?

Can I ask you what made you pick this one out?

It's for a gift, they say.

How lucky for the other person!

Whenever I see a phone booth, I have an urge to pick up the receiver. To listen. To stand there for a while by myself, taking in the chirps of the void. I've built up the courage to do it a few times. I dial the international prefix for Argentina, followed by the capital's area code, then a random number. Most of them are dead phone lines. But one time, there was an answer. Someone on the other side. A woman's voice, gravely, yet melodic. I didn't want to seem sinister, standing there panting, breathing into the receiver, but the only thing that occurred to me to ask was if I was speaking with Fabril Editora. She told me I wasn't, that I had the wrong number.

To fill the silence, I quoted one of Eliseo's favorite Camões lines:

My apologies, I messed up the entire speech of my years!

And the voice said:

I'm drawing a blank, old timer.

Then she hung up.

I stop looking at the liquidation signs.

There's a graffiti on Monte Alto, by Tower Lane: *You may not think so, but to me, you're perfect.*

Potentially Dangerous Nacho brightens my day: Epopoi popoi!

And I call back: Popoi popoi!

The phone booth is still there, out of service and in ruins, on the way to the Lighthouse. The eyes of the blackberry bramble spy through the broken glass. As for the phone, the rust has covered over the numbers of the metallic dialer. It's strange, though: the earpiece is still in good condition. Hanging with that particular stupor of devices abandoned in their prime. Some girls ride over on their bicycles. They go into the booth. They pretend to talk. They simulate conversation. They talk.

Are you there?

…

No, it's not cold right now. It's a little bit windy though.

There's the Lighthouse.

Sometime or another I'm going to have to go back up to the lantern. The last time was with her. I can't, Garúa. Yes, you can. But it's 234 steps! Just don't count them, it'll be over in no time. I'll need an Iron Lung, Garúa! There's one up there waiting for you. The Lighthouse lantern, yes. A good place to embrace, to feel your hand searching, being taken up, caressed, and lighting a torch in the origin of the world.

I wonder who's walking along the Horizon Line today.